Tinners Creek

Tinners Creek

Chris Snell

To Beryl,

Love,

Chris

Christopher Snell has asserted his right under the
Copyright, Designs and Patents Act, 1988,
to be identified as the author of this work

This book is a work of fiction and, except in the case of historical fact,
any resemblance to actual persons, living or dead, is coincidental.

Tinners Creek, the name inserted on the map, is a fictitious location
on a tributary of the river Fal.

The Priory, not shown, is also fictitious.

Paperback ISBN: 9798302421043

All rights reserved. No part of this publication may be reproduced,
stored in any retrieval system or transmitted in any form or by
any means without the prior written permission of the author.

In memory

of

great grandfather Nathaniel England on the
crew of an RNLI pulling lifeboat swamped

on

The Doom Bar at Padstow, April 1900

1

Nathaniel Hawken crewed for the local lifeboat. It was this brought him to the site he was now taking an interest in. Assessing the creek's suitability for the location of a boatyard, his attention was distracted by the half buried skeleton of an old ketch poking out of the sand. Only a few blackened ribs remained. Any planking long since parted from weakened nails attaching them to the curved struts that gave the hull its shape. The wreck immediately prompted scenes of the last shout he had been called out on. It had nearly been his last.

*

Just before dawn, a February morning three weeks earlier, the maroons had been fired calling for the volunteer crew to man the lifeboat. A full moon in a sky of fast-moving, broken clouds, produced an eerily-lit seascape of shadows alternating with dimmer, undulating tracts of faintly luminous wave crests. It revealed a two-masted trading schooner or to be precise, a now-dismasted schooner drifting towards Wreckers Reef. She'd lost her anchor and one of her masts was hanging in the water, held in place by a tangle of ropes and rigging. In fact, only one of her masts was down but the other might just as well have been, since its ripped sails were blowing like long bed linen hanging out to dry. Fortunately the trailing mast and spars acted like a drogue against the onshore wind trying to blow her more speedily onto the reef.

The rescue craft was a pulling lifeboat. Ten oars, with a low, auxiliary gaff sail to provide stability rather than thrust. It was robust to a point but, like all open boats without a deck, it was vulnerable to being swamped when side-on to a wave. It had a sealed prow and stern and a complicated system of water ballast within each, a construction that was intended to make it self-righting should it capsize. In fact, the stern and bow forms were practically indistinguishable but for the addition of a stubby rudder that gave meaning to port and starboard. This permitted the vessel to advance or retreat without needing to turn broadside-on to a heavy swell. The latter was a dangerous manoeuvre to be avoided wherever possible. The men just swung around on their seats and rotated their oars if they needed to reverse direction.

On shore the women, for launches depended on the women, turned out in a variety of garb, bearing kerosene storm lanterns. The huge doors on the boathouse were propped open by a couple of large, granite rocks. They shuddered and banged in the force seven wind, doors of two inch thick planking, to all intents and purposes behaving like balsa wood.

The lifeboat rested on a four-wheeled cradle. Each iron wheel, a foot in diameter, located on rails and kept on track by half inch flanges. A thick hemp rope, perhaps the diameter of a child's wrist, was attached to its rear timbers by a huge shackle and pin, its hard, tightly braided weave under tension, wrapped around a primitive capstan manned by four men on spars, ready to check the boat's slide down the steep, launch ramp. The spars, five feet long and a robust four by four inch section, fitted loosely into the capstan sockets. In the past runaway cradles had been known to cripple capstan operatives too slow to leap out of the way if the ratchet mechanism jumped out of its seat. Loosely fitted levers would shoot out of their sockets, at worst causing a bruise or two but not fracturing ribs or hips like their flailing, fixed forebears. Additional braking was effected by two crewmen holding the free end of the rope where, after two or three turns, it exited the capstan cylinder. It was to be a decade or so before a steel cable, on a hand-wound, ratcheted drum, would be installed. World War One would begin and end before that happened.

'Right, this one's a pig of a storm. I've been in worse but I don't want all three of you in the boat.' Andrew Nancarrow, the coxswain, addressed his remarks to Dick Trenarren and his two sons, Horatio and Joshua.

'Dick and Horatio, on board. Josh, you're on next time. Right, the rest of you,' Cox turned to the remaining volunteers, 'I'm goin' to have to take half a dozen strong pullers. We could be out in this most of the morning. Nat, I want you up front.'

Nathaniel nodded as Nancarrow wasted no time choosing the rest of the crew. Garbed in oilskins and cork buoyancy aids, one by one they climbed the platform that brought them level with the boat's waterline. Each heaved himself over the side, took his appointed seat, with a man on the tiller and Nat on the cramped bow seat. The 'pullers' checked their oars were safely inboard before a command from the coxswain would signal the craft ready for launch. The cradle was lowered to within a few yards of the water and halted. Timing was all important. Wave sequences had to be gauged. Then, with a quick final check by the launch crew, the assembly allowed to shoot down into the waves. A heavily greased cable beneath the trolley, running through two steel eyes, one front and one back, helped keep it stable, allowing the launch cradle to be recovered later, still lined up on the rails. Its timbers were lignum vitae, a wood so dense and heavy it didn't float. A wood so hard, teeth, on pinions driving the huge stone wheels in flour mills, were made from it. Many a carpenter cursed the stubbornness of the grain, a grain that resisted tools with edges sharp enough to shave with. But it outlasted any other material and rewarded its owners with years of punishing service.

Nat was not a superstitious man but for some inexplicable reason felt ill at ease. It wasn't the first time he had experienced misgivings. There were times before when he had been conscious of emerging from a negative state of mind, with no evident reason for the shadows of premonition feeding his imagination. In retrospect, seconds later, hours, days later or not at all, he remembered some earlier episode or construct of mind that had acted as a prompt feeding his unease.

This time it was a fleeting intrusion into the activity surrounding the lean discipline and tension preceding the launch. He dismissed it almost as soon as it manifested itself. It was more important to prepare for the arrest of the cradle as it hit the barrier of water surging up the ramp. If he didn't lean forward and wedge the bench between his legs and the seat of his chest waders, his spine would be rammed up against the back face of the prow.

The blunt end of the cradle slammed into the foaming sea, sending up a cascade of water. The lifeboat, held in place on the vee-shaped frames merely by friction, followed the law of inertia and shot off its cradle as the trolley's speed was drastically reduced by the mass of water it displaced. As buoyant as a duck, the craft entered the receding trough of a ten-foot wave, creating a clean bow wave that produced hardly any spray. Five pairs of oars slipped into the water simultaneously, taking advantage of the free momentum, saving them the necessity of having to pull up to speed from a standing start. It enabled them to warm-up gently and get into a steady rhythm without wasting precious energy reserves. Sometimes they had been out for ten, twelve or more hours, soaked, burned by salt and wind, weary, almost to the point of sleep. Any reserve of energy, however slight, could mean a difference between success and disaster.

2

It took them probably twice as long to reach the schooner as it normally would, had they not had to fight the wind. They were never far off shore. The reef was about a cable's length from and parallel with the cliffs. On its western end it joined a shallow platform of granite, uncovered at very low tides and connecting it at right angles to the cliffs behind. At its eastern point it marked a deep channel. This channel was hazard-free. It ended in a sandy cove at the mouth of a gently rising valley.

It was daylight when they reached the schooner. As they drew close to they could see that her deck boat had been smashed by the mast. Five men, a woman and two children, perhaps seven and ten years old, emerged from the cabin let into the deck, a sunken cabin in marine parlance. The two children rushed to the rails and waved, their childish enthusiasm at welcoming newcomers overcoming any fear of their predicament. The adults were, understandably, more circumspect but there was a noticeable change in their bearing as they traversed the deck, from one of hesitation as they left the cabin to one of relief by the time they too reached the rails.

'I don't like that.' Andrew Nancarrow was referring to the swells that threatened to wash over the deck.

The adults must have read his mind. No sooner had he said it than one of the men, probably the father, grabbed the two children and rushed them back to the cabin, followed by the woman. The schooner's hatches were still intact and, by the set of her deck, she appeared not to be taking on water. Every time a large wave lifted the ship, the mast and rigging twisted and shifted across her gunnel.

Nancarrow stood and faced the rowers, 'We're goin' to have to ditch that rigging and try a tow,' shouting above the racket caused by wind and wave.

'Somebody's goin' to have to get across and cut that mast free. Nat, you up for it?' Nancarrow must have anticipated this need when, earlier, he'd had the foresight to make him the bow man.

The Cox had noticed, right from the beginning, Nat's self-control and lack of resentment if passed-over for a practice exercise when he might have considered it 'his turn' to be selected. He'd crewed for half a dozen seasons and proved himself not only strong but agile and totally free from fear.

Nat grinned, 'Try me!'

'Right, we'll pull up to her starboard side into that mass of rigging draggin' the water. It's tempering the swell and you should be able to get several good hand holds in it up onto the deck. Jethro, you're nearest, pass the axe over when he's safely on board. Rest of you, on this side,' the coxswain indicated the port side of the boat, 'bring your oars in so we c'n get up tight to the hull. Nat, first time for any of us that we've had to clear mast and rigging like this. So leave it up to you but tie the axe lanyard to something fixed, before you start. Can you hear me?'

'Yes Cox!'

'Michael, I want you and Tim to face round, ready to take the boat back if Nat gets trapped and falls backwards. We don't want the boat ramming his back and watch you don't clash oars with the middle rowers.'

Nancarrow sat down and nodded to Dick Trenarren who'd listened to the exchange. Dick was Second Cox and needed little instruction from Andy, as he called him, on the informal occasions when not within the disciplined regime of the boat. The two had crewed for a score of years together. Those years had proved a catalyst, forging a synergy that relied little on oral communication but much on intuition and trust. Just two men, the middle two in the bank of oars, applied gentle, half strokes as Dick nursed the tiller, taking the boat up to the tangle of ropes.

Nat stood on the bow seat with his left foot on the gunnel. He was steadied by Jethro. Seeing no advantage in his choice, he shifted his stance to the centre of the short seat and crouched, waiting for the boat to sink into and then rise from a suitable trough. By the third wave surge he had got the measure of the swell and, stepping up onto the prow, half stood, then half crouched before letting his ham strings catapult him onto the tangle of mast and ropes.

The jump was perfect. A cheer went up from the crew. He landed on all fours. His boots located secure holds in the tangled loops of rigging almost as soon as his hands snatched and secured a grip on a transverse cross-spar. By this time the captain who had figured out the intention of the rescuers, had arrived to the side with the deck hands. Nat scrambled up the broken mast, managing a half turn to face the crew with a roguish grin on his face as he did so. Reaching the schooner's gunnel he pulled himself over onto the deck, kept in balance by the captain and deckhand gripping him by the harness on his cork flotation aid. He exchanged a few words of explanation with the master of the vessel who then agreed with Andrew Nancarrow's intentions.

Turning and holding onto one of the mast stay ropes, Nat then leaned out towards the lifeboat and grabbed the short felling axe proffered by Jethro. Looking about for something to attach the lanyard to, his gaze fell on a cleat alternately covered and uncovered by a piece of torn sail flapping in the wind.

Sizing up the mess in front of him, he chopped through the ropes resting on the solid timber of the mast. This released some of the constraints that were stopping the splintered end of timber sliding over the edge into the water. As the heavy end of the mast lost the support of the severed ropes, it traversed about two feet of the schooner's top rail and dropped over the edge. The shift in weight had negligible effect on the ship's buoyancy but it now posed a hazard as it floated at waterline level, still attached to the remaining, uncut ropes. Each pitch and roll of the ship had the reverse effect of a battering ram. The fractured end of the mast stayed more or less where it was, sluggishly oscillating in the swell. It was the hull which battered the ram, rather than the other way round.

Nat could hear the ominous clout of wood against wood as, with each roll of the schooner, the waterline timbers began to take a hammering. By this time the captain had realised the recovery of his boat depended on speedy release of mast and rigging. He dashed back to the cabin. From the pint-sized galley he retrieved a butcher's knife, keened it up with a couple of quick slips across a steel and sped back to the tangle on deck. The knife, now more effective than the axe, took, perhaps, thirty or forty seconds to saw through the remaining guys. The mast floated free.

Nancarrow signalled Nat to be ready to transfer back to the boat, 'Leave the axe where it is for now. We'll claim it later.' The rescue craft eased up alongside the schooner. The two vessels, because of the difference in their lengths and buoyancy, were bobbing up and down with totally different frequencies. It was going to be a risky business. For a start the lifeboat's rail was two or three feet below the deck of the Shady Maid, for that was the name of the schooner. Secondly, the lifeboat not only bobbed up and down but kept being tilted about its long axis when, from time to time, the hull of the schooner engaged with its rail at every rise and fall of the swell.

'Try to keep her back boys, free from her hull.'

For a second time Nat sat on the ship's wooden rail, just above one of the deck-wash exit holes. With the captain holding onto his collar, he swung his legs over, turning onto one hip, changing hand holds as he did so. His boots felt for the outer edge of the hole as he rested the upper half of his body inward. Both feet found a safe purchase on the planking.

The coxswain eased the rescue craft closer to the dripping hull of the Maid.

'Jethro, you ready?'

'Ready Cox.'

'Right Nat, next wave.' Andrew Nancarrow shouted across the gap separating boat and schooner.

The sleek hull of the lifeboat rose faster than its larger sister. Nat half turned, freed one hand, leaned out from the rail and held a leg over the narrowing gap between the two craft. As the boat rose to meet him, he let go, giving just the slightest of thrusts with his other foot. The timing was spot on. He landed in the space cleared by the two middle rowers and grabbed the nearest one, to check his forward flight. Despite the seriousness of the situation and the fatigue, another cheer went up from his crew mates, the nearest hands patted his back. Nancarrow gave the briefest of nods, as if to say, 'Well done, lad,' and directed his boat away from the bigger one.

Cox took the lifeboat around, downwind of the trader's bow. Both vessels were now aligned with the direction back to harbour. Jethro had been tasked with the job of throwing a line to its skipper. He was already standing, bracing a leg against one of the boat's substantial ribs, swinging the Turk's Head knot in a rhythmic pattern of arcs by the time they had lined up. He increased the traverse of his arm, allowing the cord to lengthen gradually, feeding spare coils with his left hand until the big knot at its end was just clearing the water. With one final backward swing he whipped the line out over the bank of oars and released it. The coils at his feet unravelled without a hitch as the pilot line arched over the lead gap between schooner and lifeboat. It was a perfect throw. The ball shot past the captain, dropping its line across his shoulder. One of the deckhands secured it with a temporary lashing to the foremast. Two of them then set about hauling in the heavier tow rope attached to the line. It wasn't an easy task. The rope, saturated with sea water, was probably three times its dry weight. By now the wind was gusting up to force eight but, as ever, there was a lag between wave height and wind force.

    The tow rope was of such a weave that it would absorb any strain energy imparted by the smaller rowing boat. In fact it was more likely that it would tear a towing point from the weaker of two vessels before reaching the limits of its own ultimate strength. The schooner's master had secured the one end to his bow post. The other was attached to a towing point on the stern post to which the lifeboat's rudder was attached.

3

Schooner and lifeboat now faced the long haul of returning to safe anchorage. There was one thing in their favour, they had a tail wind and a pretty strong one at that. But towing demanded a different technique. The ship dragging behind them put paid to any spontaneous, correcting manoeuvre they could effect as a free, untethered vessel. The ten rowers fell into an irregular sequence that matched the wave formations. A tiring task demanding of strength and concentration as rogue waves destroyed any chance of respite, any chance of establishing a rhythm. Their boat leaned down into each trough, righted itself and then began the opposing inclination as it traversed back up. But this was an illusion, since the waves were sliding under the boat, as they rolled towards the cliffs, not the boat over the waves.

The current, augmented by a high tide, sped along the edge of Wreckers Reef and added, perhaps, seven or eight knots to the one or two the rowers coaxed from their oars. As it passed the eastern tip of the reef, the unusually deep channel to the cove caused it to undergo the equivalent of wind-shear. When the little rescue craft cut across the cove's entrance, the effect was spectacular. The boat got caught in a powerful eddy created by the sharp end of the reef where it projected out over the chasm. It whipped around on its vertical axis. The already taut tow rope tightened like a banjo string and tilted the craft for, perhaps, milliseconds, before tearing the stern post from the hull in one, swift release of the strain energy stored in its fibres.

Handles raked across rib cages, fortunately cushioned by the cork life-jackets, as the violent change of inertia treated the oars like flimsy batons. Three men were thrown out. The schooner continued for a few metres, on course, until it too reached the Maelstrom. The effect on the vessel was moderated by its larger size. But even so, it swung around and pointed into the cove.

By this time the hull of the lifeboat was up to its gunnels in water. The crew, those still remaining in the craft, were forced to roll over its sides as it settled in the waves. All of them were now in the water. All of them were conscious but shocked by sudden immersion in water a few degrees above freezing. The buoyancy tank in the stern had ruptured. As a consequence the boat was now settling vertically in the water, supported by the still intact tank in the bow.

The Shady Maid drifted up to the men who were bobbing up and down like seals. Her captain, quick thinking, rushed to the hatch. A short ladder, used for dry boarding, was lashed beneath one side. It took him little time to release the steps. At its top end a couple of C brackets allowed him to clip it to the wide deck rail and hang it over the hull side.

Grabbing a long boat hook, he guided the crew up to the ladder. They were able to clamber up the rungs unaided. It was a reverse case of, 'from the fire into the frying pan'.

'Your best chance is to let her drift up onto the beach,' Clive Nancarrow nodded, shivering, towards the short stretch of sand piled high with sea weed deposited there by the storm and exceptionally high tide.

'She'll not suffer much damage, if any. It's a clear run in the channel, I know it, no obstacles and, it's my bet, you'll be able to get a half dozen shire horses from the farms, hereabouts, to drag her up above high tide mark. But, in the meantime, my boys need to wring out their wet clothes. It'll take her ten or twelve minutes to shore, so get 'em below decks now, then they'll be on hand for the beaching.'

The Cox followed his crew down into the hold of the schooner. Having to help each other remove boots, cork jackets and outer wear, despite the seriousness of the situation, resulted in some ribald comment. Although some of the crew were, nominally, Methodist, this didn't stop a flow of banter that would have shocked the more prissy members of their congregations. The shelter, afforded in the enclosed space, permitted their chilled bodies to regain some heat in the short time they were below. They squeezed all the water they could from their garments and re-donned the outer oilskins and cork waistcoats.

Large waves were breaking into a rolling surf onto the beach. Above deck, the ship's master used the rudder, as best he could, to stop the Shady Maid lining up broadside on for its run up onto the sand. The lifeboat crew, back on top, lined both sides of the vessel along with the schooner's passengers. Even with only one mast and torn sails the wind was powerful enough to give added momentum to the ship through the medium still afforded by the damaged tackle. The group could feel the craft gathering speed in the wash. Although frightening, the uncertainty of what lay ahead and the strange sensation of a deck tilted forward like a surf board, the surge of the hull towards land induced an irrational sense of excitement amongst them.

'Hold on! She's nearly there.' The words were barely out of Nancarrow's mouth when the unmistakeable sound of a keel shearing through bottom layers of sand and pebbles was accompanied by a smooth slide to a halt.

All were left standing. The schooner was fitted with twin port and starboard runners along the middle two thirds of her length. This, combined with a weak suction from the very fine sand, kept her upright. She stayed in place despite a strong stern wash, her mass, now a dead weight, counter-balanced by a hull no longer displacing an equal volume of water.

'Archimedes be praised!' That was Nat's response to the finale.

The captain, seeing the craft was going to remain in place for the immediate future, turned to the cox'n.

'We get 'em off now?'

' 'es. She'll be right for a while. I'll get my mob down first; only a foot deep by the ladder. If we shift it up towards the bow, we'll be able to get your wife an' daughters off without a soakin.'

'Right! Let's get moving.'

By this time a crowd, who had been watching the rescue from the cliffs, had made their way down to the beach and were on hand to give help.

'Take your shoes off and hitch your skirts up,' Andrew Nancarrow spoke to the mother of the girls, 'we'll hand the two girls down to one of the crew or one of them', Andrew nodded towards a group of men obviously prepared to wade in, 'so's we can get 'em to land without gettin' their feet wet.'

The mother, now free from the uncertainty of the earlier situation, smiled then suddenly broke down in tears of relief. The elder of the two daughters, watching and, waving back at the assembly on shore, turned and took hold of her mother in a protective hug. Her mother looked over her daughter's shoulder and croaked a 'thank-you, thank-you' to the coxswain. Meanwhile the smaller girl took advantage of the still deck and skipped up to the stern and back before she was directed to the ladder.

The transfer to land took place with no further drama. It was then and there Nat Hawken vowed that he would set about designing and constructing an 'unsinkable' lifeboat. But he would need to acquire and equip a boatyard.

He had already served an apprenticeship as a shipwright in his uncle's boatyard, his mother's brother. Working on a variety of craft, from small Cornish crabbers through to larger brigs, he had developed an insight into what constituted a well constructed and 'well behaved' boat. Outside the yard's working hours, on an unused piece of land belonging to the premises, he'd built a small craft after the style of a pilot cutter. It was about two thirds the scale of a functional pilot. Any smaller and it would not have justified having a deck. But it differed from conventional craft in that it was wider than boats of a similar length. This allowed him to give it a shallower draught, extending its range in shallow waters and giving it a few extra knots in speed for the given sail area it commanded. As always there was a compromise in that it rocked about a bit in heavier swells. But it carried a drop keel for really demanding seas, shedding deck wash through its scuppers whilst maintaining a fairly stable platform for all that. A craft built for a variety of uses it doubled as a useful little work boat during his occasional fishing sorties and provided his mother's table with the odd lobster or turbot. There were few of similar size able to compete with it in looks or performance.

4

The chattering of a magpie brought him back to the present. The bird was agitating about a squirrel dashing about in a tree near some nesting area it was eying up. It pursued the animal in branches devoid of leaves. The tree was an oak. This particular oak caught his attention. Its limbs, misshapen, offered just the kind of profiled grain that would form a natural rib in a curved hull when cut and shaped to size. Mature elm and beech grew in abundance alongside.

Nathaniel Hawken sized up the creek's potential. It lay below a loop road connecting Mylor, Flushing and Penryn. The lane down from the main road was straight and not too steep and the stream, an old, tinners' stream, would provide more than enough energy to run one of the small, new-fangled, turbine generators and power a saw, water-wheel driven. Even without long periods of rain it would provide a good head of water from three different springs. One that emanated from the quarry at the head of the valley. One out of the side of the western face of the hill above the creek and one, the most copious, flooding from a sinister looking opening that gave entrance to an adit, sinister enough to deter the most adventurous boys, who occasionally 'gamed' in the wood, from exploring its depths.

The adit, abandoned, once saw good quality tin extracted from the cassiterite and some copper, mined for perhaps half a century. Longer, if you counted the years during which centuries of miners picked at the granite strata protruding through the gorse and bracken and panned the stream. The discovery of tin, more readily recoverable elsewhere, had made the mine uneconomic.

Most of the land around the creek was too poisoned for farming, not that there was a square foot of pasture anywhere near. Traces of arsenic impregnated the soil in some places, from the days when copper ore was extracted. The contamination was not great, though enough to be considered a hazard by the locals. But, in any case, spoil from the depths of the mine lay in irregular deposits. Some were spread about and compacted forming an inhospitable layer, hostile to any form of disturbance other than by the most robust of earth moving equipment not possessed by any farmer. Other deposits formed ridges, the larger granite rocks of which were now moss and ivy covered. They had first seen the light of day a century or more ago and were now colonised by groves of twisted willow.

Nat turned his back on the slip of mud and water and made his way through dead bracken up to a granite, stamping house. The slated roof was still intact. Outside, adjacent to the wall alongside the stream, a sixteen foot diameter waterwheel was gathering moss and algae. Its massive steel axle rested in a pair of cast steel, bearing housings. Nat put down the unlit kerosene lantern he was carrying and scraped the moss and other debris from the top half of the bearing caps. The bronze bearings within had out-lived two earlier waterwheels. Their exposed end faces still looked in good fettle and were a testament to the ingenuity and craftsmanship of the Cornish engineer who had designed, cast and machined their geometry.

There were still such men about who had a feel for metal, an eye for proportion and economy of line. They were polymaths who had acquired sound reputations built on self-study, experiment and a hunger for knowledge and self-improvement. Theory was wedded to application. They were well-versed in draughtsmanship, calculus and engineering mechanics, acquired at the local night school. Few, if any, possessed degrees. They could all put their hand to a metal turning lathe or make a wooden pattern using special moulders' rules that allowed for the shrinking of the casting it was designed for. Their interests ranged across the whole field of invention, science and some of the less abstruse fields of philosophy and extended to the more technical publications put out by various learned associations. They had the likes of Sir Humphrey Davy for inspiration. A man who started off serving an apprenticeship and became president of the Royal Society. Born in Penzance, he distinguished himself pioneering the fields of chemistry and electro-chemistry, inventing the miners' safety lamp and promoting the careers of the likes of Michael Faraday, who had been his scientific assistant.

A few, instrumentalists, rather than describing themselves as trained musicians, could write a score not having received a single lesson in harmony. Their creativity derived from an accumulation of experience and intuition, playing, over the years, a range of instruments of different pitch in any one of the brass bands in their towns and villages. Nat was one such. A cornet player with a love of classical music, derived from the many arrangements for brass of numerous well-known pieces by Rossini, Berlioz and the like.

A mixture of scholar and clown, he had a reputation for mischief. The clown hid a serious side to his nature. Knowing he was not a man of letters, he was careful not to display a knowledge that might brand him a pseudo-intellectual in the eyes of those with formal academic training. He benefited from 'night school' - as it was called locally - evening classes run by The Royal Cornwall Polytechnic which had its location in Falmouth. There were those, with such academic pedigrees, who displayed a false modesty, secretly hating to be called, yet wanting at the same time to be recognised as 'clever' but who could not help declaiming, within the first three and a half minutes of encounter, that they had attended a such and such, prestigious place of learning. One of his favourite jokes was to ask any one of these 'gentlemen' from such a place of learning, 'Who discovered the Law of Elasticity?' knowing full well they would say, 'Hooke'.

His stock reply was, 'No! No it wasn't. You sure about that?'

'Yes!' they would say, 'You're wrong!' often with a superior, self-assured smirk and lift of the chin.

'You sure? Because in my bible it says, "Moses tethered his ass to a tree and walked three miles into the desert."' That was Nat! This was the raw humour of the boatyard.

5

There were two large entrances to the stamping house, one at each end of the building. Both openings lined up with the creek. They were served by carriage-sized portals sporting double doors. When open they allowed traffic, mainly horse-drawn, to enter or exit for whatever purpose suited the commerce at the time. Nat passed through a smaller door located in the side opposite the waterwheel's axle. It was a logical place for the door. It permitted room for manoeuvre in delivering and positioning or servicing the heavy steel shaft carrying the wheel.

In his mind's eye he could visualise a small jetty down at the creek's edge, complete with derrick and slipway. Ships would unload extra balks of green timber through specially constructed hatches at the waterline in their prows. A steel cable and drum, powered by the waterwheel, would haul them up to a saw powered by the same wheel, where they would be cut to some specified size. He could almost smell the scent of freshly cut timber as he visualised the location of a saw bench replacing the now defunct stamping gear.

Satisfied with the potential offered by the stamping house, he retrieved the lantern from outside and walked up to the adit. During periods when it was not delivering ore, it had been enlarged at different times and used to store all kinds of property from contraband to cattle, ploughs to pit-props. As a consequence, the entrance now resembled a cavern, rather than a mine level. The successive enlargements had been accomplished with the aim of expanding laterally, so as to keep the stream bounded by the granite wall on one side and a slightly raised floor on the other. It never flooded. The cavern extended in for about forty yards, at which point a barrier, in the form of a grating, prevented further access. Of solid granite, with no fractures in its roof, the whole space was dry and waterproof.

He was already familiar with the premises. His grandfather had been one of the last miners to work the seams and had taken him in, one day, to see a rich vein of tin that had been uncovered, a vein of tin rumoured to be one of the richest ever mined. That was a while ago. Now the site was up for auction and he was interested. He was hoping the mining potential was dead and that there would be limited interest in the timber groves as a major asset. As far as he knew, no one had ever built a boat inside a mine but he could see that with the creek, the adjacent stamping house, water power and timber supplies suited to hull and deck construction, it was an ideal site for a boat yard.

Curious to know the depth of water within the adit, he cut and trimmed a length of hazel, primed the lantern with a few strokes of the plunger, went through the tedious process of igniting the mantle and walked inside. He poked about in the stream at various points from the front to the back of the cavern. Nowhere did it seem to be deeper than twelve or fourteen inches, with just an occasional cavity no bigger than one of the wicker, crab pots that littered the quays at the many harbours in the county. The water would enable him to feed a steam box for softening and shaping the wooden rib braces and other components that gave form to the hull.

For some time now he had become increasingly frustrated by the restrictions he was obliged to observe, working for his elderly uncle Victor. Victor Lewis treated him well and paid him well but Nat had grown bored with the tedium of producing boats unexceptional in their performance and unimaginative in their design. It was time for him to branch out on his own. His cousin Jake would take over the business from his father in the not too distant future. There was a guarded working relationship between the two younger men but Nat knew the yard, as likely as not, would suffer under his cousin's management. He had good reason to believe Jake was jealous of him. More than once he had discovered his work from the previous day, tampered with. His cousin, last to leave the yard, had locked the premises each time. No one other than he could have done it. He was not someone you could warm to. Overweight and unambitious, he was prone to socialise rather than push the bounds of the business. Falmouth was a busy port that attracted all kinds of trade and selling boats, good sea-going boats, was one of them. If any trade was going to fail, boat building in Falmouth should not be one of them.

Nat now knew, in his bones, command of his own yard was where his future lay. He gave the hissing Tilley lamp a few, final, priming pumps and lifted the lantern for one last look at the interior of the mine. The roof sparkled with the flakes of mica reflecting the light thrown out by the lamp. It was a good six or seven yards from roof to ceiling, more than adequate for frameworks supporting the superstructure of any hull. A small turbine would power a cluster of lamps, more than enough to illuminate the spacious working area and the receding roof line, tapering down towards the grill, was still higher than any man he knew. He could store any amount of gear at the back without fear of running out of space. Satisfied, he lowered the lamp and walked back out of the level onto the gradient leading down to the creek. His boat, hitched to an overhanging branch of oak, had ridden up a few feet on the rising tide. Before returning to it he extinguished the lamp and set it down by the track leading to the water's edge.

What remained of the existing jetty was unsafe. Some of the more robust timbers might be salvaged but most of the rest were fit only for burning and the sight of the boat riding purposively alongside, in the wash of seaweed and tidal flotsam, prompted him to examine a nearby ridge of spoil extracted from the mine workings. Plenty of stone lay about. A stone jetty would be easy to construct and, wherever there were boats, it benefited their owners and other users if quays were solid and easy to moor alongside. There wouldn't be the problems encountered when building breakwaters on unprotected coasts, this creek was sheltered. It was ideally sited and such a jetty, to suit his requirements, wouldn't need to be too high nor too long.

He clambered about. There were blocks granite, blocks of a size easily handled by one man and easy to transport down to the creek. A few tips of looser debris containing sedimentary rocks would provide paving, should it be needed. The track, originally used to bring Norwegian pit props up from the holds of shallow-draft schooners, was still clear. A horse with a flat bed cart could transport really big stuff. He could rig up a tripod sling-crane to raise the more bulky pieces and a flat bed cart would be easier to manhandle heavy rocks from than over the sides of an enclosed one.

Satisfied, he retrieved the lantern and strode off down to his boat swinging about its line on the incoming tide.

6

The auction was advertised only in local newspapers. Because the mine was no longer viable and the timber reserves, although substantial, not worthy of serious commercial exploitation, the property would only attract attention from a few amateur speculators and one or two local farmers, maybe. Nobody, except Nat, had the savvy to see its potential as a boatbuilding facility. The farmers would consider the outlay a rather costly, non-productive asset, merely to be used as a storage facility for cattle or machinery. Walking down to the boat, his mind was considering a number of issues that were crowding in now that, mentally, he had committed himself to owning the site.

If he managed to buy the mine he would remain in his uncle's boatyard until he'd built the jetty, equipped the stamping house and put double doors on the entrance to the adit. Time would tell! In the interim, he would say nothing until the auction. The auctioneers had quoted an estimate of a hundred and fifty guineas. He would be able to cover this, finance enough second-hand machinery to make a viable business and still have a tidy sum left over.

He untied the line and pulled on the boat until it grounded by a large rock, coiling the rope as he did so. Stepping up onto the rock from a pile of damp seaweed he stopped to look once more at the terrain either side of the creek before tossing the line into the bow. He heaved himself across her topside timbers, picked up a long boat hook and pushed himself away from the eddying piles of weed. A few yards out into the wider strip of creek he paused again, stopped poling the boat and listened. He drifted quietly under the momentum of the vessel in the flooding tide. For a second time he heard a strange cry from a gull. But it wasn't a gull, as he'd first thought. It was a human voice and panicking, coming from further down the waterway.

He turned the boat around, pulled on the halyard raising the gaff sail as he floated against the incoming tide.

Again he heard the voice. He yelled, 'Hello!'

'Help!' It was a woman's voice. Nat took the tiller as the sail filled, now that it was out in the main watercourse and picking up a light breeze. He let the boat sail a little further down the reaches of the creek before he answered again.

'Hello! Where are you?'

'In mud. Below the big house.'

The 'big house' was Trelogan. He'd never visited it but had seen it from a distance a number of times. It was the sort of building you couldn't fail to notice. It stood out on the hillside on a level clearing amongst the trees. As he passed the overhanging branches of the low oaks, trimmed like bobbed hair by the high spring tides, his boat rounded one of the many sedimentary rock faces that prevented the wooded escarpment from disappearing into the river. It marked the entrance to a wide, open creek. It accommodated a partial mudflat bordering a wetland area fed by yet another river, a river much larger than the stream at Tinners Creek where the adit lay and one that provided refuge for huge sea trout and salmon.

A spaniel, up to its belly in mud and in obvious distress, was not far in front of a young woman who was holding skirts above her knees. Her knee caps were just visible. As she tried to lift one leg the suction pulled the other leg further into the morass.

'What's your name?'

'Jenny.'

'Right Jenny, don't lift your legs. I've got some planks. I'll throw a rope but let me get parallel first, then we can get you aboard.'

'What about my dog?'

'I'll put one plank down, then another on top with the rope attached. You can drag the top one to you and lever yourself onto it. Pick the dog up when you get to him and let him walk the plank, so to speak,' he gave a laugh as he said it, which eased some of the tension.

'I daren't get any closer or I'll get stuck myself.'

Nat judged the sense of the current and location of the boat in the channel, dropped the sail and threw an anchor over the bow. The boat swung around under the influence of the river's flow to line up with the edge where water and mud met. He lifted a plank from the deck, balanced it on the gunnel and waited until the boat oscillated back towards the bank. As the hull reached its closest point to the bank, before beginning its swing back, he shot the plank forward. It landed almost in line with the dog and its owner, just feet from the dog. The latter sensed rescue and stopped struggling.

'Get ready to catch.' Nat waved the coiled mooring rope at the girl then tossed it across to her.

'I'm going to unhitch the rope now and tie it to the other plank.' It took only a few seconds to secure the plank and, again, balance the timber on the boat's edge.

'You ready?'

'Yes.'

'Right, pull when I say,' Nat judged the next swing towards the mud flat, 'take up the slack. Pull!'

The girl yanked on the plank. It shot over the side, landed on the plank below and slid up the surface of the one already in place. A few further pulls saw it conveniently in place just in front of her.

'Toss the rope forward and bear down on the plank with your hands. Now lift one leg free. That's it. Put your knee on the plank and lift the other leg out. You know what to do now.'

The girl, on her knees, worked her way along the plank until she was within reach of the dog. She grabbed the loose skin at the back of its neck, steadied herself and slowly pulled the animal towards her. As soon as it reached the plank she dragged it on in front of her. No longer distressed, it stood up, shook itself, jumped across onto the first plank and trotted towards the boat where Nat leant over and hauled it on board. The girl continued forward, dragging her long skirts through the mud either side. She eased herself across a foot or so of mud separating the two pieces of timber, got shakily to her feet and traversed the remaining distance without mishap.

'Stay there, where you are. Pick up the rope and pull the other plank up alongside and stand on it. Before you do, so's you know what you're doin', I'm goin' to ask you to lift the free one up and pass it to me so get the other in the best position before you do. That alright?'

'I think so. I'm not stupid.'

By this time a little group of people, hearing the ruckus from below, had appeared from the big house. They cheered as the girl reached the side of the boat and passed the plank to her rescuer before sliding her body across the threshold of the swinging vessel. Her cheeks flushed with embarrassment but she quickly composed herself with a pointed stare at her audience.

'I'm going to sluice down your dog. Can you stand him in the half barrel and hold him?' All this said as Nat picked up a pail from the deck of the boat, 'Then you can dangle your feet over the side and swill them off.'

The girl pulled her pet over to the barrel. It was a cask that had been cut length-wise and looked more like a bath suitable for washing an infant in. She lifted the dog and held him in place as Nat dipped the pail into the river. It took two or three bucketfuls to free the animal from the stinking ooze. The dog shivered in the half-butt. It wasn't cold, it was, in fact, a warm day but the animal up to his belly in river water already opaque with sediment and disturbed by his experience in the cloying mud, was nervous and uncertain as to what further treatment this stranger was going to mete out in surroundings it had never before encountered.

'Hold him still. Why hasn't he got a collar? It'd make life a lot easier for all of us if he did.'

'None of your business and I'd be grateful if you put us on the bank so I am no further obligated to you.'

'Oh, little Miss Fancy Pants are we? Suit yourself.'

At that moment the dog released itself from his mistress's grip, leapt from the butt onto the deck and shook himself. A shower of muddy water sprayed the two of them. The dog shot off and raced around the cramped deck at high speed. After completing three laps and a reversal of direction the dog was finally cornered in the stern. Both adults looked at each other and broke into fits of laughter.

'I'm sorry. I didn't mean to be ungrateful. No knowing how long I might have been stuck there if you hadn't come along. Nobody ever goes past to the end of the creek. Leastways, not whilst I've been about in the garden. Is it impertinent to ask why you were?'

'No! That's alright, I was just going to have a look at the old mine. My grandfather worked there as a miner and took me in one day to see a new vein of tin they discovered. It's up for sale, so I was curious to have a look for old times' sake so to speak.'

Something cautioned him not to mention his interest in possessing the site.

'Look, why don't you tie up over there on our jetty? I'm Jenny Bennallack, I teach at the local village school. You can come up to the house for a clean-up. My father will be pleased to thank you. What's your name?'

'Nat Hawken,' and as an afterthought, 'Nathaniel.'

'Pleased to meet you, Nat Hawken; very pleased and thank you,' she put out a grimy hand, which he took. The grip was gentle but the contact something else. Shaking hands was something you did without giving much attention to the fleeting, physical act. Not this time. The two paused suddenly conscious of the novelty of this forced and almost ridiculous, unplanned meeting. For the first time each viewed the other not as rescued and rescuer but as free agents of no particular qualifying status other than that of being male and female. This put a wholly fresh take on their encounter. Jenny, normally self-confident almost to the point of being arrogant, suddenly was at a loss as to how to react. Both fell quiet.

'I'll get the anchor up and put you off onto the jetty.'

Jenny smiled, 'You will come back to the house?'

'If you want me to.'

'Yes, it's the least I can do to thank you. I was getting pretty desperate.'

'Right then, can you grab the tiller whilst I free the anchor? Then steer her into mid-stream whilst I get the sail up.'

Nat pulled on the anchor rope. The boat traversed the slack, against the current and freed itself as the anchor disengaged from the silt below. He raised the sail and then took over the tiller. Within a couple of minutes they were at the jetty. Nat tossed a pair of sisal, rope fenders over the land side of the boat. Before he'd tied up, the dog had leapt onto the short spit of land created from a few facing blocks of granite, filled in with rubble and earth and grassed over a century or more, ago. A substantial iron ring, linked to an equally substantial bracket, provided a secure tethering point for the prow and a large wooden stump for a stern line. Nat jumped across the short gap and held out a hand to his passenger.

The dog, by now, was at the front entrance to the house and barking with the kind of excitement typical of its breed, dashing from one person to another of the small group of people – a gardener, an odd-job man and a domestic helper who all were non-resident - earlier watching the spectacle.

Nat and Jenny Bennallack made their way to the top of the rise where the gravel path ran onto a wide frontage. There the girl strode ahead to a man who advanced from the small crowd of onlookers. She took his hand and led him forward to meet Nat.

'Father, this is Nathaniel Hawken. I've invited him back so he can clean up. Nat, meet my father, Captain Bennallack.'

Nat put a hand out and was greeted with a grin and short but firm, hand shake.

'I see you've managed to stay cleaner than my daughter. Rex, that's the dog if you don't already know his name, will come to a sticky end if he's not careful. Not the first time he's nearly met with disaster.'

'Oh Dad, he's not that naughty.'

'Well, he got stuck on a ledge in the old mine last year. That's why we had to put the grating up. Can't seem to resist going down any hole or chasing a duck or two into the marsh. If you hadn't seen him this time he'd have not been missed for hours and would have drowned. Anyway, let's get Nat into the rod room. He can give himself a bit of a sponge-down there. You'll stop for a bite to eat after?'

Nat was not expecting so much hospitality but knew from the past that Capt. Bennallack's father owned the old mine and had a reputation for generosity to his miners, not common to many mine owners in the past. There was no reason why the son shouldn't be as hospitable.

'That's generous of you to offer, Captain but it would be putting your wife to added responsibility preparing for an extra mouth.'

'Not at all! Jenny will see to it with my housekeeper, Betty. My wife died some while ago. Come on, let's get you cleaned up.'

*

An early supper, for that was the time of day, was a meal of sea-trout cooked in a long, earthen-ware pot, garnished with oysters, also from the river, precooked in a pastis sauce.

'Nice little craft you have there. Rides nicely on her haunches so to speak. Unusual lines if I may say so.' The Captain nodded down towards a view of the jetty through the dining room window.

'I'm pleased with her. I ought to be. Built her in my spare time and wanted something compact and shallow enough to navigate the lesser creeks but large enough and stable enough to ride the seas outside the estuary.'

'Ah! I've got it now, you're part of the boatyard further down the estuary. Recognise her, seen her tied up off their slipway. Jenny says you were looking at the old mine. Odd sort of thing to do, someone of your metier. I've put it up for sale, did you know that?'

Nat now knew there would be no problem admitting to knowing it, 'Yes, that's why I went to have a look.'

'You're interested. I can tell by the way you're holding back.'

'Oh father, you're putting him on the spot.'

'No, it's fine. Your dad's right. I was wondering how suitably it would lend itself to conversion to a boat building business.'

'Well, that's a novel idea. I've visualised all kinds of scenarios it might lend itself to but that's the least likely one I would have put my money on. You think it has potential?'

'I do. It's got something most of the other yards don't have and that's water power. But there's another reason. I was in the lifeboat that capsized going out to that schooner a while back. Maybe you heard about it. I think I could design and build a boat of more reliable construction, more storm-worthy than I've seen elsewhere in my travels.'

'Look, I don't want to be rude but you know it has a reserve of a hundred and fifty guineas on it.'

'I do and you're wonderin' if I can afford that sort of money.'

'Well, there aren't many lads your age can scrape together fifty let alone a hundred and fifty.'

'Yes but there aren't many who've been to South America and done a bit of fruitful prospecting either. My grandfather, before he married, went to the Andes as a silver miner. Ever since hearing his stories about the wildness of the place I couldn't wait to finish my apprenticeship and work my passage across to see it all. I signed up at a mine soon after arriving, learnt some useful skills and then went off on my own to Brazil. Knew the geological indicators that might offer prospects of semi-precious or even precious stones and set about looking. Not very rewarding, initially, in terms of time spent. I kept myself solvent by doing a lot of joinery work on the side but I did find a lot of low grade gem stones and developed an instinct about terrain. Then I got one lucky find but it was a one-off. An emerald crystal that had formed in an amethyst pipe. By some freak of geology the pipe had leeched from a mineral-rich seam and a few grains of some element must have infused that single crystal to give it its colour. It was a freak chance. Anyway, I didn't know for certain if it was emerald, could have been olivine. Took it to a reliable merchant I had been dealing with and he gave me a fair price. The amethyst itself was of superior quality and quantity. That alone made a sizeable sum.'

'How d'you know what was a fair price?'

'I didn't. But I guessed that if I got a third of the price he was selling pendants of a similar carat for, then allowing for cutting and other costs I shouldn't be far out. And even I could tell it was a stone of particularly blemish-free clarity. Anyway, he was expecting further business from me and it wasn't in his interest to do me down. He also did trade with some European dealers and always welcomed premium grade stones.'

'Sounds exciting,' Jenny, who had been absorbed in Nat's account of his sojourn in the southern hemisphere, leant forward on the table, 'I would love to see South America. Why'd you come back?'

'I was missing the sea and being knee-deep in wood shavings.'

Captain Bennallack leant back and observed the other two oblivious to his interested gaze. He wasn't a fool as far as being a judge of character. Nat had piqued his interest. He had already sensed, in this short encounter, a shrewd but altruistic resoluteness on the part of Nat with his intention to improve the safety of his fellow crewmen going to the rescue of victims threatened by the sea. But more than this he could see the attraction the two younger adults were developing towards each other, each unaware it was happening to the other ... maybe. There was a pleasant innocence about Nat's typically, male openness that Jenny showed herself attracted to.

The captain made a snap decision, 'Look, I know it might seem premature on my part but how'd you fancy taking a chance on paying the reserve price and taking over the site? I'm pretty certain it would fetch more at auction, but not much more. It would please me to offer it at that figure. Although I'd be missing the chance of a higher bid, I wouldn't have to pay auctioneer's fees. We'd both be gaining. What'd you say?'

Nat looked at the other man, glanced sideways through the window at his side for a brief few seconds as he weighed up the proposal.

'That's a generous offer, sir. Since you've been fair with me, if I take it up and don't make a go of it, it could be put up for auction again. I take out my one fifty guineas and we split any profit.'

'Fair enough. I'll sort out the legal thing in the next few days. The title deeds have already been drawn up. You can have a look now at what's actually on the plan, if you want but are you expected back by anyone? It'll be dark in an hour or two.'

'My parents know I'm not out in the bay so won't be worried. Sometimes I tie up off the boatyard, sometimes off the rocks below their cottage.'

'So you're not married?' This was Jenny.

Nat grinned, 'I didn't say that. But no, I'm not. Had someone for a while but she wanted to marry and have babies as soon as I finished my apprenticeship. I know it sounds unkind but I always found her a bit docile and clinging so decided it was kinder to her to finish the relationship and let her find someone she would be happier with. That's when I went away. Stayed away four years, been back three.'

The expression on her face revealed a trace of the satisfaction she felt, reflecting her pleasure at hearing this.

'Anyway, I'd best be going. Thank you for supper. Can I come back sometime then to have a look at the title deeds for the mine?'

'That'll be fine. Why not tomorrow? Sunday here is a pretty leisurely affair. Look, why don't you come for lunch? We don't have visitors very often and I'm sure Jenny will be pleased to entertain you.'

Jenny looked none too disappointed at the suggestion, 'Yes, please come. I want to hear more about South America.'

With that Nat put his napkin on the table, stood and shook hands with the Captain.

'I'll see you down to the boat. Rex,' she addressed the dog which had sensed a chance to run out, 'you're a naughty boy. Stay!'

The dog recognised the tone of his owner's voice, stopped wagging his tail and slunk off behind a leather settee.

Nat bid good evening to the Captain and called into the kitchen to Betty, thanking her for a splendid meal. The two then left by the front door of the house and headed down to the quay. The tide that would have threatened the dog had now risen to cover the mud and the little cutter was now only a foot or so below the grassy tongue of the quay.

Nat jumped across to the deck, 'Thank you again for supper.'

At the boat Jenny unhitched the ropes as Nat lifted the boat hook from the planking. As the craft picked up on the turbulence caused by the protruding jetty, Nat steadied his balance and spoke to Jenny, 'What time should I turn up tomorrow?'

'Will you come up the road or by boat?'

'By boat.'

'We have lunch at one o' clock. Come early. Ten o' clock, ten thirty, doesn't matter, I'll show you around.'

'Tomorrow then,' he said as he shoved off from the edge of the quay. He crossed to the sail, raised it quickly then turned to watch, hand on tiller, as she stood observing his passage out into mid-stream. She stayed there until he was almost out of sight around the head of trees that marked the point known as Cask Point. One single wave of her hand marked her response to his signal as he pointed out a heron that took off from the shallows of the bank opposite, just before he disappeared. She stood for perhaps a minute, hands in the folds of her dress, before turning and traversing the length of the quay back to the path.

*

The trip back was quick but he didn't tie up at the mooring, instead he took Pol-Pen, the craft's name, outside the river mouth and headed towards Helford Passage. Just beyond Stack Point he slackened off the jib and coasted up to a cork marker sporting a short bamboo baton with a piece of orange cloth fluttering from its top. Grabbing the boat hook it took him, perhaps, eight seconds to trap and haul up a lobsterpot attached to the cork. It broke free of the water. He did a quick hitch round a cleat to secure the rope and leant back over the side to inspect the contents. There was movement. Three good sized lobsters and a large crab were trying to escape their funnelled, wicker trap. The dripping, bee-hived shaped pot was not heavy but the tarred, willow frame, now pretty full, took some effort to haul over the top of the boat's rail.

'You little beauties,' Nat voiced his pleasure at the sight of the catch dribbling its runnels of sea water over the deck. He dragged the half barrel towards one of the scuppers and tipped the muddy, river water out. Grabbing the bucket, he slung it over the side and sluiced out the barrel with sea water. A few more bucketfuls transformed the staved container into an aquarium.

The lobsters and crab were soon transferred to their new prison. A piece of fishing net completed the incarceration, fixed by copper nails round the edge of the oak cask. His job was not done. He looked towards the west. There was, perhaps, half an hour maybe three quarters of an hour of light left. Taking a line out of a small box he inspected the lead weight and the five hooks on the paternoster. White feathers were fixed to the hook's shanks by fine-threaded whipping. He tossed them over the side and felt a tug almost immediately. Mackerel were abundant in these waters. It was a time well before foreign factory ships would cruise the bay sucking up every living creature, large or small, that could swim or crawl on the sea bed - edible and inedible - forcing local trawlers to sail further afield for smaller and smaller catches.

Hauling in the line he slammed the catch down on the deck in one, swift, well-practised arc of movement. The stunned fish wriggled a bit. He took a wooden priest and clouted each over the head then hung them over the funnel of the lobster pot. A couple of quick jerks and they were freed from the hooks and lying ready bait for the next visitors to the wicker trap. Usually he liked to let them rot and stink before releasing them onto the sea bed. They were a more potent attraction for the lobsters when in a carrion state of decay but he was in a hurry and that would have to do. He dropped them over the side and watched until the pot was out of sight, always fascinated by its slow descent as it dropped in graceful, almost balletic, swirls into the green gloom.

A bit of a breeze was blowing up, adding white horses to the seascape. He tightened the sail with a few hauls on the jib rope and turned the boat towards Falmouth. His timing was good. Tied up and ashore in the little dory he used as a go-between, with still enough light to pick his way easily up the short, rocky rise to his parent's cottage, he dumped a small Hessian bag containing one of the lobsters on the kitchen table.

'There you are. Dinner! I'll just have some bread and cheese.' He nodded towards the sack as he greeted his mother.

'Crab or lobster?'

'Blue gentleman.'

His mother gave him a peck on the cheek, picked up a large pan and placed it, half-full of water, onto the compact, blackened, cast iron range heating the kitchen.

7

Nat was up early the next day. Sunday, as ever, was a day of quiet. Local boys weren't allowed out to play for one of two reasons. First, their parents were pillars of the Wesleyan chapel or, more usually, they weren't pillars but the father daren't antagonise the local employers who were. Employers, some of whom were hypocrites to a degree, engaging in all kinds of profitable commerce that saw competitors subjected to the most un-Christian of practices. So offspring were kept in until at least after lunch or dinner as the meal at that time of day was referred to. The Sabbath had to be observed. Sins of the previous six days had to be given a veneer of respectability.

He went outside to the tap in the yard, chest bare and sluiced his face with the cold water. Reaching up, he took a bar of carbolic soap from the top of the granite wall that separated the yard from the back lane. Soaking a flannel, he rubbed the not unpleasantly smelling block a few times across the dripping rag and washed himself under the arms and across his chest. It was late March but the sub-tropical shelter of the Falmouth estuary was at least four or five degrees warmer than most other parts of the county. A brisk towelling added colour to the goose pimples that had resisted the previous onslaught of cold water. He'd washed his hair the previous evening, occasioning curious glances from his mother. Back inside he took a soft linen shirt from a chest of drawers. The cream-coloured fabric accentuated the colour of a day or two's worth of dark growth on his face. Above all it accentuated his raw masculinity and he knew it. The soft linen was not at odds with the enigmatic, almost threatening aura his presence commanded. In fact, it gave contrast to his appearance in the way deep bass notes of an orchestra complement a dynamic passage in a Mozart piano concerto.

'You've got a maid at the end of a line, Nathaniel Hawken. You can't fool me.' His mother stood with hands on hips, head to one side and challenged him.

Nat just grinned, 'Shan't be here for dinner,' and that was all he was prepared to let out.

He lifted the double-breasted, three-quarter length, serge jacket off the back of the chair. A dark navy. It was one he had acquired in Lisbon on return from South America. Of a style favoured by captains of packet ships, it had tortoise shell buttons and a heavy, indented seam bordering the lapels.

'This, or the Guernsey?' He held up the oiled, woollen sweater in his other hand and tendered each garment in turn to his mother.

'I know what I would wear if I wanted to make an impression.'

'The jacket then!'

He slipped it on, gave his mother a peck on the cheek and grabbed the leather satchel from the well of the bow window overhanging the limpet and mussel covered slate of the harbour foreshore. He was down at the little dory within ten seconds. It was the first serious boat he'd made as an apprentice. He'd been allowed to keep it on the understanding that the cost of its materials was deducted from his stipend. It was bigger than it needed to be for the purpose merely as a go-between but not big enough to justify a mast and sail. Untying the craft, he pulled it into a narrow cleft covered in algae until it wedged itself between the faces of the v-shaped gully. Dropping the satchel into the bow, he steadied the hull against the wash of a large schooner passing seconds before. Then, with both hands on each side of the boat, he thrust off, feet swinging over the stern to land in the boat all in one, smooth move.

Picking up an oar he pushed off further. Legs astride, he located the oar in a recess on the edge of the stern timber. The first few sculling strokes took him across water still rippling from the passage of the larger boat. The steady rhythm of the blade as it went this way then that, parting the pulses of water and creating a trail of eddies, set him off thinking about the design of the saw mechanism at the waterwheel. It wasn't long before the rhythm aroused other thoughts, as his body began to respond to images of Jenny, fresh in his mind from yesterday. He stopped sculling and let the craft glide quietly for a few yards as this rather pleasing distraction diverted him from the dynamics of water-mill mechanics and boat propulsion. The dory rocked as another large ripple caught it side-on causing him to return to the task in hand and resume his journey to the larger of his two boats.

Pulling alongside Pol-Pen he shipped the oar, tossed the dory's painter over the top rail and followed it in one deft move to the deck. Safely hitched to the rear stern post, he gave the dory a tug and satisfied himself it was a safe distance from the stern. He checked the two lobsters and the crab and added a fresh bucket of sea water to the half cask. Lifting the long boat hook, lying along the scuppers, he snatched the mooring rope from the inky water and unhitched it from the iron buoy it was tethered to. Before the boat had chance to drift far he untied the dory, hitched its rope to the buoy in its stead and then set about unfurling the sail. A light breeze soon gave the canvas shape as he pulled the gaff up the mast. The pulleys - for he'd rigged the peak and throat points on the sail with an integrated system of ropes - gave the pleasing hiss greased, wooden wheels on steel centre pins do when reaching a certain speed of rotation. This rig enabled him to handle the boat without the need of a second pair of hands. Soon he was out in the main course of Carrick Roads, the wide estuary that made Falmouth one of three deepest, natural harbours in the world. He took pleasure in the feel of the deck under his feet and the sound of the rush of water as the hull separated the salty mix into the foaming, vee-shaped wake that caused little rowing boats to rock as he navigated between their mooring buoys before reaching mid-course.

The trim little craft scudded towards the inner reaches of the Fal. It was exhilarating to feel the force exerted on the rudder. The deck leaned over, perhaps just enough to prevent friction liberating the loose items on deck - the half barrel, a couple of wicker crab pots, a few coils of rope and other bits of marine equipment to be found on such a boat - from sliding down towards the lower of the two gunnels. He kept an occasional eye on the proximity of the bank or rather the trees lining the water's edge and thought about the time he had sailed up the lower reaches of the Amazon with the skipper of a small trading schooner.

*

Then, both banks were a good couple of leagues from mid-course. The foliage of the tropical trees might just as well have been clothed in the more temperate growth of European oaks and beech that lined his current course, for all that he could distinguish of their appearance at that distance. The skipper was making for a fairly new settlement. It had attracted a mixed bunch of speculators chancing their arm at brief forays into the tropical forest in search of mineral wealth, recently uncovered at a number of different locations thereabouts. He carried a mixed cargo, tools, provisions, cloth and other items that go to providing for the demands of frontier living.

Nat had already discovered a few low grade stones at a site further down the banks of this mighty, South American river and knew, in his bones, that the news filtering through suggested richer pickings further upstream. The little port, where he'd befriended the master of the trading vessel, would turn out to be paradise compared with what he would encounter at the isolated collection of huts clustering around the rickety, timber landing stage stilted over the slow-flowing Amazon. The schooner's captain had called Nat up to the wheel.

'Just 'round that rock, stickin' outa the trees, below that hill, is where we're landing. Here, take the glass.'

Ralph Jago handed Nat a telescope from the cabin roof in front of him. Only a keen pair of eyes would have made out the jetty unaided, it was so far off but the scuffed, leather-bound telescope magnified it to the point where he could see the vertical, rough-hewn piles supporting the thin-planked decking. Nat handed the optic back. He had only been two days sailing on the schooner but knew her timbers intimately. Jago had had his craft hauled up onto a stony patch of bank a few feet from the water's edge when Nat had arrived in the little Brazilian township downstream. It needed no explanation to know that the hull needed attention. Sensing an opportunity, Nat made his way to the tavern where the vessel's master was said to be looking for assistance.

'You Ralph Jago? The schooner yours?' The Cornishman greeted the only European in the tin-roofed bordello, for that, virtually, was what it was. He was seated at a table with a tin mug of rum in front of him looking as though he was anticipating but not hopeful of, company.

' 'es, an' if I'm not mistaken yer from civilised parts west of the Tamar, boy. I'm from Portscatho.' The master of the Greyhound, so-called because her sails were grey, stayed seated but extended a hand of welcome.

'You're right there. Falmouth. Nat Hawken,' the younger man put out a hand, 'I hear you're plannin' to go up river. I could do with passage.'

'Well, pull up that chair. Sam,' Jago called across to a mulatto who was trimming a green coconut, ' 'nother one of these.'

Sam picked a mug out from under the roughly sawn bar top and poured a generous measure of rum the colour of ripe chestnut. It was obvious Nat was expected to go and pick it up because Sam resumed chipping away at the huge nut he'd retrieved from the bar.

'You're best having some of this in de cup,' Sam stopped hacking and pointed to the nut with the machete, 'dat stuff not good for de kidneys man,' he said, tapping the tin with the flat of the blade.

Nat waited for the nut to be opened and some of the coconut water added to the rum. He made his way back to the table just as a heavy, tropical downpour released stinging globs of water onto the corrugated iron roof. The noise was like a meet for frustrated snare-drum enthusiasts. He put his mug down and sat side-on to his newly-found compatriot, waiting for the downpour to end.

'Your boat needs some attention. I've served my time as a shipwright. If I sort out the timbers for you will you give me passage up river?'

'Well, that's the best news I've had for months. Sure. Happy t'oblige.'

'I had a quick look at her. Most of her timbers are in good shape, at least where it matters most. But you've got a rogue plank just on the waterline. Take a knock somewhere?'

' 'es. Hit a log. Dark, didn't see it. Just lucky to be close to this place when it happened, so didn't ship much water gettin' here.'

'Well I reckon we can save most of the plank. Can cut out the splintered area and splice in a butt strap. You carry some ironware?'

'Got a bag full of coach screws. Different lengths and the tackle to do easy repair jobs.'

'That should do the trick. Look, there seems to be plenty of mahogany and other timber about. I reckon there must be a mill around, even out here, where we can get a patch.'

'I bin tradin' hereabouts two or three years, there's plenty of logs, rough hewn but you need wedges and an adze - which I got - to trim 'em to size.'

'Alright then. Reckon I can do the work in a day, two at most.'

'Fine! I guess you'll be happy to fill a hammock on board. I burn a slow rope with tar to keep the mosquitoes out of the cabin at night. Bleddy scourge! I 'ate 'em.'

'That'll suit me fine. I'll ask Sam about wood. The tavern keeper knows all the business round here, I'll be bound. I found a stone dealer through one at the last place I was prospectin.'

'You're into a bit of fossickin' then?'

''es. A lot of jewellers in the capitals, London, Paris, St Petersburg, are keen to buy any good quality stones. I've got a good trade goin' with a dealer who also cuts and mounts his own stones as well as sendin' gems across to London.'

'Soun's an interestin' business. That's one area I know only a bit about. Had the odd passenger who was into the game but you don't get much out of 'em. Tight-lipped mob, 'fraid of bein' robbed. Anyway, we can set about sortin' the boat out tomorrow.'

The two men took their time finishing the rum, waiting for the last of the downpour. Nat took the mugs back to the bar and questioned Sam about timber.

'Sam says there's a mill at the edge of the township, not far out. If we follow the track back alongside the tributary we'll hit the mill. They use the water to power their gear. I'm pretty sure they'll let me use their equipment if we sweeten the sawyer with a quid or two of tobacco as well. But Sam says we ought to take a pistol with us. It's a bit wild out there.'

'That's alright. I'm carrying a dozen Beretta, Stampede Old West Marshall, Colt-style for sale or trade. They're the short barrel model, three and a half inches. Got 'em from the Pietro Beretta manufactory direct. Tell you what, you sort the boat out I'll give you one at trade price and throw in a box of shells.'

'Suits me. I nearly bought a revolver the last place but the store wanted top dollar for it so I stowed the idea.'

'Right then, let's get back to the boat before it tips down again.'

8

Back on the boat Jago introduced Nat to his brother Tim and the only other crewman, Zeke Hunkin, a stocky mining engineer from Camborne. Zeke had hitched a lift for no other reason than to escape unemployment and seek better prospects in South America. He was typical of the Diaspora of Cornish miners who were scattered all over the globe, many of whom had gone to Australia, South Africa, Canada and anywhere there was a hole in the ground, at the bottom of which would be a pick and shovel.

'We'll have a bite t'eat before we check out the mill. Zeke's bin lucky with line and hook, got some tasty Amazon fish, ugly blighters but good eating. Don't know the name. The locals seem to survive well on 'em but let's find a space to dump your swag first.'

Nat was led to a tidy area in the hold not occupied by merchandise.

'I'll rig up a hammock 'cross those beams. You'll be more comfortable here than the fleapits ashore. That suit you?'

'First rate but I'll take a few measurements of the damaged area before we eat.'

Nat foraged in his swag and produced a notebook and pencil. He also retrieved a folding rule which he slipped into a slot stitched in the side of his trousers.

'I shouldn't be more than a few minutes over the side.'

'Right then. I'll see about gettin' some grub on the table.'

Meal over, Ralph Jago took Nat into a small, locked store room separate from the main hold. He hung the kerosene lamp he was carrying, on a hook, one of many fixed to the roof beams.

'Grab the rope and pull that out,' Ralph pointed to the thick rope handle attached to a chest under a shelf supporting spare canvas.

Nat obliged. The chest slid easily across pine decking smooth and polished from the numerous substances, tallow, rum and the like, that had been spilt over the years. Ralph groped around in a small, sunken cavity in the side of the hull above head level, took a key from the recess and unlocked the box. A piece of cloth, smelling of light machine oil, covered a pile of neatly laid out wrappings. Ralph lifted one out and put it on top of the folded sails.

'There's your pistol. See what you think.'

Nat unfolded the wrapping. The gun sported a mahogany grip and the film of oil on the metal parts glistened in the light of the kerosene lamp. A lot shorter than the one he'd previously been interested in, it felt more comfortable as well as lighter. Ralph reached down and felt about in the reaches below the remaining guns and produced a small carton of shells.

'Load her and we'll make our way to the timber mill. You don't want a machete as well do you?'

Nat shook his head, 'Got one in my swag.'

'Should've guessed. Can't do much explorin' fer stones without havin' to cut your way through bush sooner or later.'

Nat could see one or two handles of what were obviously machetes also occupying the chest. He wondered what else lay inside. He put the pistol back on the sail, cylinder broken open and perforated the seal on the box of ammunition with his thumbnail. It was a box that slid in a sleeve, much like a matchbox. Opening it just enough to expose a few shells, he turned it upside down and shook them into his hand. The shiny cartridges added noticeable weight to the pistol as he inserted them carefully into the bored housings of the cylinder. They looked like little miniature targets, the red, copper percussion centre like a small bull's eye within the brass rim. Snapping the chambers shut, he felt the difference in balance. The bullets added mass to the weapon, providing additional stability through the inertia the blunt, lead tips gave the gun. He sighted along the barrel and nodded to Jago, signalling his satisfaction with the pistol as at the same time he slipped it into his waistband.

'Right, I'm ready to hunt down some planks.'

Jago closed the lid, locked it and replaced the key. Nat picked up the carton of shells and slipped them into his pocket then knelt down and pushed the chest back into its hiding place. Back in the tiny saloon where they ate, Ralph took a pot out of one of the cabinets up against the hull wall.

'This time of day you'll be glad to put this on your skin.'

'Mosquito killer?'

'Well, dunno about that but seems to keep 'em away! I've seen too many bites go septic in this neck o' the woods. Gangrene'll set in and that's it, you've lost a leg or arm. Here, put it on. Won't hurt you. Camphor and tallow. Mixed it meself.'

Nat took the lid off a tin that originally sported a 1oz quid of chewing tobacco.

'Smells alright,' he commented as he took the piece of rag, used for applying the gunk, from the top of the mix. It didn't take them long to put on a protective coating and don the waxed canvas jackets that were common to most of the sea-going fraternity at that time.

'It'll be dark in three or four of hours. Let's get goin'.'

9

Tim and Zeke watched the other two disappear between the buildings fronting the waterside. The leaves had stopped dripping. Nat was used to the noises of tropical Brazil, like his companion who had traded at a few ports both sea-side and river-side over the last year or so. The two men passed the bordello, watched from the colonial style balcony by a mixed bunch of miners, gamblers and other bar flies as they headed out to the edge of the township. They picked up the track where it bordered the tributary. Away from the stone-paved reaches of the town, the track was rutted in places where the heavy buffalo carts had churned up the top layer, a soft, leafy mulch that rested on a firmer mix of gravel and stones deposited over centuries by the shifting banks of the river. They wore stout, sea-going boots. The oiled leather uppers were supple but stiff enough to stay well up on their calves. Both wore felt bush hats after the style of what was to become the famous, Australian, Akubra brand. The insects buzzed around them and although they could feel an occasional wing beat, none actually landed.

They walked for a while in silence until an armadillo ran across the track, 'Probably don't need to tell you but watch out for leprosy, 'specially don't eat armadillo meat.'

'Never tried it. Don't like the look of the stuff. I've heard you can get infected from it.'

' 'es and anybody sneezing with the disease.'

At the next bend the course of the river straightened out and a couple of hundred yards ahead they could see some buildings.

'That'll be it. Nearer than I expected.'

They had barely set eyes on it when some movement, followed by agitated barking, left them in no doubt the place was guarded. The dog was pulling on a length of chain. They could hear it rattling even from that distance. As they got closer they could see piles of logs stacked in front of an artificial creek dug into the bank. A wire cable, the permanent set in its coils giving it the appearance of a gigantic, helical spring, lay between creek and the door-less entrance to the sawmill. Its obvious use was for dragging logs from the water. There was no sound coming from the interior.

'Hallo! Hallo!' The dog barked louder and became frantic as Ralph shouted to anyone in range.

'Whadda d'you want?' A short, swarthy figure advanced from behind a stack of timber situated in a small clearing a few paces from the building. He covered them with a revolver and shouted something in Portuguese at the dog. It stopped its tirade, uttered a few frustrated yelps and growls and commenced pacing to and fro before squatting to watch from the roughly constructed shelter it obviously lived in.

'We wish you no harm. I own the schooner pulled up on the bank at Sao Pedro. Need some planking.'

The wary mill owner, at least they guessed it was his mill, seemingly reassured, put the pistol into a holster at his side and gave a shout. A trio of mixed blood came from behind the same stack bearing machetes. It was clear they were taking their cue from the sawyer and ambled across the clearing at a leisurely pace, eyeing the two white men with no sign of apprehension. A second man then appeared from inside the mill sporting a rifle, which he still carried in a defensive way across his body.

'I take the precaution. There are evil men about. We keep the eye open along the track.'

Nat was familiar with the dangers posed by the remoteness of any of these small towns from centres of more civilised settlements. There was a collective atmosphere of law observance but not enforced by any official judiciary. Occasional occurrences of robbery posed problems because it was easy for felons to melt into the wilder parts of the terrain and avoid being caught.

'Come through. This is my son Jorge, I am Luis de Sousa. You can have a look at what is already sawn. It will be easy to mark out and cut to your needs.'

The group went into the mill and were taken to an area in the rear where planks in different woods were stacked. A system of belts and pulley wheels was connected to a small number of items of wood-processing equipment. Nat lifted a plank or two and inspected the grain. He wandered about sizing up what was on show.

'You've got some good stuff. Just the right thickness. I was expecting to have to come back tomorrow after you'd had time to separate some planks from a fresh log but one of these'll do the job.'

It was no surprise. Numbers of boats on the rivers, on and off the Amazon, were in regular need of repair or modification at some time or another. Luis kept a stock of planks he knew would be in demand for just such a purpose.

'Right! Come and have coffee before you pick out your pieces, then we can sort out transport. You prefer to cut to size here?'

'That would save us a lot of trouble.'

There was one long plank, serving as a table, supported on a pair of trestles. A number of logs, end-on, provided seating. Luis' son went to a box-like structure hanging from a rope. A sticky ring of tar, where it entered the top of the box, protected the contents from invasion by ants. This swinging larder contained, amongst other things, a jar of molasses and a small, hessian sack of roasted coffee beans. Luis placed a pan of water over a brazier of smouldering off-cuts and put clean cups on the table. Jorge brought the sack and jar over to the table and tipped a measure of beans into a small grinder. Nat had seen similar coffee mills on some of the Breton fishing boats that occasionally put into one of the Penryn or Falmouth yards for repairs. They were universal. Compact items, furniture almost, common to Mediterranean households but a rare instance in most Cornish kitchens. Jorge turned the little handle and pulverised the kernels, giving the contents a bit of a shake every so often.

Whilst they waited for the pan of water to heat up, Nat and Ralph caught up on local news.

'You must be careful. There is no law where you are going. You should take someone with you if you are looking for stones.'

'I been thinkin' about that,' Ralph looked at Nat, 'why don't you take Zeke with you for a few days? Can spare him whilst I do trade and load up with other goods. He'll be glad to get off the bawt for a spell and he'll have some idea, then, whether he wants to stay or go back with me.'

'Good idea! Don't too much like the sound of what Luis has to say.'

At this point Jorge chipped in, 'If you want more company I will come with you. My father can manage here without me. Not a lot for five of us to do for a time. That alright?' He addressed his father.

'Yes. Not so many logs coming down river over the next few months. But don't come back empty-handed. Find some gold and stones to bring back.'

The pan started to bubble. Jorge poured some of the water into an earthenware jug, gave it a swirl around, let it stay in long enough to feel its warmth reach the outer glaze then tossed it out. He shook the coffee into the jug, dribbled hot water slowly into it and set it on the table to steep. The brew smelled good to the two visitors. They waited for a spell as the powdered beans released the residues concentrated by the roasting process. Jorge poured cups for everyone and pushed the jar of molasses along the plank. Everybody added a spoonful of the sticky sweetener and relished what was an exceedingly good brew.

'What sort of yield are we talkin' about.'

'Gold or stones?' Jorge held his cup at shoulder height away from his lips as he turned to face Nat.

'Well, either but I would prefer to look for gems. Unless you come across free nuggets, too much complication involved separating the yellow stuff from ore.'

'There have been some good finds of sapphire and emerald. Plenty of lesser stuff, like amethyst and rose quartz. You're going at a good time. News won't have reached the big cities yet, so there won't be a mob of chancers like there was in California. The gold being brought out here is alluvial, which means there must be content to extract from ore, if you can find the sources. That's why the time is right now, before the 'heavy brigade' get there with their dynamite and sluices, tearing up the forest and hillsides and making life difficult with their armed protection trying to muscle in on claims.'

'How'd you know this?'

'Went up to check out some stands of timber. Nobody feels threatened if a sawyer turns up to size up the timber growing in a newly opened-up camp, which is what it is, little more than a colony of tents. I stayed overnight on the boat that took me up. Safe enough on board. The prospectors were staying under canvas rigged up over a pole supported on Y posts. Some were lucky enough to own army issue and were sleeping four to a tent. But it is pretty rough livin'.'

'How many people?'

'Hard to gauge. Around the river bank perhaps twenty or thirty at dusk, with two or three making a living preparing food during the day but the ones inland, who knows? Can't be more than roughly the same number though. There's a pier, bamboo and log affair that comes out by a pair of small tributaries. Not very deep water. Can wade in it except that there are alligators to watch out for. The gold panners are mainly within close reach of the smaller streams further into the jungle. But the gem hunters are usually lookin' for hills with exposed rock faces. That's the dodgy thing though, can get lost if you don't take note of where you're trekking into. Two metres into the bush, off the track and you can't see where you've come from. Snakes? You've got to watch out. Don't reach up to a branch to steady yourself without seeing where you're putting your hand. Fer-de-lance are the worst, curled up on a limb. Caput,' Jorge drew a hand across his throat, 'if bit by one of those.'

Nat looked at Ralph, 'Sounds about what I'd expected, the prospectin' that is.'

'Right my friends, let's finish the coffee and sort out your needs.'

Notebook and rule in hand, Nat soon sorted out a couple of planks and marked one up for cutting there and then.

'We'll take the other as a spare. There's another of your planks, above the waterline, needs replacing sometime. Warped! Can't have been seasoned properly but not rotten; no immediate threat in calm waters.'

As Ralph had agreed to take Jorge upstream, Luis only charged his client a nominal fee for the timber and cutting.

It would be dark soon and as it wasn't far back to the boat the three decided to set off carrying the planks between them. Jorge went to an inner part of the building and returned with a small canvas swag and his rifle slung across his back. The group, assisted by two of the machete-carrying locals, hoisted the lengths of timber and trekked back to the vessel.

10

It was immediately apparent something unwelcome was going on around the boat. Two men, standing on the foreshore of the river bank, shielded from view of the settlement, were reaching up to a third who was handing down what was obviously one of Greyhound's spare sails. The canvas was bunched like a huge money bag, tied at the neck by a length of rope. Concentrating on the effort of releasing the rope and contents of the sail gently over the gunnel, the three did not notice the appearance of the group from the mill.

'Give me your rifle.' Ralph Jago held out his hand towards Jorge.

Jorge de Sousa, well acquainted with life in these regions, didn't need to be told the three at the boat were hostiles. Like Ralph, he knew a soft approach was not the form of greeting to be extended to unwelcome visitors of this kind. He slipped the weapon over his head and handed it to Ralph, simultaneously loading a cartridge from the magazine into the breech.

Ralph took careful aim at the ships bell and squeezed the trigger. The bullet hit the bell full on and shattered into a multitude of fragments. Detonation from the cartridge arrived at the boat before the resonant chime had faded and compounded the shock experienced by the unsuspecting thieves as some fragments of shrapnel buried themselves in the body of their criminal partner totally exposed on the open deck. The agonised scream he let out, more from pain rather than from injury, totally unnerved the other two who high-tailed it in the opposite direction and pushed off in a small boat pulled up a short distance downstream. The third man half clambered half jumped over the edge of the boat and landed badly as one foot, taking his whole weight, made contact with a sizeable rock. His shin bone fractured. The crack was heard by all five who must have been a good hundred paces away.

Ralph rushed to the boat and clambered aboard concerned for his brother, ignoring the injured thief moaning in pain and now retching and vomiting on his side. Aboard the boat no damage had been done but Tim Jago and Zeke Hunkin were tied up and lying in the hold on sacks.

'What took you so long?' Tim was obviously not overly traumatised by the experience, as he joked with his brother in the kind of harbour banter Portscatho fishermen or indeed any port-dwellers, were accustomed to. A welt where the rope had been was the only injury the two men suffered.

'What happened?'

'We were sorting out some tack in the galley when this half-breed appeared with a pistol. His two mates behind him. Took us into the hold and tied us up. That's about it.'

'Just as well we left when we did. This is Jorge. His father owns the sawmill. Comin' with us upstream,' Ralph nodded to the new 'passenger', 'but let's get out and sort out that bugger below before his mates come back for him.'

'I doubt they'll appear.' Jorge spoke as he stepped forward to shake hands with Tim and Zeke, 'We'll drag him up into the town. They'll more than likely hang him. People here don't take kindly to their possessions being stolen by force. Straight theivin' and they're lucky just to get away with a beating but violence means ...,' Jorge drew a hand across his throat.

'Where'd you learn your English, boy.' Zeke used the term boy as title accorded to any Cornishman, one to another. It didn't seem to offend their new Portuguese friend.

'I picked it up on English boats trading in logs. Done a number of trips up and down. Even been to the USA a few times, up as far as the boat yards on Mystic River. They like our mahogany.'

'Well, welcome aboard.'

Greetings done with, they moved above deck to sort out the injured number on the gravel bed. He'd dragged himself a little way up the slope. There was no bank as such, just a gentle gradient up to the beginnings of the small township. His way was blocked by a gathering of locals attracted by the shooting. He was not known locally and, according to one of the group, had come down river a short while earlier and wandered into the town with the other two. Without any pity, the man was grabbed by the wrists and pulled screaming in pain up to the first level piece of ground. A rope materialised from somewhere and was slung across the branch of tree overhanging a small, watery inlet. Two of the larger members of the population held him down as a noose was tied and put around his neck. Three or four men then took hold of the end of the rope. Without any show of mercy they dragged the choking, threshing form across the rough ground.

Even in the throes of agonising pain, caused by his now badly swollen leg, survival instinct took over. In a futile effort to ease the tension in the rope he used his arms in an attempt to sit upright. But the speed at which he was now being dragged forced him to raise his hands to his neck in a reflex action as his brain, deprived of oxygen, ceased to record these further stages of execution. Unconscious and now totally supported by the rope, he swung out over the pool of water and was raised another few feet to dangle and twist out of reach of any alligator chancing its luck.

This was the first time Nat had experienced such rough justice. He'd seen one or two fishermen beat up the odd boat thief but nothing compared with this. Jorge could see he was shaken by the whole event. He took him by the shoulder, partly in an act of kindness but also with a steely expression on his face and a kind of grim determination in his stance.

'This is frontier territory. You'll get used to it. That's why we had you covered when you came to the mill.'

'Yes,' Ralph nodded to him, 'I've seen worse along here. He was lucky not to be roasted first. The people depend on us traders and treat us like their own. They don't like traders interfered with. Come on, let's get back on board and have a hot grog. I'll give these one of the cheeses. It does to repay service of this kind, brutal though it be, with a sweetener.'

He beckoned one of the crowd, one he obviously knew from the past and told him to wait below the boat's rail whilst he went to fetch one of the hard cheeses. The muslin-wrapped prize was the size, roughly, of the crown of a Panama hat and was received with pleasure by the small crowd. It was taken to a tree stump, used as a mooring post. A machete was produced and the cheese, a rare treat for these tropical dwellers, divided up to the satisfaction and appreciation of the excited group.

The sail was dragged back on deck and its contents examined for damage. In their hurry to rob the boat and get away before risking detection, they had only collected a few articles from the galley and the main hold, some clothes and one of the small kegs of rum.

'Well, a large price to pay for so little profit. Come on, let's stow it and get some supper.'

Ralph waved to the few remaining at the stump and together the crew carried the retrieved spoil below deck just as the mosquitoes and tree frogs signalled the onset of tropical dusk.

They were up early the following morning, eating by lantern light. Nat got the tools ready on the open deck and got busy sawing, notching joints and shaping the main repair plank as soon as the sun appeared on the east-west stretch of water.

11

A pair of swans, taking off ahead of his boat, brought Nat out of his South American reverie. He was not far from the big house, in fact he could hear Rex barking. Slackening off the jib a fraction, he brought the little cutter across towards the next bend where the current had kept the river bed free from mud. Rounding the large oak overhanging the river, pendants of debris, left by the last spring tide, bobbed up and down as the bow wave passed under its canopy and lapped the bank. Jenny rose from the wooden mooring stump that had been her lookout and waved. The dog, catching sight of Pol-Pen, stopped barking, uncertain about the presence, yet again, of this floating bath tub. Not taking any chances he gave one woof and shot off back to the safety of the house.

Nat lowered the two fenders over the side and threw a line to Jenny. Within seconds he was ashore and tied up. They both started off for the house

'Wait a minute! Nearly forgot.'

Nat retraced his steps and jumped back on board. Picking up the bucket, he unfastened the net securing his catch and dumped them in.

Back on the jetty he held up the bigger lobster, 'A contribution to the pantry.'

'Betty will be delighted.'

Up at the house, greetings dispensed with, Jenny took Nat on a tour of the grounds. A horse whinnied.

'That's Skim. If he hears my voice he calls.'

'Why's he called Skim.'

'He got into the dairy, as a very young foal, where he was reared. There was a bath of milk from a cow with a new-born calf. Farmers often let the cream from the first 'take' thicken up on top of the milk. He got in, skimmed the ream off and was christened Skim by the farmer's daughter. We'd better go to see him. He'll keep on else.'

The stable was two-storey and long. A third was dedicated to its original purpose; the remainder had been partitioned off and had been converted into some kind of studio, laboratory and workshop.

'That is what father calls his 'hell hole'. He used to retreat there to get out of mother's way. I'll show you but let's see Skim first.'

The horse was in a well-proportioned cubicle allowing him to turn round or lie stretched out on a generous layer of straw. His face registered unmistakeable pleasure, ears forward and bright, black eyes, even in the half light, giving the impression of an intelligent and spirited character. The floor outside the cubicle was as clean as stables in a royal mews. Jenny went across to a chipped, enamel bowl perched on a hay dispenser fixed to one of the large wooden pillars supporting the mezzanine hay loft and used for everything, it seemed but hay. The horse stamped twice with one of its front legs as Jenny held out the carrot she had taken from the bowl.

'Certainly is a fine animal. I've never ridden a horse. Like them but never had an inclination to get on one.'

Jenny rubbed her pet's forehead, spoke a few affectionate words to it then turned towards Nat. She stood with one hand on the horse's neck stroking it slowly, stopped then seemed about to say something but half turned back to the horse, gave it a couple of pats and led Nat out.

'Let's see the rest of the place, 'I'll take you into father's side. He doesn't go there much these days.'

The door to the converted part of the stables was locked. It was a large, coaching double door that had had panes of glass let into the upper panels. She produced a key. It was not dark inside. He had expected it to be gloomy but the thick, granite walls had been given a white wash. This reflected light and contrasted with the darker interior of the part they had just left. There was a window opposite the door and this looked out onto an orchard separated from a field by a hawthorn and briar hedge.

'That's where I take Skim for a gallop.' She nodded in the direction of the window.

Nat wandered around the room. The original coachman's fireplace had been restructured and furnished with a small, rectangular, cast steel stove sitting on four Queen Anne, scrolled legs at each of its four corners. Two solid oak tables - one sporting various books, instruments and a drawing board, the other clear - were furnished with an assortment of chairs. A glass-enclosed book case showed the owner's interests. There were books on bridge design; mining; ingenious mechanisms and inventions; astronomy; a whole range of books with encyclopaedic titles. It was a treat for Nat to discover such a selection. With a hand on the door fastener he looked at Jenny as if to say, 'Can I have a look?'

She nodded. The smell of carefully curated leather bindings wafted into the room as he slid one of the books from its shelf, a book on schooner design.

'Now why would you pick that of all things?' Jenny gave a mock frown, then, smiling, set about clearing some space on the table for him to set the book. She sat and watched him absorbed in its contents as he stood leafing through a few pages in different sections, pausing here and there to examine, with greater interest, some detail of construction that caught his eye.

'Well I can't keep you sitting there while I indulge myself in this.' He put the book back, closed the door and watched as she slid off the chair.

'Anything else you want to see? Up there is where my father relaxes with a cigar and sometimes a brandy.' She pointed to a steep set of steps leading to a floor constructed from long, wide planks of sweet-smelling pine that spanned the whole plan of the coach house, 'Could have a look, we've plenty of time.'

The layout was an intriguing mix of club room comfort and lecture theatre formality. There was a collection of studded leather wing chairs, a sprinkling of low tables, a locked cabinet and a blackboard on one end wall. The sloping roof was insulated with strips of pine narrower than those on the floor. Because the area had no columns of the kind used below to support the floor they were standing on, the whole space felt much larger than its footprint at ground level. Ingeniously, the Captain had contrived to run the cast iron flue, from the stove downstairs, diagonally up and across one of the walls before it exited through the roof. It was obvious there would be a comfortable heat given out by its unshielded surface. Its extra length slowed the draught, ensuring coal, coke or seasoned timber would not burn too quickly.

'Father gets some of his cronies up here to listen to a talk given by one of them or some invited guest from outside the area. He's a big supporter of The Royal Cornwall Polytechnic in town but now and again likes the independence of being able to organise his own events here. Means he can select an audience and subject of his own choosing.'

Nat sat on one of the wing chairs, 'Comfortable!' he looked around the room, 'I can see why your father likes to retreat here.'

'He's got it exactly to his liking. If you think that's comfort see what he's got the other end.'

She reached for his hand and led him out of the chair over to a curtained recess at the opposite end. Pulling aside the heavy curtain she invited him to follow through. A wash basin and jug stood on a small dresser at the foot end of a large, single bed shoved side-on to the wall. Still holding his hand, she sat on the edge of the bed and pulled him down to sit by her. She kissed him on the cheek then got up quickly.

Slightly taken aback but not totally surprised by this turn of events, he followed her back into the room and, gently, caught her by the arm, turning her towards him. They stared at each other for little more than two seconds before giving way to a passionate embrace. They kissed, savouring the soft, sensual pleasure of lips on lips, each enjoying the frisson of long-dormant emotions.

She smiled as she held him away at arm's length, pleased at the expression of pleasure on his face. They embraced and kissed once more before she released herself and led him to the stairs.

'Let's see the garden.'

The two made their way back down, Nat leading. At the bottom he waited and lifted Jenny off the last step. She wrapped her arms about his neck, both enjoying this last opportunity for contact before going to lunch.

Outside the sun had penetrated what only fifteen minutes earlier had been shadow. There was a definite hint of spring arriving at last. The walled garden which, by its very nature, had been sheltered from some fierce gales blowing in from the south west, reflected the relief other parts of the estate had not enjoyed. Cordon fruit trees were displaying buds and there were plots given over to cultivation of crops that on open land would be at least three or four weeks behind in growth. They spent a few minutes wandering about. She tidied up a few areas as they passed – raspberry canes that needed pushing back under a strand of wire freeing the path from obstruction; bamboo canes that had fallen from a wall against which they had been stacked and other trivial but unwanted infractions that irritate a serious gardener.

'Better make our way back. Betty will be serving lunch in a while and I'm sure we'll be offered a glass of something first.'

12

You like my retreat then, Jenny tells me?' The older man pointed his pipe in the direction of the stables.

'Yes Captain. First rate collection of books too. I had a look at one, the volume on schooner construction.'

'That was written by a naval constructor not far from here, a Devonport man. Spent time in the States, Mystic River, and brought back some ideas when he returned. Spot anything of interest?'

'I did as a matter of fact. There was a section on prow design, a sprung, if that's the way to put it, stem that'll push its way through light pack ice without serious damage to the strakes. Never seen one here even though we get the odd Newfoundlander putting in from time to time and, whilst we don't get ice, the lifeboats do get a hammering from the waves more than the fishing boats because they don't put out when it's bad.'

'Let's get into the library, more comfortable. I still keep the library here in the main house as it's always been. The books in the coach house are mainly technical and Jenny likes to use the room here for a bit of sewing as well as reading, allows us to get out of each other's way. She'll be in to let us know when lunch is ready. We can have a drink and I'll get out the deeds of the mine to look over.'

Nat followed. The room was L-shaped, overlooked the creek and sported a reference area where book cases were set into the 'blind' section around a mahogany table. James Bennallack walked into the shadowy area enclosed by three walls of books. The shelves in the middle section rested on built-in cabinets. Keys were in the doors and one of them was glass-fronted, revealing a sherry decanter and glasses. The captain opened this and an adjacent solid door. From the latter he retrieved a file of documents and placed them on the table, then bent to bring out the decanter and two glasses.

'It's actually a Madeira, not sherry,' he lifted the glass stopper and sniffed the contents, 'I prefer it to sweet sherry. The French make an aperitif - vin de noix - not dissimilar in taste but made from red wine, rosé wine, pure alcohol and walnuts. Stimulates the appetite.'

He filled the glasses to within half an inch of the lip and passed one to Nat.

'Well lad, here's to a fruitful future - in more ways than one!'

Nat raised his glass in response puzzled by the 'more ways than one'. It must have shown on his face.

'I've a ... ,' James Bennallack grinned, 'I've noticed a sudden change in my daughter's mien in the last forty eight hours. You two are poor at concealing your feelings for each other. But none of my business!'

Nat blushed, 'I don't know what to say.'

'Don't say anything. I'm pleased. The son from the boatyard was paying attention to her but she wasn't impressed. I must say the one time he turned up here, unannounced, I wasn't particularly charmed either. But of course, you will know him.'

'Only too well! He's my cousin. I keep the peace for my uncle and mother's sake but under the surface we don't get on.'

The Captain nodded, 'Families! Less said the better. Let's have a quick glance at the deeds, before we eat. We can look more closely after lunch.'

The older man sat and gestured for Nat to take the seat at his side. He selected one file, tied like the others with pink tape; laid the unwanted files aside and opened a folder with the single title 'Mine'. There were parcels of land, delineated in red, some contiguous with each other; others were juxtaposed in various solitary positions further from the main house. Even though the room was damp-free the map smelt of age and had lost its original clean, light cream surface. Tiny rust marks peppered its surface, ingrained from decades of unchecked, chemical action from salts in the paper. James Bennallack spread the chart out, pushing the other documents across to the centre of the mahogany table. The map contrasted sharply with the patina of the highly polished wood.

'There it is! That's what you're letting yourself in for.'

Nat leant over the document. He felt a surge of excitement as he gazed at what would be, for the first time in his life, ownership of an asset that meant more than just the sum total of gorse, granite and bracken that characterised the creek. This was an ancient ground that had yielded up treasure long before the Christians had built their hermitages and then their churches and later their Wesleyan chapels. He was neither superstitious nor religious but he did have an inner respect for what might be explained as a spiritual affinity for 'The Land of Saints', by which Cornwall was known. Like a lot of Cornish before him, he had seen a large part of the world few others had ventured to risk visiting. Like most of them he had gradually lost the parochial mindset that infects people who never move from their comfort zone. People encountered anywhere, in any tribal or nationalistic group.

Nat recognised the stamping house immediately.

'What's that?' He pointed to an outline situated further down towards the water's edge. It was obviously another building.

'It's a small foundry. Didn't you know? Walls are still up, roof intact as far as I know but it's screened by quarter of a century's growth of willow and other trees. It was busy at one time turning out castings for the navy, back when Boney was a threat. It's not far from the quay, what's left of it. Used to be a track across to it. Both for shipping metal in and for shipping castings out.'

'Could it be brought back to life?'

'Depends on whether you're prepared to spend money on it. There's still some casting sand and mould boxes there and the roof is sound. The roof cross-beams are pretty substantial. There is an overhead track, single rail, for shifting all sorts of equipment and castings about.

The longer building there, between the mine and the foundry, is a pair of miners' cottages.'

'Yes, I saw those.'

'Why'd the foundry stop working?'

James Bennallack pursed his lips, 'Dunno really. Some believe it was the foundry at Charlestown, owned by the China clay industry around St Austell. They expanded their premises and started taking in work from other clients. Brunel's railway made coal delivery cheaper than it could be bought for here and so, gradually, the foundry fell idle. You think there's potential there?'

'Maybe. I know my uncle says the castings he's buying for fitting out his boats are costly. There's certainly a demand now that would keep a few men in work if the costs are pitched right. Bronze propellers particularly. You'll know that they last longer than steel and lower casting temperatures make for lower costs. But it's still a bit of a novelty for small craft like we build. Still a big demand for sail. Can't see that changing for a while, 'specially round here. But there's always a market for small bespoke castings on pleasure craft built for rich clients.'

'You mentioned a dam. Where'd you propose to put it?'

'Not sure. I thought there,' Nat pointed to a spot where the lane narrowed between a V-shaped cutting, 'but I need access for a horse and dray. That means digging out a track above or, at least, clearing the bushes growing alongside.'

'You've got plenty'a ballast to construct a substantial gravity dam. Wouldn't need to be more than five or six feet high. It would hold back enough water to give about twenty foot of head if the turbine's sited far enough below, enough to run a good sized turbine generator if you built it there,' the Captain tapped the plan, 'I take it you'd want to house the turbine in or alongside the stamping house?'

'Not sure. Depends on the noise it'll make. A small bunker outside on the same wall as the waterwheel will make it easy to divert the outflow into the big wheel race. Any extra flow of water can only be good.'

'Good point. I think this'll be a profitable venture. Got a feelin' about it. Don't want to cramp your style but am willin' to put some money into it if you need that kind of assistance.'

'Well sir,' Nat got no further.

'Look, my friends call me Jim. That's what I prefer.'

'Yes sir,' they both laughed, 'Jim then. What I was going to say was I want to get as much done off my own back first. Then when I can see where I'm heading, so to speak, I'll start considering what assistance I need to take it onward.'

'Well, keep it at the back of your mind.'

'Hello you two. Lunch ready in five minutes.' Jenny called from the door.

'Right! We're ready,' James Bennallack put the title deeds back into the folder, 'I think you've seen all you need for now. Get Jenny to take you up there after lunch. You can check out the foundry then. There's a good path, in fact it's more of a lane, up to the mine from the house. She takes the horse or dog up that way from time to time. Anyway, let's eat!'

13

Jenny Bennallack helped Betty serve the food whilst James Bennallack sat quietly finishing the glass of Madeira he'd brought from the library. The housekeeper also joined them at the table. There was little conversation during the early stages. Nat was preoccupied with different images of the terrain at the creek, going through his mind. At one stage of the meal, when the housekeeper was fetching a dish from the kitchen, Nat suggested that his purchase of the mine be kept secret.

'I intend to use the evenings and weekends to clear the site. I don't want my cousin to know. Don't trust him, sorry to say.'

'You can speak in front of all of us. It won't go any further. Betty's family, almost, was a friend of my late wife and came to help out when we had guests. Her husband was lost at sea. I asked her if she would take on the job of housekeeper some time after. A great comfort to Jenny when Antonia, my wife, died. Almost a surrogate mother, in fact better than that – a friend.'

Jenny nodded and then returned to the subject of the site. 'I'll help you clear it.'

'Good idea. Get her away from the house,' the Captain grinned.

'Let's go to have a look after lunch. You can tell me more about your time in South America, on the way.'

'I'm glad you said that. Your father thought you might show me the way up from the house.'

'It's a good quarter of a mile but pretty level going, the lane drops down above the stamping house. I take Skim up sometimes but more often walk with the dog. It's a good track.'

'Yes', the Captain nodded, 'somebody kept it in good fettle over the years. The track benefits from a slate and, in places, granite surface strata where they took the trouble to make a cutting in a place or two. So I reckon it's seen some traffic in its time.'

'Father reckons it might have been used for smuggling. Most of the revenue men expected cargo to be landed in coves but we know some made its way up the estuary, deep into the county, on small cutters landing in creeks like this one.'

'Old Bill Tangye used to let a word or two out. Did a few jobs for me around the estate every so often. That jetty down there has seen a few lanterns in its time, he's told me. He's still goin' strong, well over eighty. I send Betty with a basket of saffron buns from time to time and a bottle of brandy at Christmas. Anyway get yourself up to the mine after this and have another scout around. Check out the foundry. Jenny, there's a key in the key box, big steel thing. Don't know if the door's still hangin' on its hinges, was last time I looked but you'd better take it in case.'

*

The two set off after lunch. Nat recounted his adventures on the Amazon up until the time of the robbery on the Greyhound.

'I'll tell you the rest on the way back.'

14

'Father said the foundry was very close to the quay. Let's get down there and look for the track.'

The two made their way down to the old jetty.

'I don't know why I didn't spot the track when I was here. It's pretty obvious when you know.'

'With your mind on rebuilding the jetty it would be easy to miss.'

The track was not badly overgrown but, nonetheless, willow and sycamore screened the building effectively from casual view. They weaved between the trunks. The foundry stood on a level piece of ground, its roof much higher than that of the stamping house. There was no chimney. Casting took place in a couple of small furnaces that vented their toxic gases to atmosphere in the darkened recesses of a secondary upper roof, reminiscent of the architecture of a whisky distillery. The huge, arched portal sported two solid elm doors with a locked, access door of normal proportions, let into one of the halves. Jenny tried the key in the lock. The mechanism moved with a smooth toggling action against the resistance of some hidden leaf spring guarding the tongue. Stepping across the raised sill onto the granite flagstones of the foundry floor they could see the interior clearly in the light from small-paned windows high up in the walls. A bird flew out through the vertical struts supporting the upper roof. This signalled a general exodus of what turned out to be pigeons which had colonised the cross beams.

Nat drew the bolts securing the top and bottom of each door. The hinges, as must have been the lock, had been liberally greased and the big doors swung inwards with hardly any sound. There were small bays with various grades of casting sand; one sported a small heap of naval bronze ingots, another wooden boxes of scrap metal of indeterminate, metallurgical provenance. The latter was probably a feeder for the chief founder who would toss, perhaps, a small lump of zinc or antimony into the melt to reinforce a particular property of the finished casting.

Jenny, mature in a way that girls are compared with boys of the same age, smiled to herself as she observed his obvious pleasure at the various discoveries he was making. The two explored the rest of the floor area. Unusually, the premises possessed a large-bed lathe that was driven by a system of multiplying pulley belts that appeared to take its power from a shaft through one of the walls.

'There must be a waterwheel the other side. I did see a channel and sluice gate up near the stamping house. Didn't think much of it at the time. This must have been where it was headed for. Let's take a look.'

Outside, a tangle of yet more willow guarded a small race. A rusting, steel waterwheel, obviously designed for speed rather than great power and much smaller in diameter than the wooden one, looked as though it might still function, given a little attention.

'I reckon this could be put to good use again. There's a demand for castings since these new petrol engines have started appearing in boats, 'specially for bronze propellers.'

'Is that what you want to do? Put a motor on board?'

'Well, I know the propeller driven jobs'll get to a boat in trouble faster than a dozen men pulling their guts out rowing. I've got plenty of ideas to try out if I get the chance.'

Nat climbed down into the race and removed dead leaves and other debris choking the lower vanes. Once cleared he stood and pulled on the top of the wheel. It moved. It moved so easily, in fact, that he almost fell. Having expected to meet with a lot of resistance he was taken by surprise at the fluid movement of the wheel and its system of connected pulleys and axles.

Nat climbed out, 'That's better than I expected but there'll be some work to do clearing that lot,' he nodded in the direction of the channel.

'Let's finish looking around inside.'

Back in the building they checked the various corners, cupboards and shelves. There were tamping tools for the casting boxes; jugs for whetting sand too dry to cohere; a multitude of engineers' tools that were obviously required by the lathe: steel cutting tools neatly laid out on a shelf; measuring callipers, depth gauges hanging on a board fixed to the wall; a vernier height gauge still in place on a cast steel, marking-out table - much of it totally meaningless to Jenny. One more piece of machinery complemented the equipment. Behind a partition they discovered a large pillar drill. A selection of drill bits stood upright in a rack and, on a wooden dais set into a corner, out of the way, wooden patterns were laid out carefully, each sporting a label identifying its purpose and part number.

'God, this is a bonus.'

Jenny smiled again at his pleasure in discovering the various items positioned around the furnaces.

'All it needs is a few belts replacing and proper lighting and we've got the makings of a machine shop as well as a foundry. Let's get up on the walkway,' Nat looked up at the mezzanine landings going around three of the walls.

Ten feet above the floor they could see better the layout and could imagine the activity that would have taken place below. Each mentally pictured the glow of a furnace; the sparks as molten metal was discharged into the top half of the mould; the smoke and steam driven from the risers; the clink of iron handling-cradles as men in leather aprons sweated against the heat as the crucibles discharged their fluid content. At that height they were level with the rail holding the primitive, travelling, crane head. It was a simple affair. A chain loop raised or lowered another chain, with a solid-looking hook attached to it, through a system of reduction gears.

'That looks substantial enough to raise an elephant. Come on, let's get down. I've seen enough.'

The two reached the floor, both encouraged by what they'd seen and exhilarated by the prospects of an exciting future and a profitable relationship.

'Shall we have a look at the mine?'

'If you like but we haven't got a lantern.'

'Well we don't need to go in far. I haven't seen it for a long time. Now that I know you want to build boats in it I'd like to see it and imagine you in place working. Then we can go back and you can tell me the rest of the South American adventure.'

The two took a brief look around and turned back on the track to the house.

*

'So what happened at the settlement?'

'When we arrived Jorge made contact with some loggers he knew. Most of the action seemed to be invested in alluvial gold and there seemed to be as much demand for craftsmen as there was enthusiasm for prospecting. I could have spent my time building sluices and other construction work. Skills in boatbuilding lend themselves to any number of different jobs. Anyway, to get back to the emerald, that is quite a story. Zeke Hunkin was eager to get off the boat and into the ground, so to speak. Jorge decided to join a group of Portuguese so we parted company.

We set off along a track up to the hill. Didn't carry much with us, machete each, revolver, small hammer-pick and a day's provisions in a canvas bag. It got though, that we found it easier to build shelter at one particular spot rather than keep trekking to and fro daily from the boat. Used a piece of canvas over a branch and rigged up a couple of makeshift hammocks. Had to watch out for snakes. Fer-de-lance everywhere, although they scurry away if they feel the ground vibrate but those were the least of our problem. The ones curled up on branches were the ones to watch out for. Most of the bites around the camp were from out of the trees.

It was about the third week I was hammering at a piece of alluvial rock above a small tributary. Bit of a gorge, although that's an exaggeration since the sides were a slope you could just about clamber up on all fours. A large chunk fell away and tumbled down the slope into the river below. Zeke turned at the noise, he was a few yards away having a go at a quartz vein hoping to find gold. He shouted, 'There's somethin' in that rock. I seen it glitter.'

I'd seen it too, so I slid down after it. Water wasn't deep. Managed to drag it to a bit of a beach, if you can call it that and found it had a cavity. Opened it right up, found the amethyst inside and a bit of a quartz run. That's where the emerald was, sandwiched between quartz and slatey stone. I knew right away it was a beauty, just a bit bigger than a thrush's egg. It must have been our lucky day, just one of those coincidences, because Zeke let out a whoop just after. He'd uncovered a small nugget, reckoned it was worth three or four month's wages.

'We don't tell anybody about this,' he yelled out. He didn't need to tell me that. I certainly wasn't going to broadcast it to the world. After our experience with the thieves at the Greyhound I was wary and suspicious of anyone at the settlement. Anyway, I chipped away any surplus rock and carried the find back to the boat, well before nightfall.'

Jenny stayed quiet as they continued along the track, giving Nat's hand a squeeze every so often or uttered a brief 'go-on' as he looked to see if she was still interested.

'We stayed in the same area for a few more days. Then, when we'd exhausted all the promising outcrops with the slightest trace of quartz, we upped camp and moved further inland. Zeke had found a further one or two smaller nodules of gold but we reckoned that was about all we were going to get from the hill, after that. Inland we went down to the river course. Both of us had packed pans and Zeke showed me how to pan gold from river gravel. Took our boots off and just got on with it. Got a few grains but reckon it had been worked already. So we moved into a side stream in some dense jungle, thinking it was worth a try. A bit better but in the end decided we were wasting our time. I think we each recovered another three or four months of wages all told. Ralph Jago was only staying for a few weeks trading his goods so we called it a day; left our tarpaulin and hammocks to a couple of Cornish miners we met and went back to the boat. Both of us had had enough of the mosquitoes and the lack of dry clothing. I gave Ralph Jago enough of my share to make a decent sized gold ring.'

'What did you have for food?'

'River fish and crayfish and a few yams. The yams were pretty stringy but when they're roasted in embers they soften up a bit. Ralph let us have a small ration of flour. We eked that out each day. Made a short length of dough, coiled it round a stick and baked it over the same embers.'

'And the emerald, you got a good price for the emerald?'

'A really good price but I had to wait 'til I got back to the big town in Brazil. That's about it. There was only one time we encountered trouble, the last day. Zeke was ahead of me going back on the main track, just out of sight. Couple of prospectors, I'd seen 'em around, had come out of the trees with staves. As I came around the corner I could see Zeke backing up. They hadn't reckoned on me being armed. I always kept the revolver in my bag, out of sight. Confrontation a second time in little more than a month, I was beginning to wonder if every other character was a criminal. Anyway I got the gun out and fired in the air. Seeing I wasn't going to aim at them they just leapt back into the bush and disappeared. That was it!

We'd already decided to finish and go back with Ralph. That episode clinched it.'

'Did you see any snakes?'

'Only once. Dropped out of a tree in front of me.'

'Could have bitten you.'

'No! It had the tail and back legs of a lizard sticking out of its mouth. Reckon it needed to be on the ground to swallow it.'

'Horrible!'

Their conversation was interrupted as Rex, having heard their approach, appeared from somewhere in the garden where he'd been foraging. He dashed up and danced around them, yelping and barking.

'I take it for granted you'll stay for tea?'

'Well, not if it's going to be trouble to anyone.'

'I think father is expecting you to and Betty seems to be pleased to feed you up.'

'That settles it then. She's a good cook; don't want to disappoint her.'

'Disappointment my ass. You're just a pig.'

'Not very lady-like. Where'd you learn that kind of language?'

'Old Bill Tangye, if you must know. If it's good enough for a man it's good enough for a woman.'

'Alright - woman!'

She gave him a shove, which got the dog even more excited. They linked arms and went through the garden into the house.

*

'So what do you make of the foundry?'

'Well sir,' Nat still found it difficult to call the Captain Jim, 'I think that could generate some income and provide work for a few people.'

'That's good. Thought you'd find it interesting. So I'll get the notary prepare the paperwork accompanying the deeds and we should be able to transact the deal in the next week or so. In the meantime, feel free to carry out improvements.'

'Thank you. I'll probably get going on it this week. Can't wait.'

15

On the Monday, at the boatyard, Nat was preoccupied fielding ideas that flashed into his mind. Ideas that had multiplied in number since the dream had become reality. He reckoned to keep working there until either momentum forced him to engage full time at the creek or relationships at the boatyard soured once his cousin knew of the enterprise. His uncle wasn't a fool. In Nat's mind he must have realised that his son lacked the drive and demonstrated few of the skills that went into the making of a successful businessman. But that would not debar him from taking over when Victor decided to retire. Jake had no eye for form nor instinct for the finer points of design. Nat knew damned well patience with his cousin would give out sooner or later over some issue of practice related to construction. A shout from the recesses of the timber store made him realise he'd been so engrossed in his thoughts that he'd stopped planing the bilge stringer he'd been working on.

'The old man's having a heart attack'. It was Sam Karslake, one of the more skilled carpenters in the workforce. Sam marked out the templates and was capable of working out the incremental adjustments to be made to the planking at each level above and below the waterline. He or Nat gave shape to the profiles of the boats that left the yard. Nat dropped the plane onto the bench and hurried through shavings, ankle deep, to the back of the shed. Victor Lewis was slumped over a heavy bulk of timber he and Sam had been lifting. He was conscious but wincing in pain with each intake of breath.

'Let's get him flat on that door,' Nat pointed to the door lying propped against the shed wall, hinges still attached but long since ceasing to function as a piece of furniture, 'hold him in place while I get a pair of trestles.'

Nat placed the trestles alongside his uncle, laid the door across and kicked one of the A-shaped supports into a more stable position on the earthen floor. With help from another workman the three men manoeuvred the old man onto the door.

'Send the boy for doctor Trueman and he might as well try the Chisel and Adze to see if my cousin is there,' Nat addressed Sam. The 'boy' was the apprentice. That done, the three held a council of war, so to speak, after one of them had laid a coat over their employer. They went into the main part of the boat house where, whilst out of ear shot, they could still keep Vic, as they called him, in view. As ever, Jake Lewis had taken himself off earlier to one of the taverns in Falmouth on the pretext of drumming up business or some other barely plausible excuse.

'He's not going to be able to work for a while, if at all so what's next?'

'We've got work for the next six or seven months and these days he doesn't make much more of an input than Jake so I reckon we carry on as usual for the time being. Can't do much else,' said Nat.

'That's alright,' this was Sam speaking, 'but I've got mouths to feed and if I know Jake, we won't be seeing our wages on time every week. Might have to look elsewhere for a job.'

'I'll see to that. The bank manager is secretary and treasurer for the lifeboat crew. He's a ... ,' Nat chose his words carefully, 'he's a ... familiar with Jake's commitment to the business.'

The third man laughed at this irony, 'There's plenty'a work to be had round here. Shan't bother my head about it too much and I don't think you need to either. The docks are building larger dry docks to take on some of the big liners. I know that for a fact. They'll need carpenters as well as steel men.'

Sam nodded to Nat, a gesture more of gratitude rather than assent, 'Yes, if we hadn't got you here we'd have been in a bit of a mess long before now.'

'I'm goin' to brew up a tea. It'll be a while before the doctor gets here.'

Victor Lewis lay motionless, initially afraid to move. Whilst the men were drinking their tea his colour began to return to normal and he started to fidget with discomfort on the hard, panelled door.

Victor raised his head, 'Get me up and give me a mug.'

'No! I reckon you're safer lyin' flat. Wait 'til the doc gets here to see what he says. You could have another attack. Don't know much about it but I know they say to rest.'

Victor stopped agitating, sighed and dropped his head back onto his temporary stretcher. The arrival of the doctor gave some focus to the enforced inactivity. Pulse taken; stethoscope examination; temperature read, the old man - who was in his early sixties and appeared, outwardly, in good health - was eventually loaded onto a flat bed cart and transferred to home and an alarmed wife. The son could not be located and would only have been a hindrance anyway - sober or inebriate. Back at the boatyard Nat took charge. As nephew he was regarded as a controlling party until Jake was to arrive.

'Right, I don't think it's any secret to the rest of you, from what you must have observed, that Jake and I are not comfortable with each other.'

Sam laughed, 'Don't think any of us are comfortable, as you put it, with his lordship,' the latter said with some dissonance.

'Well, as long as we get the present contracts fulfilled we should be in paid work for at least half the year. After that ... ,' Nat let the words trail off.

'I can't see him coming back and if his boy is in charge, I don't relish the idea of working for that bugger for the rest of my life.' Sam, again, expressed his misgivings in no uncertain terms.

'Don't worry about that for now. I happen to know there are opportunities in the offing that'll see us through to further contracts. Shan't say any more. So don't ask me and don't say anything to anyone, particularly Jake and Victor. They know nothing about it.'

Sam Karslake looked on the point of challenging Nat but then thought better of it. Nat knew the two men well enough to know he could say that much without revealing anything about his new venture and that they in turn would respect his request. The apprentice, David Tresize, was a quiet lad who looked up to Nat. It was his father, Bill, who served on the lifeboat with Nat. David could be trusted to keep his own counsel. Nat had intervened on his behalf a number of times when Jake had taken to baiting the boy in a particularly nasty way that was beginning to sicken everyone.

Nat helped Sam to re-position the bulk of timber on the trestles where Victor had lain, leaving him to mark out a series of ribs, top futtocks as they were referred to in the trade, ready for cutting.

'What the hell's goin' on and why did that bleddy boy come lookin' for me in the Chisel?' As ever, Victor's son announced his arrival with the usual bluster and undeserved presumption of authority that always manifested itself when he'd drunk too much.

'Your father's had a heart attack, that's why.'

'Well I don't like being told by my friends there's a boy lookin' for me. Where's he anyway? I'll teach him a lesson.'

'I think you'd be better employed going to see your father.'

Jake swayed in the direction of Nat just as David Tresize came out of the wood shed.

'Come here you,' Jake picked up a slat of wood from the bench.

'Stay where you are David,' Nat stepped between Jake and the boy.

'Put the wood down. Put it down!' Nat caught Jake's arm in mid sweep as he, ignoring the latter's injunction to drop the slat, swung the piece of timber, instead, at his cousin.

Having learnt to defend himself in some of the dodgier lodging houses that were his lot travelling the world, Nat bent his cousin's arm back over his shoulder and stepped forward, backing the move with the momentum of his own body. The pain of an arm in torsion at the shoulder combined with the flat of a hand against his face, left Jake with no option but to sprawl backwards over the keel of the half-built boat behind him. The fire in his shoulder was exacerbated by the pain in his legs as the muscle at the back of his shin bone contacted the unyielding edge of the solid, oak keel. Nat let go. His assailant fell back with a screech across the spine of the vessel. His fall was arrested and yet more pain inflicted as his shoulders collided with a pair of keel ribs on the other side of the boat's skeleton. With too much liquor in his belly and trapped in the gap between the ribs, he was unable to lift himself off the frame.

'Get me up!'

'No! You can lie there 'til you sober up.'

'Karslake, get me up!'

'Mr Karslake to you and you can stay where you are, you little shit!'

The rotund, struggling man gave up.

'You're without a job. I'll see you and yours in the workhouse.'

Sam Karslake turned back to the abusive form standing below him and stood looking down, all solid six feet two of him, a pillar of cold rage. Nobody risked threatening Sam, ever.

'You two,' he half turned towards Nat and David Tresize, 'lose yourselves in the timber shed for a couple of minutes.'

The two complied. Nat knew Sam could be threatening but not violent so wasn't concerned for Jake's safety.

Jake Lewis stopped struggling, an expression of fear on his face, 'What are you going to do?'

Sam didn't answer. He went to a little cast iron pot full of fish glue bubbling away on the Turtle wood stove. Lifting it off he turned back to the now desperately struggling man and put one foot on his chest. Slowly he tilted the pot over the man's groin.

'What did you say you would do to me and my family? Hey? What did you say?'

Sam let one small trickle of glue drop onto Jake's fly front.

'Come on, I want to hear,' he poured another little trickle, a bit more than before.

'I didn't mean it.' Jake could feel the warmth beginning to seep through the worsted fabric to his skin.

Sam took his foot off Jake's chest, 'Bring your wallet out. Open it. How much is in there?'

'Fifteen pounds.'

'Right! Take it out and give it to me.' Sam still held the pot over his abuser.

The helpless man had no choice or rather he did but didn't like the alternative. Sam took the notes, pocketed them and took the pot back to the stove. He walked to the other side of the boat and clamped Jake's head between his legs, pressing his ears until the man winced.

'Just a little warning. If you try any way to cause me further grief I'll have a word with a few fishermen friends of mine and we'll sort you out one dark night. Is that clear?' He gave Jake a savage clap between his two legs, 'Clear?'

'Yes!'
'Say it again.'
'Yes.'

Sam called the other two back in, 'Jake's just given me a month's wages in lieu of notice. So I think we can let him up now.'

Nat looked at his cousin, 'I don't like you, I never have but try any more of your dirty little games with my work and I'm off. I know you've been misaligning some of the strakes I've put in place ready for fixing when I've gone home at the end of the day. Now your father's sick you need me. Don't forget it and keep Sam on for the remainder of the time it takes to finish this boat and stay out of our way. Sam, give me a hand to lift Mr Lewis up,' this latter said with no little measure of sarcasm.

'And one more thing, you show any more aggression to David Tresize and you'll end up back down there. Understood?'

The dishevelled figure said nothing, just turned and left the boat shed leaving the group satisfied with their response to a period of unpleasantness, endured for too long and delayed for too long, from the departing scion.

16

There was no immediate act of retaliation from Victor Lewis's son. Victor, after a week of convalescence, turned up at the boatyard in a pony and trap. If he was aware of the episode he said nothing. He stayed for an hour sometimes but more often left after ten or fifteen minutes in the following days. Jake turned up late most mornings but apart from that behaved as though he were none other than a paid employee with no claim to ownership. The atmosphere was no different to that in any field of employment where relationships were bad between employees and any yard dog, as working foremen were known, where underlings were bullied, except that barely a word of communication passed between Jake and the rest. He still absented himself at least once or twice a week, mostly at lunch time and for the remainder of the afternoon. Victor's input over the last year had been dwindling anyway, in terms of physical work so that measurable progress in boat construction seemed unaffected by his absence and was certainly little affected by Jake's continued, sullen presence.

As the evenings lengthened and weather improved Nat spent more time at the creek. The documents had been signed and approved giving him ownership. Because he referred to the creek so frequently he had decided to name the property, on the actual title deed, 'Tinners Creek' in line with the name for the actual inlet, written on local maps. His focus, initially, was on the foundry. He knew he could get it into a working enterprise over a far shorter time span than it would take for the long, drawn out process of designing, acquiring materials and building a boat. There was a demand for small bronze castings, particularly for propellers. Aluminium alloys were also beginning to appear; it had a relatively low melting point compared with most metals. Corrode in sea water it might but Nat knew that new generations of metallurgists were beginning to discover ways of alloying the metal so that it was more corrosion-resistant in salt water. He hadn't told Jim Bennallack how much he'd received for the emerald but the residue after buying Tinners Creek left him with a considerable reserve. It would allow him adequate margins to experiment with a non-traditional hull design.

Jenny Bennallack, infected by Nat's enthusiasm, put herself wholeheartedly into the regeneration of the premises. She spent some of her spare time there hacking down brambles, bushes and other obstructions at weekends. Their frequent visits to the creek on his boat meant that she was soon becoming a competent sailor and began to enjoy being on the water as much as in the saddle.

'Would you like to be co-owner of this boat.' Nat handed her the tiller, almost as a way of emphasising his offer, one day as they sailed up river on one of their visits to the foundry.

'What'd you mean?' She looked at him as though all his sheep were not in the top pen.

He laughed, 'I mean, will you marry me?'

'Well why didn't you say it?'

'I am saying it.'

'That depends.'

'Depends?'

'On whether you think more of me than you do of Pol-Pen.'

'Well?'

'Yes!'

Abruptly their frivolous repartee was silenced as the significance, the immensity of the situation registered with them. There was a sudden release of pent up sexual energy. She let go of the tiller. They each took the other in an embrace that saw them sink to the deck, further liberated in the knowledge of their being in an isolated, safe stretch of the river.

The boat, no longer being steered, swung around and floated into a mass of branches overhanging the slow moving river. Caught by the mast, it stayed gently oscillating in the current. Passion was given full license. They stayed in each other's arms for some time, savouring the warm, close comfort of each other's bodies.

It took them a while to free the boat from the branches. It was deep at that point. The boat hook wasn't long enough to touch bottom to act as a punting pole. Nat managed to wedge it into the fork of one of the more robust limbs of an oak tree. With much giggling, pulling and pushing on branches between them, the two freed the vessel with no harm having been done to the sail and rigging.

Tying up at Tinners Creek, both were silent, lost in thought at the consequences of their new relationship. They combined each visit to the creek with the opportunity to transport some essential item for future use. This time the mundane activity of unloading bags of coke for the foundry, contrasted with their recent, intimate activity on the boat, made the circumstances almost surreal.

The two furnaces were not yet ready for charging with ingots but the landing jetty was now fully functional and sported a small jib crane he'd acquired, cheaply, from the owner of a derelict wharf.

'I shall have to build a larger one,' when Nat saw Jenny looking at the crane, 'but it'll do for the time being. Let's get this dragged across to the foundry. I'll come back for the pulley belts later. I want to try out the wheel before anything else and will need you to open the new sluice when I shout.'

Jenny nodded, glad to witness some real activity in the early stages of the foundry's regeneration. Cutting down bushes and clearing undergrowth was satisfying in a physical sort of way but it lacked the visual appeal, the dynamic, of a functioning mill race. The small, steel waterwheel was now, effectively, a free-running cylinder in its freshly greased bearings. Nat gave it a full turn to check its movement.

'I'll walk along the leat with you first, though. I want to check nothing's likely to jam in the slots.'

The two walked along the levada-like channel to a point where the leat joined the stream that fed the larger, wooden waterwheel. The channel was clear all the way up and at the sluice there was no debris waiting to foul its easy opening and closing. Nat left Jenny in place and retraced his steps back to the small foundry wheel.

'Can you hear me?'

'Clearly.'

'Open the sluice.'

Nat stood above the wheel watching out for the flood of energy to appear around the only bend in the channel. The undergrowth had been cleared all the way along the leat allowing sunlight to catch the first rippling gush of water pushing with it a fluid matrix of dried, brown leaves, twigs and a handful of small stones. It hit the lowest plate with a muffled clang. The wheel reacted instantaneously, not hesitating but picking up speed until it settled into a hum of steady motion.

'Alright,' he shouted, 'do you want to come to see the wheel?'

Jenny appeared quickly. Together they stood watching the flood piling up behind the plates, exiting at a slower speed in the shallower channel down towards the creek. Floating debris eddied and whorled, stopping and starting in its journey towards the salt and seaweed of the lower, near-static, body of water. It was fascinating to watch.

'That's good,' satisfied with the outcome Nat turned to Jenny, 'I'll go with you to close the sluice. Then we'll fit the new drive belts.'

*

Back in the foundry the two looked at the results of their improvements to the interior.

'I think we can rig up two generators. One from this drive shaft and the other where I originally intended to install it but I want to get a furnace going first. '

'You've got some business lined up in that direction?'

'Not a specific order. No! But one of the men in the band, euphonium player, works in Hayle foundry, says they're turning away work so I thought there was a chance there to take the surplus and give this little enterprise a start.'

'Who're you going to get to do it? You don't know anything about casting. Do you?'

'Not a lot but I've watched a pattern being set in mould boxes and the melt being poured in. I know what has to be done. Could employ two people. An apprentice and a skilled man. The foundryman I was telling you about, Ralph Hooper, has to travel between Lanner and Gwennap to get to Hayle. Finds the journey a bit of chore, especially in wet weather. Cycles to catch a train at Redruth. Would welcome being that much closer to home, working at the creek, I'm pretty sure. Making a pattern is what takes the time. I could make patterns but would be a lot slower than a regular, skilled pattern maker. I would expect customers to provide patterns already designed and made, to start with. The rest, casting, is a day's work. When I get it up and running I can tout for work from the Admiralty and Falmouth docks.'

Jenny nodded, not specifically interested in the trade of pattern-making and moulding, per se. But, like her father, she was alert to the mechanics of profit and loss. Having grown up steeped in a family tradition of enterprise, the stages of production and commerce were meaningful to her, second nature, which was why she was unable to resist challenging Nat over these stages.

'What about wages?'

'I've got reserves that'll see me past the casting stage.'

Jenny let it go at that, content just to be a sounding box, for now. The two made their way back to the boat. Downstream, passing the trees where they had made love she could still feel a sensation of his presence inside her. There was no discomfort, just a lingering sense of a physical encounter that aroused her again as they sailed past the 'obliging' oak tree.

'You're going to tell Jim?'

'When I drop you. Yes?'

'Yes. He'll be delighted, I know.'

17

Back at Trelogan the two eventually discovered Jim Bennallack relaxing with a glass of brandy, upstairs in the coach house. He put the glass down.

'Had a fruitful trip?'

'Yes. The leat is clear and we got the foundry wheel running. It's going to be a real asset.' The response sounded a bit stilted.

'Good! But that's not what you've come to tell me, is it?'

Jenny let out a short laugh, 'No. You're a cunning old fox!'

Nat took her by the hand, 'I asked Jenny to marry me.'

'No you didn't. You asked if I wanted to be co-owner of your boat.'

The Captain gestured with a wave of a pointed finger in the direction of a brandy decanter, 'Fetch a couple of glasses from the cupboard and let's celebrate, unless of course she said no.'

'No sir, the glasses are in order. I take it I have your approval.'

'You certainly do. I've been expecting it. Thank you for taking her off my hands and becoming co-owner of her horse.'

They all laughed. Nat fetched the glasses. Jim Bennallack poured a splash of Cognac in each glass and topped his own up.

'Here's to the both of you. I'm delighted.'

They took a sip and, invited to sit, joined Jim around the table.

'Have you given thought to where you are going to live?'

'It's all happened a bit sudden. Have to say we haven't.'

'Well, Trelogan's a bit of an empty box these days. There's more than enough room for the two of you to set up camp in the east wing. What'd you say?'

Jenny got up and hugged her father.

'That's very generous of you sir - Jim,' Nat still felt uncomfortable at using his name, 'but you haven't really given yourself time to think about your offer.'

'I have, long before you knew what was happening. You can see how my daughter reacted and I don't think you believe it's a bad idea either.'

Nat leaned forward, looked at Jenny and smiled, 'Looks like two to one!'

'He is a cunning old fox, I told you so. But I love him.'

'That's settled then. I'll get Betty to give it a spruce up and you can make what changes you like. And, since we're on the subject, you can use the room below to work on your boat designs. That's if you want to. I'll say no more. That's enough surprises for today!'

'Well, I have to say, that was going to be a problem finding somewhere to work on drawings and store the plans. I really am grateful. Now I've got to justify your generosity.'

'I'm pleased it'll be put to good use again. I've never given a reason for selling the mine but there's another parcel of land, Tregennza farm, adjacent to this, the owner has died. Traditionally the owner takes the title of squire. My sources tell me there are no close heirs and the only claim on it is a distant relation in Australia who has made it clear he's not interested. He's instructed a local solicitor to dispose of it. I've done a deal. The property is more useful to me than Tinners Creek so it makes sense to use the one to help finance purchase of the other. I'm well covered but don't want to overstretch my resources.'

'So that's why you're selling. I wondered but didn't think it polite to ask. Will you work it as a farm?'

'Yes but with a manager in place.'

The little group talked for a while whilst finishing their brandy.

'So you'll need to tell your parents the news.'

'Yes. They haven't met Jenny yet. I'll take her next Saturday to meet them. My mother knows something is 'going on' but I've avoided saying anything about either Jenny or the mine. She thinks I'm cruel but I don't want anybody at the boatyard to know about the creek until I'm ready to tell them, as you know.'

'Fair enough! Well let's see what Betty has in the kitchen. You'll stay?'

'He'll stay.'

'Petticoat government already and you aren't even married yet. You need to watch that one. She'll be putting a saddle on you next.'

'I don't think so. The way she handles a boat,' he got no further, she gave him a mock-ferocious look that ended any further ribbing on his part.

*

'Hello?' Nat stood in the doorway to the living room of his parent's house.

'I'm out here.' 'Out here' meant outside in the back yard. Nat waited. His mother appeared. She had been to town and had not yet changed into clothes more suited to the usual chores of running a home.

'Someone here for you to meet.' Nat stepped aside from the doorway and gently pulled Jenny through to meet his mother.

'This is Jenny.' The older woman had already caught a glimpse of someone standing behind her son and had slowed her advance across the living room. Both women took an instant liking to each other in the way that first encounters can generate either instant reserve or immediate rapport. The two greeted each other with a handshake.

'So you're the civilising influence on my son,' Mary Hawken continued to hold Jenny's hand, 'come and sit down. I take it you'll have a cup of tea.'

'That would be nice.'

'Nat's father is still at the chandlery. He should be back soon. In fact I'd just put the kettle on before I went outside and thought it was him when I heard the door go.'

'Does he have a boat too?'

'No. He's part owner and Saturday mornings, early, for some reason, are always busy. Anyway you can talk while I make tea.'

By the time it had been brewed Bill Hawken had arrived and Jenny again introduced.

'You live at Trelogan then?'

'Yes.'

'I know it. Visited it when my father was there in the days when tin was still taken out of the ground, further up the estate.'

'That's what we've come to tell you about, or partly,' Nat took Jenny's hand, 'I've asked Jenny to marry me.'

Mary looked at Bill Hawken, 'I told you there was a girl in tow. Well, that's good news but what do you mean, 'partly'?'

'Well, I've also bought the old mine at Tinners Creek. I'm going to start my own boatbuilding business there in the adit. There's a cavern at the entrance big enough to take a boat. Captain Bennallack's let me have it at the reserve price for the auction and offered us the east wing of the house when we're married.'

Mary Hawken took a sip of tea and looked at her husband over the rim of her cup, holding it still to her lips as she swallowed. Bill Hawken smiled. He knew his son would make a go of any enterprise he took on. The father got up and shook hands with the son.

'Your mother and I were wondering if you'd ever settle down. Congratulations. We're delighted. That means you won't want to take over my share in the chandlery, when I give up.'

'Well, not really my cup of tea selling rope and tallow candles to sea captains. You know that. But you're not thinkin' of giving up yet are you?'

'No! But I can't go on forever.'

'You could put a boy in to replace you and just go down to keep an eye on trade from time to time. I would get my rigging from you and other fittings.'

'Yes,' Mary joined in, 'I can't see you liking not being occupied. I don't doubt Nat'll be glad of a hand now and again if he hits a busy spell. Anyway, that's good news, the wedding. It'll be nice to have another woman in the family. Are you staying for dinner?'

'Hadn't given it a thought.'

'You fibber. I know you turned up because it's Saturday, pasty day.'

'Yes, stay. Jenny, you happy to put up with us for a couple of hours?'

'Yes Mr Hawken.'

'Call me Bill. Everybody else does. Let's go down to The Chisel & Adze whilst Mary's making the pasties. You happy with that Mary?'

'Yes but bring back some clotted cream from Hicks' dairy when you go past. I'll do some stewed apple to have after the pasty.'

*

Back from the Chisel and with a good lunch inside them, the four discussed possible wedding dates and potential guest lists. Jenny diplomatically pointed out that her father would expect the reception to be held at Trelogan. Also that although not one of the family, Betty was as good as and that the Captain, who would be responsible for giving away his daughter, increasingly relied on her organisational skills. Mary Hawken understood and was secretly pleased that the arrangement would enable excuses to be made for the non-inclusion of some who might have expected to attend. She was also aware of the potential for disharmony that might be caused by her nephew if he attended, although unaware of the episode that occurred at the time of her brother's heart attack.

18

Nat enjoyed the greater scope afforded by the facilities in the coach house. Later hours of daylight provided time, after his daily spell in the boatyard, to work up at Trelogan. He visited various harbours around Cornwall where he knew there were lifeboats. Many of the boats suffered the same characteristic feature - an open deck in which the oarsmen sat. Various schemes for self-righting. Some, simple and more effective than others, were incorporated into their main frame timbers but none left him with any confidence. Steam-driven boats needed twenty minutes or more to raise power. Close, inshore rescues could not afford to be delayed by that length of time. There were dangers additional to those faced in an open rowing boat: steam-driven boats that capsized trapped the stokers and engineers below deck. There was little, if any, chance of escape.

Nat was intrigued by the potential afforded by the new petrol and diesel engines appearing in various vehicles and elsewhere in other applications. This, in his opinion, was the route to explore. He knew there were crew members who resisted any kind of change. He would have to overcome hostility by demonstrating the superior performance of an engine-powered boat over one that was solely man-powered. To do that he would need a team, in the first place, willing to crew such a boat. But before that he would have to build his boat.

The coach house was a sanctuary as well as a design studio. He spent more time there now and fewer evenings with his parents. Each day at his uncle's boatyard seemed to pass in sterile conformity but for the fact that whilst his hands were shaping wood his mind was shaping ideas unrelated to the task in hand. Each rib and stringer, each stern post and stem, each carlin and strake took on a different significance to the time when he was merely assembling the pieces into the skeletal structure of any old boat. Now he paid attention to potential weaknesses of construction: the particular joints and methods of pinning needing to resist the forces of the Atlantic rollers but, above all, major changes to traditional modes of construction necessary to accommodate an engine. He was in uncharted territory.

He could visualise, in his mind's eye, the response of such a boat to waves that arrived buffeting the timbers as it was launched into a matrix of surf and cascades of pebbles. In other scenarios he could see the consequences of huge wave formations lifting a boat thirty feet or more onto its crest then releasing it, keel practically vertical, to hover then slide with sickening speed down into, then beneath, the watery trough into which it was descending. This was dreaded. Side-on swamping did at least provide a chance of survival. But in the former oars snapped or worse, broke backs of oarsmen in front if they didn't, as the boat submerged at speed, stern first. The oars were arrested as they engaged with the water. Forced to rotate in the rowlocks they acted like blunt scythes as the hull tomb-stoned down into the green depths. This was a foaming hell.

The whole scenario, by its very nature, was played out in slow motion. Gravity resisted by the watery brake gave the men seconds of mental agony as they rested poised on the cusp waiting for the boat to rotate, then drop two or three storeys down the wave front. It was as horrifying as that experienced by balloonists who, rising beneath the path of a higher balloon, have the top seam of their balloon ripped off, the basket above dragging across the inflated skin of heated air supporting them. They would plummet down with increasing speed as the reservoir of hot air escaped, rapidly depleted the buoyancy of the balloon.

As these images played out in his mind he began to formulate other images, structures, profiles that took on the form of a buoyant, purposeful craft. There would be the problem of a surging engine as a propeller, denied the resistance of water, was released into air on a freak wave, cavitating as it again hit water. There would be the problem of ensuring continuity of gravity-fed fuel from a nearly empty tank sloshing diesel or petrol about with every pitch and toss of the boat. These thoughts did not dismay him. A simple solution to the latter had suddenly presented itself to him one night, in one of those wide-awake spells when an overactive mind evades sleep. He welcomed the design challenges they posed, stimulated by the eureka moments when a simple solution to a seemingly intractable problem suddenly presented itself.

*

At the next band practice he sounded out the euphonium player when the band broke off for a few minutes respite. Some lighted pipes or cigarettes. Others discussed local news or told ribald stories of their times in military service. Some of the younger players – learners promoted from the youth band – went outside on the chance that they might see a 'piece of skirt' pass by. Often as not there would be no-one; that was usually the case but it did not deter them from looking.

'Like to go for a pint after rehearsal? I've got a proposition to air I think you might be interested in but I don't want it to be public knowledge, for the moment.'

Ralph Hooper looked at the younger cornet player with interest.

'I've got fifteen minutes or so to spare. I told my missus I'd be back normal time, depending on what time Cecil decides to put down his baton. Takes me twenty minutes on the bike.

'That should be long enough. We can go to the Admiral Nelson.'

'After practice then.'

*

'Right! I'm all ears.' Ralph Hooper put his glass down on the ring-stained, oak surface of the pub table.

'I've got an old foundry. Just acquired it up the Fal. Place called Tinners Creek. Been unused for some years but intact and still equipped with its original furnace, in fact two furnaces. Mould boxes, moulding sand and ancillary equipment, the lot. Need someone to operate and manage it. Interested?'

Ralph lifted his glass then put it down without drinking, 'Bit of bolt out of the blue but I must say it sounds attractive, first off. Course, you'd need more than just me there.'

'That's what I guess and that's the reason I'm sounding you out. You've got 'on site' experience and knowledge. Also I know you would be square with me. You would be in charge and I'd rely on you to recruit whatever assistance you needed.'

'How'd you propose to go about drumming up trade? I've got a few contacts but I don't want to antagonise the owner of Hayle foundry by taking away trade from there. Having said that he's turning away work. We could try out some of the new clients he's put off. With them there's always a risk over payment until you get to know which customers are reliable and which not. A government contract or two is always a sound bet, if you can get one. You have to accept admiralty pricing policy and put up with delay in payment but you do get your money, eventually.'

'That's the sort of thing I was hoping to hear you come out with. I'll leave it with you for now. Think it over. I'm looking at, perhaps two, three, four months before getting it going. We'll need to talk more once I can see my way to doing a pilot run with the furnaces. Could be sooner.'

'Tell you what, let me have a look at it sometime. Earlier the better. Help me get a handle on it. Can make a few suggestions that might save you some bother in the meantime.'

'That would be welcome, goes without saying. Alright then. Let's say Saturday – if you're free.'

'That would suit me.'

'Saturday it is then. Come over to my parents and we'll go from there. They live across the water from the quay at Flushing. Crabber's Cottage, right by the old gig boat house. Nine o'clock suit you?'

'Yes.'

'Right. See you then, then.' The two men shook hands, downed the remains of their beer and went outside back to their homes.

*

The two men disembarked at Tinners Creek. Up at the site Ralph Hooper took in the various features and content of the foundry.

'You'll be better off re-locating the furnaces closer to the main doors and having your moulds in the middle. That way your moulds and castings are not going to be in the way of the furnace men transporting coke and scrap metal to the furnaces and crucibles. Light's not too bad there either. I'm pretty certain you can make a go of this. I'll take you up on your offer but I'd like to buy into a share of the profits.'

Nat wasn't expecting this but neither was he surprised, 'Let me think about that. On the face of it I'm ready to say yes. Amounts to a vote of confidence in me. No mark of flattery on my part. Just hesitating, for now, because I'm getting married. It's no secret but not widely known. But I've a lot on my mind and my prospective father in law might also put money into the venture so I would need to get him on side with your proposal.

'Congratulations. Good enough excuse for anybody,' they laughed. 'Still count me in. I'm pretty sure things'll work out whatever. It has the feel of success about it.'

'Whilst you're here what'd you think about those miners' cottages?'

'Let's have a look at them.'

The two pushed through stinging nettles and cow parsley to the door of one of the granite-built houses. The door was unlocked. Inside a few items of furniture and other artefacts of no value littered the small rooms. A kitchen sported a large, white, glazed earthen ware sink. Unusually it was serviced by a tap. Most such cottages obtained their water from an outside source, often a well. The sink lay below a four-paned window and they could see a galvanised steel pipe emerging horizontally from the bank a few feet away. It entered through the two foot thick, granite stone wall and jutted out about four inches over the sink. Ralph gave the brass cross bar of the tap a tweak. It resisted.

'Seized up! Give me that old sauce pan.' Ralph pointed to a decrepit, enamelled pot on the black kitchen range. He took the vessel, put it upside down on the floor and stamped on the base. The rivets pulled away separating the handle from the pot. He put the hollow end over one arm of the tap handle. Giving it a few careful jolts it gradually began to shift. Water started dripping onto the dust in the sink.

'Well that works. I better not force it any more 'case I can't close it.' Giving it some torsion in the opposite direction he put an end to the trickle of water. He opened the door of the cupboard supporting the sink. The drain pipe was sealed with cement into one of the Delabole slate slabs that paved the kitchen and living room floors. It drained to a cement channel along the foot of the outside wall.

Upstairs the bare timbers of the two bedrooms were dry. The ceilings were still sound. Wall paper had been put on by an occupant hoping to give the dwelling something of a more homely feel. It had the stamp of a woman about it. The pattern of flowers showed taste. Nat could imagine a woman with an interest in art having selected the rolls of paper.

'It won't take much to restore this. Plenty of people would welcome it as a home. Looks like there's a vegetable garden at the back, too. Wouldn't take long to clear it and it's away from the mine spoil behind that wall so free from arsenic.'

Nat nodded, 'I had been thinking a workman might be glad to have it on a nominal rent. Anyway, that's something for the future. Might as well be getting back now. Nothing else you want to see?'

'No. Let's get back.'

19

The day of the wedding passed without incident. Jake Lewis did not attend. Jake Lewis did not want to attend and if Jake Lewis didn't want to do anything then he made sure Jake Lewis didn't put himself in the way of doing it! Instead, he went to his local watering hole and, with a hatred that had been simmering ever since, brooded on some plan of retaliation for his humiliation at the hands of the boatyard employees.

Victor Lewis and Irene, his wife, went to the church service and to the reception. They knew nothing of the incident at the boatyard. Irene was an overfed, overweight creature who bordered on the lazy end of the domestic spectrum. It was from her that Jake inherited his hedonistic traits. But it was his maternal grandfather, a man with a reputation for violence, who added the further, unpleasant dimension to his nature, vindictiveness, the characteristic that demonstrated itself in his bullying attitude towards the apprentice.

At the reception Nat's turn came to give the customary groom's speech.

'Thank you every one for your good wishes and gifts. I ... ,' Nat continued with the usual cordial platitudes and jocular comment expected of him. After enough such comment he stopped, looked around at the guests and smiled.

'There is a piece of news I would like to share with you,' Jenny sat up, an expression of consternation on her face. Nat was the only one who knew she was pregnant. Six weeks into her term and there was no outward sign yet of her pregnancy. She wanted to be the first to tell her father before he got to hear from any other source and was aghast at the turn Nat's speech had taken.

'I have decided to go into business,' Jenny sat back in her seat, the tension dropping from her shoulders. She almost laughed out loud with relief, 'a few months back I bought the foundry at Tinners Creek.'

Nat looked at his uncle Victor, 'I don't intend to leave my uncle in the lurch so won't be leaving the boatyard until he's found a replacement. I have to thank him for teaching me the difference between a mast band and a massed band,' this was an 'in joke' that would be appreciated by those guests with a knowledge of the mast rigging on boats and those guests who played in the brass band, 'I've enjoyed my time building boats but want to extend my interests in other directions.'

His parents were as surprised as anyone. Not in the sense of being surprised at such an announcement – he was prone to drop bombshells out of the blue, this was nothing new to them – but in the content. He had always kept his activities a matter of his concern only, even to the point of not informing them of the most unimportant and insignificant of commercial and social transactions. He was used to being cautious, aware of the nosiness of Methodist abstainers – don't smoke, don't drink, don't swear. Nat's father had been baptised into the Church of

England but his mother was the daughter of Wesleyan chapel-goers. With the latter there was a culture of 'looking out for the wellbeing' of one's fellow communicants. That, in principle, was a good ethic but, with some, bordered on an almost tyrannical obsession with moral rectitude that degenerated into a form of bigoted reporting of misdemeanours to the manse.

Sad because there were good souls within the Methodist congregation. But the most obnoxious rejoiced in a form of false naivety; of smug banter affecting a self-deprecating form of virtue-signalling not dissimilar to that manifested by the most bigoted of some Welsh Congregationalists. They were as bad, in their way, as their counterparts in the Anglican Church. Those who affected a disdainful attitude to what they perceived as the intellectual inferiority of lesser beings not blessed by the scholarship of their university-trained vicars and the near, high church purity – as they perceived it - of the Catholic Church, to which it was distantly related. But, again, there were exceptions: men of scholarship and humility amongst these who, with a sincere concern for their fellow human beings, put those less pleasant brethren to shame.

The usual protocols were pursued until there was a natural end to the festivities. People left in groups. Promises between groups of relatives to: 'We must meet sometime', were made with no expectation of fulfilment. Whilst everyone was occupied making such promises or waiting whilst members of their particular group were fraternising with others, Jenny turned to Nat, 'I thought you were going to let the cat out of the bag then.' He laughed.

When all had gone except Mary and Bill Hawken, Jim Bennallack ushered the four into the library for a family, celebratory drink whilst Betty supervised the clearing of the tables by itinerant staff in the large dining room. They were later expected to remain for a light supper and to stay the night. The Captain had already put out glasses and motioned them to sit down whilst he poured measures from his regular stock of Madeira.

Jenny waited until the drinks had been handed round, 'We've got some more news for you. You are going to be grandparents.'

The Hawkens and Jim Bennallack, still relatively new to each other's company, were engaged in polite, exploratory conversation. When the significance of the news began to take hold and the brief silence greeting it was broken they were up, smiling, shaking hands and hugging Jenny, voicing pleasure at the news.

'Another toast in order. Nat, ask Betty to let the hired people take care of the clearing up and tell her to join us. Betty will be pleased to hear the news. Looked after Jenny when Antonia, my wife, died. She's pretty well one of the family.'

Jim fetched another glass.

'Betty we've some news for you. Jenny, you tell her.' He handed her a glass of the Madeira.

'Don't need to. I can guess. Seen the signs.'

'You wily old fox. That's two of you in the house.' Jenny got up and led her to a chair, Betty put down her glass and gave her a long, gentle hug that said more than words could of her fondness for the younger woman. She had no children and Jenny had provided a welcome distraction when she found herself, suddenly, without a husband.

*

Later, before the evening meal, the two young ones treated Mary and Bill to a tour of the east wing where they were going to start their married life. Jenny had been just as busy converting the east wing of Trelogan for occupation as she had been to improving the site at the creek. She had put up new drapes and rescued carpets from other little-used rooms elsewhere in the house. The existing furniture was complemented with extra bits and pieces again 'adopted' from other rooms. One room, originally a staff kitchen, had been renovated and equipped with more up-to-date equipment and new utensils. If Mary Hawken had been a jealous kind this would have made her green with envy. Instead she was pleased, as any mother would be, that her new daughter-in law would not be strapped for cooking facilities. Tour over, the little group returned to the dining room for supper.

20

Nat stayed at the boatyard as promised. Victor introduced a new employee, he came recommended by Jake. Although affecting a disdain for the owner's son the other workers were wary of saying anything in front of him. His negative observations didn't quite ring true and they suspected Jake of having instructed him to report back on anything that might prove of future use to him. Nonetheless they treated him cordially and he was otherwise pleasant enough to work with.

*

In a second discussion with Ralph Hooper, Nat agreed Ralph's request to a share in profits if he would lend a hand on clearing the miner's cottages. The two men set about the work at weekends and evenings. Nat also enlisted the help of David Tresize who was soon to complete his indentured time at the boatyard. The lad was glad of the extra cash Nat was able to pay him. During one of the evening sessions Nat sounded him out on the prospect of his joining him at Tinners Creek. David's training had been entrusted to Nat by Victor almost from the beginning of his apprenticeship. He also knew Sam Karslake would probably jump at the opportunity of joining, that's if he didn't seek work elsewhere before Nat got up and running. Sam and David between them, he knew, would make a good team. He could rely on both of them to work with the minimum of supervision whilst he alternated, according to need, between the responsibility of overseeing and helping out at both the foundry, the boatbuilding and other site work.

By the time the last boat Nat would ever work on, at his uncle's yard, was complete, Nat had already got the foundry established under Ralph Hooper's skilled eye. There were orders coming in from a variety of clients. They had pitched costs so as to attract custom. Not so low as to anger some of the larger, more powerful foundries but in a costing range that accommodated a more bespoke approach towards their clients. They were willing to accept, in fact encouraged, clients to submit work of more complex, intricate design than other companies were willing to undertake. This would become their metier.

Ralph had taken a liking to one of the cottages. With its closer proximity to Penryn and nearby Falmouth than it was to Redruth, it held a particular attraction for Ralph's wife Jean. They moved in soon after the premises were cleared. Nat installed a network of cabling, primitive by modern standards but modern by local standards, ready to be linked to the turbine generator when it was up and running. Most local homes were illuminated by paraffin lamps. Their white, incandescent mantles hissing under the conversion of the kerosene and air feeding the flame. A few had gas lamps.

Before he embarked on the actual construction of a new lifeboat or indeed any boat, the building of the dam, the ancillary infrastructure necessary for running a turbine had to be addressed before winter. To get maximum advantage from the foundry he needed to extend the working hours that otherwise would be curtailed by dark, winter evenings. Lighting that first, the cavernous entrance to the adit would be the next priority.

Jim Bennallack, with extensive knowledge of civil engineering projects and Nat's experience in the South American mines with sluices, pipe work and levadas, enabled them to lay out such a system. It served two goals. One, its primary function, light and power generation. The other a means of stopping the stream from flowing for short intervals, permitting Nat to dig out a deeper channel in the stream's bed down to where it entered the creek. This would enable him to transport a boat hull from mine to creek more easily but this would be a long-term project requiring temporary manpower to complete.

*

The results of the activity never went unobserved. It was now common knowledge that Nathaniel Hawken had opened the old foundry at The Creek. Jean Hooper, out at her washing line, did not see Jake Lewis nor did Jake Lewis see her. His latest self-indulgence was a motorbike. The hatred he felt for Nat had case-hardened into an obsession. It was the convenience afforded by the bike that had driven him to motor up to observe the site a number of occasions from the cover of the willow trees. This time he was bent on causing damage. It was Saturday afternoon and he'd seen Nat go out to fish in Pol-Pen and had assumed the site would be unoccupied. His observations had not detected occupation of the cottage on previous sorties. Shielded from the foundry by gorse and shrubbery it was screened from the industry going on around it.

Tracking down the lane he reached the newly constructed dam. No gate had yet been slotted into the base of the sluice. The dam was merely an un-submerged wall at this stage. Taking a crow bar, lying across a pile of stones, he set about attacking the pristine facing of concrete sealing the granite mass that would hold back the water. Jean, hearing the abnormal noise and thinking it a group of boys up to no good, slipped out quietly from the garden. She was shocked to see an adult causing the destruction, someone unknown to her. Wisely she crept away and got Ralph and her son Simon who was visiting. The two men crept around the back of the cottage. Simon spotted the motorbike pulled in amongst the trees further up the lane.

'That's what he came on, whoever he is. I'll go up and put it out of action. You go and keep an eye on him but wait 'til I get back down. Don't approach him on your own.'

Simon sped up to the motorbike. He turned the petrol drain tap on, pulled the ignition wire off the spark plug and jammed a twig into the inner-tube valve of the back wheel, releasing the air. This done he ran down the lane to the dam. Ralph seeing it safe to challenge the man in front of him picked up a fair sized rock and hurled it at

Jake catching him between the shoulder blades. It hit him just as he was about to have another good stab at a particularly large boulder he'd uncovered. Overbalancing, Jake dropped the bar and fell forward onto the rubble of rocks and stones he'd dislodged. Simon jumped down the bank on top of him.

'Right you bugger. What d'you think your game is, eh?' He knelt on him.

'Have you got any rope anywhere? We can tie him up then and get the police.'

'Yes, there's some in the old stone pig sty, we've cleared it out and use it for storage. I'll get it.'

'Keep still you bastard,' Simon gave Jake a cuff across the back of his head, 'or I'll break yer bleddy arm.'

The face-down victim had no chance of retaliating and was forced to accept the pain of sharp rocks sticking into his rib cage. Ralph appeared with the rope.

'Do his ankles first. Good and tight. I'll do the rest.'

That done Simon took the end of the rope.

'Right you kneel on him now.'

Simon bent Jake's legs up at right angles and slipped a full loop from the free end of rope around Jake's neck. Jake started to panic and screamed he would be throttled if he straightened his legs.

'That's right! That's what I intended and you'll stay like that until I've roped your arms. We don't like men who destroy another man's means of livelihood.'

The two men pulled him up onto his knees and bound his arms firmly to his sides. Simon then slackened the loop round Jake's neck leaving just enough tension to threaten him, with a pull, if he attempted to cause trouble.

'What are we going to do with him?'

'I suggest we put him in the pig sty.'

'Can the door be secured?'

'Yes. It's a substantial door. Had to be to keep some of those big boars in.'

'Right let's get him there.'

They dragged their catch to the sty and pulled him in onto the bare earth to lie amongst an assortment of posts, rope, coils of wire and other items. They pulled the door to and secured it with a cross beam wedged into a pair of slots.

'I'll bike to the police house in Penryn. They've got rid of their horse carriage and got one of those new motorised vans. If he gets out, which I doubt, he can't use his motor bike. I've seen to that. Let me get going.'

*

'Hello!' Simon shouted. He, a police sergeant and a constable were half way down the lane. They had left the police vehicle up on the road, its narrow wheels too fragile to risk the bumpy ride down the rough track. Ralph appeared from his perch on the wall by the sty.

'All fine. I've checked him a time or two to make sure he hadn't strangled himself. He's quiet. Can't be much else.'

They lifted the bar from its slots and opened the door. Jake Lewis was sitting against a barrel of caulking tar, like an inanimate bundle, still but sullen and expressionless.

'Right! Undo him.' The sergeant addressed the constable.

'We'll take over now. I think it'll be a while before your next client seeks accommodation.' He laughed at his joke. Jake Lewis was pulled to his feet, led away and his motorbike loaded alongside him into the modernity of a non-horse-driven police van.

*

Out of consideration for his mother Nat did not press charges but insisted his cousin make good – by whatever means – the damage to the dam. He wondered if this time Jake had learnt a lesson but was uneasy. There was a nagging feeling at the back of his mind, one of unfinished business, vendetta.

21

After this episode Nat stayed one more week at the boatyard. Jake kept away. The foundry was making more than enough money to pay him a living just with one of the furnaces operating. Because of this he decided to offer work to Sam Karslake and David Tresize on the basis that they alternated initially on helping in the foundry, outside site work and, as occasion presented itself, fitting out and equipping the adit until he could employ them full time in boatbuilding, the work they were trained in. This suited the two. They were pleased to acquire experience foreign to their recognised trade. Any additional skills made them more readily employable in the labour market. Nat encouraged David to try his hand at simple pattern making. There was always demand for pulley blocks. The wheels could be cast in the lighter, lower melting aluminium alloys. These were easy patterns to make and David found the novelty of changing the gearing on the lathe, setting up a wood blank, turning it to size, a welcome diversion.

Sam Karslake, glad to be away from Jake Lewis, had not realised how oppressive the effect of working in his company had been until liberated from the yard. The work at the creek gave him a renewed interest. Entrusted with a number of separate activities, loosely connected with boat design and construction and encouraged by Nat's interest in the subject, he began to explore the mechanics of wind, wave and buoyancy and their interaction with hull profile dynamics, outside working hours.

With so much help now on site, the dam and the primitive hydraulic controls associated with it, were completed sooner than Nat hoped for. The turbine generator was located in a little, granite turbine house built especially for it and, following that, lighting installed in the foundry and the antechamber to the adit.

Nat was not at liberty to invite anyone into the coach house neither was he inclined to seek Jim's permission to do so. This was a privilege he was jealous about guarding. There he applied himself to his interest in propeller design. Most of the screws he'd seen on the very few boats that yet had motors were two-bladed. Two blades would be hard enough to replicate in a casting box but the symmetry demanded from three introduced manufacturing complications out of all proportion to the addition of just one extra blade.

Complex, algebraic parameters governed the profile of the three-bladed screw. The few, written specifications existing had been derived from empirical successes and failures. It was beyond the wit of most people to associate any kind of mathematics with the specification of a blade shape let alone comprehend the added complication of defining the twist in a single blade's geometry. Too much twist and the blade caused cavitation, bubbles of gas that caused erosion. Too little and too little thrust was generated.

All his design attempts started as sketches. He kept them all, even those rejected on the basis of some failure of mechanics. Others he rejected because of impossible manufacturing techniques. Still others when, intuitively, he knew the intended outcome would not be successful. But these were diversions, essential but secondary to his main motivation: the design of an unsinkable lifeboat. The very act of working on a problem allowed other ideas to germinate in his subconscious. This was how he thought; this was how his creative output materialised. Solutions appeared out of the blue, pushing aside any secondary thought.

At one such moment, late one evening, he abandoned his thoughts on propellers and turned to the whole purpose of the enterprise: the lifeboat. Sitting back from the big oak table, littered with books on hull design, he considered the prevailing, unchallenged assumption that the boat would have a single keel. He wasn't concerned with twin hulls. An inverted catamaran was virtually impossible to right. Not good! They were fine - until they capsized but the idea of a twin keel, in a single hull, suddenly displaced all other images in a eureka-inspired moment. A madcap idea; he would later wonder why he allowed himself to entertain it. A parallel, dropped, double keel would still permit a propeller shaft to exit the hull along the boat's centre line. More importantly the dropped keels would provide a protective channel for a propeller vulnerable to submerged hazards.

This sudden revelation brought with it another image that would give counter-buoyancy in the event of capsize: a sealed superstructure running along two thirds of the deck. It went against his original intention: to design a boat which was simple in construction. He was, however, beginning to tire of stereotypical methods of construction years of conditioning had planted in his mind and craved the novelty of a fresh approach. It left him uneasy, though, knowing the old methods to be sound and well-proven. But then, they applied to sea conditions less challenging than he was expecting his craft to withstand.

Knocking up a few sketches to fix the idea, he flipped through the pages of his notebook before getting down from the table. It was time to turn in. He was getting stale. He would discover, later, looking at some ideas, that they were rubbish. Unrecognised fatigue had been accompanied by unjustified optimism.

*

In the house Jenny had lit a fire in their living room. A gale-damaged apple tree provided the logs fuelling the fire. The hiss of sap turning to steam, apart from the occasional crack as the green timber split, was the only sound in the empty room. Nat guessed Jenny was in the kitchen. He crept up on her and drew his finger down the back of her spine. She gave a shiver of masochistic pleasure, resisting it yet wanting the experience repeated.

'You tormentor,' she turned with a grin towards him, 'you leave me for hours then abuse me. What kind of husband does that to his adorable wife?' Said with all the mock seriousness she could muster, she hugged him with her hands clasped around his waist and gave him a peck on the lips, leaning back out of the reach of his mouth as he tried to make something more of the contact.

'Who said you are adorable? Just because the children at school like you and the mothers think you are wonderful and I think you are the loveliest little lobster in the sea ... .' He got no further.

'Loveliest little lobster in the sea? You could at least liken me to a rose.'

'You can't eat a rose.'

'Oh give over Nat Hawkens!' They left off the banter. Nat helped her carry food to the kitchen table where they ate a supper of crusty, home-baked loaf, pickled onions for which she'd developed a craving since becoming pregnant and cheddar cheese so yellow it almost glowed with the intensity of its deep colouring.

'How are you getting on with the boat?'

'It's coming along. 'have some ideas that look promising. Going to sleep on it; 'give it some time to sort itself out in my mind. Jim still in London?'

'Got back this afternoon. Went into Truro straight away to see his lawyer. There was some minor issue over mineral rights in the deeds of Tregennza farm. Nothing serious. The meeting with the Duchy Land Agent went alright. He's not exercised about anything at the moment other than farming. Anyway, it's sorted out, whatever it was. There appears to be some flexibility written into the deeds over its use so he's happy at the outcome. Just a matter now of lawyers on both sides signing.'

She returned to the subject of the boat, 'The boat - it'll cost you something. I know it's close to your heart but will you try to get people interested in it? Public subscription towards the cost or something?'

'Don't know! Once I've got a solid proposal for the design then I can think about financing. It looks like the demand for castings is not just steady but expanding fast with the sabre-rattling that's going on in Europe. The income generated by one furnace is enough to free me up to pursue the boat project. In fact we're so busy we need to get the other furnace going and, another thing, there's a dearth of machining capacity in the county. A lot of the castings are being left with us longer than they need to be because the clients can't find machine shops with spare capacity. There's room for a metal-turning lathe and a small milling machine in the foundry. We could take on that kind of work easily. Perhaps take on an apprentice, even. Would need to increase the diameter of the iron waterwheel to give us greater torque. Drill a few holes in each paddle and bolt on extensions. That would do it.'

'What's torque?'

'Well, sort of leverage. Sort of adding more power to the pulley system. Like when you have a longer handle to a crow bar you can apply more force, more leverage. Waterwheel's just like a rotating ring of levers. Extending the paddles is like using a longer crow bar. There's also room in the old stamping house for one or two machines even after fitting it out with a saw bed. Would only need to add a few extra shafts and pulleys off the big wheel to do it.' She cut him a slice of saffron cake and pushed a dish of clotted cream towards him.

'Anyway, I've come in to see you and leave work behind.'

'I like to hear about it.'

'How was school?'

'We got the scholarship results today.'

'How'd you do?'

'Again: better than most. Nearly half the ten year-olds have places at the grammar.'

'That's pretty good. How'd you do it?'

'Drill! Constant drill! Doesn't hurt them. Most of them, even the ones who don't get a place, can turn out an essay of sorts. It's the maths paper that floors a lot of the schools in the county. That's where the hard work pays off. Too many teachers haven't the patience to discipline themselves, let alone the children, to drill their charges in a diet of repetition: constant exposure to simple exercises then gradual exposure to more testing-examples of the same. Children don't mind it. They aren't bored by it. Quite the contrary. They love to settle into a routine of problem solving and getting it right, getting lots of red ticks. They develop intuition, a confidence handling figures that only comes with repetition, practice, like with a musical instrument.'

'The village school will miss you.'

'Suppose they will but I'm looking forward to being at home and keeping house for you properly. Baking, cooking for a change, instead of preparing lessons. I enjoy cooking, it's so relaxing. Allows my mind to roam.'

'You won't have a lot of time for that with a baby.'

'Yes I will. I've asked Betty if she'll be a godmother. She is crafty. Do you know what she said? Only if she can be a part-time nanny.'

'She's a godsend. Jim would be lost without her.'

'Since Jack was drowned at sea this has been her home.'

'I'm surprised they haven't married.'

'So am I! Both seem to enjoy a comfortable companionship about the house. Dad's made provision for her in his will but I wouldn't be surprised if they still do tie the knot. I've a feeling the purchase of Tregennza might be more than merely a financial investment. He's taken her with him a time or two to look it over.'

'What do you mean?'

'Well, although he doesn't own it yet I've overheard both of them talking about serious work on the farmhouse and discussing improvements, like a married couple setting up their first home. Really serious as though they would move in and put a manager in the larger of two farmhand's cottages. The farmhouse is older than Trelogan and used to be part of a priory that was supposed to be connected by tunnel to the church. In fact dad calls it The Priory. It's quite a beautiful building. You can see the ecclesiastical influence in its make-up. Maybe we should walk over on Sunday to have a look.'

'I'd like to see it. I know roughly where it is. Went to a wedding at the church once but never been up to the house.'

'That's settled then. Let's rinse this lot. I'll get up early to wash it properly. We both need to get to bed, been a long day.'

22

The following evening Nat returned to his note book. A triple keel idea was gnawing at him. He didn't like it. A third keel running the whole length of the hull would provide horrendous problems of construction and sealing. But he wasn't convinced. It was against his instincts. He returned to an earlier design.

The next task he set himself was to build a half model. Normally this would be carved from a solid built from layers of stacked wooden boards. This time it would have to be a miniature of the real thing, made from thin strips of wood simulating the ribs, strakes and stringers. His sketches needed structural proof. Form was not enough. Time to seek a few opinions.

The next working day he took the notebook in with him. The men broke off mid-morning for a 'bit of crib'. It could be a yeast bun or some part of their lunch, a corner of a pasty, maybe or mouthful of cheese and a piece of bread cut from a hunk using a folding knife, the blade always honed to a fine edge. Ownership of a pocket knife was almost a rite of passage for young boys and it carried through and on into adulthood. It came from observing their fathers, grandfathers, uncles. They would take a knife, cut a short length of young sycamore, cut a ring round the bark and tap it gently along its length to loosen a tube of the sap-filled layer. Blowing across the top, whilst sliding the stem up and down, produced a flute-like sound to the pleasure of their young watchers. The younger the watcher the more intrigued but the more frustrated when their first attempts resulted in bruised and split tubes of bark. Older boys would go on to cut more mature growths of Y-shaped sycamore or ash, to make catapults. Using a length of a tyre inner tube for elastic, they were able to fashion a pretty potent weapon.

A huge, cast iron kettle with a wooden handle fixed between its two, upright arms, would always be simmering in any winding house, foundry or clay kiln somewhere throughout the county. The men took turns to brew-up. On this particular day it was David Tresize who filled an assortment of enamelled, half-pint mugs from a large, enamel teapot. Invariably a spoonful of sugar was added to the mix of strong tea and milk. Foundry work wasn't always hot and grimy but it was thirsty work. With the huge doors open the atmosphere was constantly replenished from a draught through the end window. The occasional whiff of the creek – seaweed and mud – together with the more subtle scent of gorse and bracken, mingled with the gases from the risers as the melt from a crucible was poured into the moulds.

Nat opened the notebook and laid it on an impromptu table, an old tea chest one of the men had turned up with one day. There was an assortment of logs cut to knee height and used for seats. They grabbed their mugs and sat around the inverted box, enjoying the break in the matey kind of way men can, switching off from work and finding immediate relaxation in discussing anything from ferrets to philosophy.

'Here's what I was on about earlier.' He put a piece of riser, cut from one of the castings, across the open pages to stop them closing.

'You can see what I'm getting at that's different, in that sketch there.' He pointed to the re-entrant hull - one of three different views, one that showed skeletal detail mainly of the ribs and the knee they slotted into. 'What'd you think?'

Ralph Hooper, the foundry-man looked on as Sam Karslake and David Tresize bent over the drawings. Sam pulled the book towards him, rolled the riser off and lifted the drawing to give it closer scrutiny.

'Your weak points are going to be at the ends where the two keels meet the bow and stern sections. But you've already recognised that from what you told us before.' Sam took up a piece of dowelling and started sketching in a thin layer of casting sand at his feet. He did a few strokes, scrubbed them out with his foot and started again. Stopped, paused, surveyed the lines, shook his head and scrubbed them out again.

'Like you, I don't like it.'

David Tresize studied the sketch, 'That section there is the weak one. Takes all the hammering,' he pointed to a cluster of joints, 'almost needs a Y-shaped stem knee and stem post cut from a single piece of oak.

You'd have a job finding a growth that shape that's uniform.'

Nat pulled the book towards him, 'You've given me an idea. Ralph, how easy is it to cast a profiled plate in aluminium that we could bolt timbers to?'

Ralph had been following the discussion between the three boat builders and had come to a similar conclusion almost at the same time.

'Shouldn't be difficult. I've seen some pretty complex shapes cast in my time. But you're not forced to do it in one single casting. Bolted assemblies make them easier to repair.'

The three men now looked at the design from a different perspective.

'Your main problem though is that this new metal corrodes. Bad in sea water.'

'Any way round that?'

'Well, some boat builders put a zinc bar in contact with it. Have to replace it every so often because it sacrifices itself. That's the whole point of it. That's how aluminium or steel is preserved. Never pure aluminium anyway. The chief metallurgist at Hayle tosses a handful of silica sand into a melt, gives it a bit more resistance and strength. But the bugger should weigh it out accurately. Two melts never the same when he's in charge of a casting.'

'Right then,' said Nat, finishing his mug of tea, 'I'll give this another look.'

The men got up, washed their cups outside in the stream and turned back to what they were engaged in previously.

23

Jim Bennallack received confirmation that week. Documents giving ownership of the farm were signed and the financial transaction completed.

'Jenny says you would be interested to see The Priory.'

'Only when convenient.'

'Betty and I are walking across early Sunday morning, then back for a late lunch. If you'd like to come with us you're welcome. I've got a couple of brace of pheasants. Local gamekeeper tossed them through the kitchen door, couple of weeks ago. They're well hung and ripe for roasting. Why don't we make a day of it and you come into us for lunch, after?'

Nat looked at Jenny and there was a mutual, unspoken 'yes' communicated to the Captain as they both beamed smiles of assent.

*

A leisurely walk to Tregennza took about twenty minutes. Before visiting the house the four of them had a look at the condition of a walled garden. Placed on the east side and just forward of the south-facing house, it benefitted from a full day's sun. Like most gardens of its kind it was built on the side of a hill. The lowest part contained a carp pond – long since abandoned. Allowed to silt up, its remaining weed-choked pools making a froggy heaven for newts and frogs. Rex, the ever adventurous Rex, always ahead of the pack, put up a heron chancing its sentinel patience hoping for an amphibian to show itself amongst the reeds. The witless dog dashed straight into the mire yelping and attempted to leap the ten or fifteen feet the heron had put between it and the ground.

'Not again! Rex!' Jenny yelled at the dog, trapped up to its belly on spongy weeds.

Nat strode over to the struggling, now panicking dog, 'Hola Senior Perrrrro,' Nat rolled the rs with theatrical exaggeration, using a still-remembered smattering of Spanish from his South American days, 'Como esta?' He reached over, grabbed 'El Perro' by the scruff and dragged him out onto the grass. This time only his legs were muddy. Nat grabbed him by the lose skin at the back of his neck, marched him over to the trickle of a stream feeding the pond, the dog's front legs not touching the ground and dunked him up and down in one of the shallow depressions of the feeder. The others clapped. Rex, embarrassed in the way dogs can show, didn't even shake himself to start with but stood briefly with tail down, one paw up, whites of eyes showing, suffering the laughter. Then, listening enough to the offending abuse, scattered the water with a few good shakes and took off for a race around the garden. Like any dog, nursing not the slightest grudge towards mankind, he caught up with them, acting as though nothing had happened, as the group ambled off stopping and starting to take in various other features in the vicinity of the house.

The front door was set into a gothic arch, not unusual considering its clerical past. Robust to a degree, its weathered mass was supported by exterior hinge brackets extending a third of the width across, fixed to the two-inch thick oak timbers by heavy-duty, coach screws. It opened into a small antechamber. Granite formed a short flight of steps leading to a glass-panelled inner door, steps smooth from centuries of footwear, perhaps even that of armed militia in the civil war or later; or the boots of smugglers hiding contraband in some secret, hollow place like a priest's hole.

The panelled door opened into what had once been the prior's private chapel but was now a dining room. Doors led off to a kitchen and a corridor, the corridor leading to various side rooms and, at its end, a stairway to a series of chambers that once housed guests of the prelate. Previous owners had been respectful of its provenance. Little had been done to alter its interior. But this was unsurprising, the craftsmanship reflected in the panelled wall carvings invited respect. The four were quiet, silenced by the ghosts that, in their imaginations, walked the passage.

'I never realised this was such a beautiful house,' Jenny spoke to her father, 'had you been here before, when the previous owners lived here?'

'A few times. With my father when the old squire lived here and once or twice with your mother, before you were born.'

'Do you think there is any truth in the story about a tunnel?'

'Yes. There definitely is but it was never, for obvious reasons, marked on any deeds or maps.'

'Why are you so certain it exists then?'

'There is an allusion to it in some document held in archives over at Bodmin but it gives no indication as to where it is accessed or exited. Not even that it is connected to the church. It's possible the church story is just a blind to put the authorities off and that the real exit is down to one of the faces overlooking the river, amongst the trees.'

'So it could have been used for smuggling then?'

'Yes! More than likely but could also have provided escape for protestant or catholic believers, depending on the resident danger, during the religious wars. But it might not have existed that far back. Nobody knows. Somebody digging it or using it might have let slip something of its existence to a relative or friend. Legends grow!'

The four visited all the rooms, Nat and Jenny now alert to any oddness of feature that might indicate the existence of a tunnel's whereabouts. They were looking in the wrong place for the wrong clues. They would never discover it using the kind of thinking suggested by a romantic perception of false panels, secret tunnels and smuggling haunts. The tunnel's builder was more cunning than that.

*

Squire du Plessis's forebears were Huguenots who had escaped persecution from France. One branch headed to Franschoek, South Africa the other to Cornwall from Brittany. Robert du Plessis, a bachelor, was a frequent visitor to a certain inn on Customs House Quay, in the port of Falmouth. There he conducted business with a close eye on the door and watchful interest in any face new to the usual clientele. Although of French descent and it being only three years since the defeat of Napoleon Bonaparte, he was not regarded with suspicion. Well known to the 'Free Traders', as the local smugglers termed their profession, he had contacts across the Channel in the port of Roscoff. His fluency in the Breton language eased the negotiations that facilitated safe transfer of contraband – mainly brandy from the Cognac makers further south - to the schooner captains plying out of Falmouth.

His father had bought the Priory. It was a thriving centre of activity that so far had not attracted the attention of the revenue men. But times were changing. Faster revenue cutters, firearms, modern for their time and possessing greater accuracy, were proving disastrous for this clandestine trade. It was true, those getting caught were not observing the same caution his band of free-traders practised but even so he was uneasy at the rate of success the government men were achieving.

Samuel Bray stood in the doorway and peered into the blue smoke coming from a score of clay pipes. Sam was du Plessis's main choice for a run. His boat, the Agnes, was fast and his crew trustworthy. Informers were always the main risk, especially since the authorities had upped the reward money for information. Du Plessis spotted him and pointed to a pewter tankard next to his own as Sam finally caught sight of him in a corner on a raised dais away from the main body of drinkers.

'Thought I'd get here early and secure a quiet spot.' Robert pushed the full tankard towards his visitor forcing him to sit opposite rather than alongside him on the wooden settle. That way, with Sam blocking him from the view of other clients, he ran less risk of some nosy lip-reader knowing his business.

'Problems Squire?' Sam picked up his tankard and addressed Robert with a quizzical look, 'We're not due a consignment for a while.'

'Not yet! That's not what I want to talk about. Drink up! I've got another proposition.'

Sam took a long pull on the ale, set the mug down and put both fists on the table.

'We've been lucky but we've been careful and I want it to stay that way. I've got it in mind to run a tunnel from the house to the river. The two shore men from Redruth, who sail with us sometimes, are miners. I'm willing to pay them to put a 'rat run' between the two but since I'm taking the longer-term risk against a search, receiving and storing the goods, I need to defray the cost, a bit, from the proceeds. Now,' du Plessis put his hand up at Sam's immediate attempt at an objection, 'I'm guessing you were about to object. Now, to put your mind at rest, I also recognise that you as schooner owner are also taking a risk, as is everyone. The crew with their lives and the shore men as well. So what I propose is that first we don't accept any increase in cost from the suppliers for at least a year. Last grape harvest was good and they've distilled more Cognac than they know what to do with. I don't think they'll be too put out by that because demand here is increasing and they'll benefit from the extra trade we can shift from them. Second, we put prices up this end to our customers. I'm pretty sure they'll accept because they'll be aware of the greater risk to us that increased rewards for information is bringing. Third, we pay every one of us more per cargo, splitting the extra profit equally amongst all bodies with a separate, additional bonus to the two of us.'

Sam nodded, 'Yes, when you put it that way, everyone our end will be happy. Nobody complains at an extra bit of income and the prospect of continued, future 'commerce' will be a deterrent to turn informant.'

He took another draught of ale, then paused with tankard in mid air, arrested by a more serious thought, 'There is a problem. How are you going to explain a lot of digging activity if anybody challenges you?'

'I've sorted that one out. Tregennza doesn't have a smoke house. I'm going to build one between the house and the river and drag it out so completion takes as long as building the tunnel. Make it look like that's what all the earth moving's about. No one person casually passing the farm will be daily observing progress. It's unlikely anyone will be aware of when the project was started or at what stage they are witnessing its development. Visitors are a rare occurrence. Those who do come rarely come twice and as far as the two farm hands are concerned, they know which side their bread is buttered. I look after them better than any on the farms around. They're in on the job anyway and will benefit from the extra split in the profits.'

'A smoke house will be one of the first places revenue men would search if that's where you propose to exit the tunnel or store goods.'

'I do propose to exit the tunnel through the smoke house but not store goods in it.'

' Well there you are then. They'll dig and discover any cover you're hiding the entrance with.'

'Who said anything about it being in the floor?'

'So? What d'you propose? They'll spot any disguised access in any wall. They're aware of all sorts of tricks.'

'That's where the mouse beats the cat. I will make sure a fire is lit the same day as the moonlighting so that any patrol on the scent sees a fire going. They will see smoke coming from a chimney. What they won't see from ground level is a chimney that is double channelled. One small hole for smoke, another going all the way down to the tunnel and wide enough for small casks or crew to get up or down. Even if they put out the fire, start searching and go as far as digging, they'll be disappointed.'

Sam slapped a thigh, 'Best one I've heard yet. It should work. What about the other end?'

'We follow a route that takes us to the overhang where the river's deep, rather than using the strand either side, as we've risked doing the last few times. We can transfer cargo to a skiff, push under the tree branches and offload into the entrance. It's always a couple of fathoms deep even at low tide. We can dig right to the water's edge and practically float in on a high tide. The trees will hide the opening from view. It's an impossible place to land as far as any revenue man is concerned. In fact it might be a good idea to open up the first ten or fifteen feet to make a wider, flat staging just inside a smaller entrance so as cargo can be offloaded speedy-like.'

The two, satisfied with their proposal, carried on talking about nothing much in particular after that, finished their ale, then left to see to other business.

24

A few weeks later Robert du Plessis and Sam Bray met at their usual watering hole.

'My contact at the consulate in Penzance, informs me Gaston Lefevre has two dozen quarter casks waiting at Roscoff as well as a consignment of baccy off-loaded by a Virginian trader. How are you fixed for mid month? No moon and should be clement weather, if the last four years are anything to go by.'

'Depends on the actual day. There's a spring tide about then. Means we could go further upstream to unload, if you wanted. When d'you reckon the tunnel's goin' to be finished?'

'Haven't started yet. Only just put down the slate floor to the smoke house and a foot or two of wall. It's less than a third of a furlong to the river's edge. The terrain is slate, soil and stone aggregate. Won't be difficult to dig out and more stable than plain earth but will still need shoring up in places. We'll have to be six or seven feet below. Tree roots are a nuisance. Any shallower than that and we'll get a suspicious looking avenue of trees dying off all the way to the river.

I'm going to put down a slope from the chimney, not a shaft, with a short, level, bit of a platform outside, enough for one or two men and a few casks to stand on actually below the lip of the chimney itself. In fact, when I say I haven't started the tunnel, not quite true, I have cleared the level and built a sort of solid, stone ante room.

We'll need it for long term storage where the rain doesn't seep through. That much I have done just to get a handle on the effort involved. The roof over the level is about a foot below the surrounding ground-level and I've already covered it with earth again.'

'Fair enough. I've got a consignment of Norwegian pine pit props to fetch and deliver to Devoran. I'm banking on a fair wind this time o'year but it'll take me five days to get to Kristiansand. Two days to load, maybe. Five or six back. Another two to unload. She's a fast craft but we're talkin' about a fortnight's delay. That'll take us to about when you want to fetch your cargo.'

'Will just have to chance it. I don't want any of the other captains doing this run. Too much at stake with the tobacco. Can't afford to lose any cargo but at least, with brandy, the charge isn't as high as for baccy that's already bin transported half way cross the world. The premium on that one is too much to risk.'

'Should only take twenty four hours or so to get to Roscoff. I'll sail out of Falmouth early morning, just before dawn. The customs crowd will notice we've up-anchored and gone but not which direction and if I turn round by dusk at Roscoff – that'll give me twelve hours to load and give the crew a rest - should get back into the estuary well after dusk, twenty four hours later. Can drop a man off at Rosemullion Head and he can be on horseback to Falmouth before we get there, to warn you.'

'Fair enough. We'll have to rely on some Penryn men then if that's the case. The Helford mob will have to miss out on this one. Tell you what, I'm of half a mind to go with you. We can leave with an extra couple of men on board. Won't need to waste time dropping a man at Rosemullion on the way back nor having a bunch of men hanging about not knowing when the boat was due. Might be able to pick up a few yards of Breton lace; I have a contact who can get his hands on pretty well anything local at short notice. The gentry always like to sweeten their ladies with a bit of haberdashery and I fancy a visit to the old country now things have quietened down.'

'It might be just as well. I've always thought it risky dropping it off at Port Navas or Gweek. Too much small boat activity; then moving the stuff overland in dribs and drabs just adds more risk. If we unload at the strand below Tregennza we cut out more middlemen.'

'Whilst you're at it, you might as well hang onto a few pit props. I've got a stack already from the saw yard but not enough. We'll need quite a bit of timber to shore up with in the tunnel so it might as well come from your consignment. Can you 'half-inch' a few?'

'No need to. I'll get the stevedore at Kristiansand to put a small stack on deck. He'll be only too glad to if I throw in a couple of bottles of rum. Alcohol costs an arm and a leg up there Squire, that's if you can get it even. How many you likely to need?'

'Don't know. How long will they be?'

'Five, six feet, maybe.'

'I'm guessing props won't be needed all the way along but I want to put a couple of small storage bays in a third the way from each end. Pretty sure we can use some of the stones to support parts of the tunnel but will need some cross-slats as well, against the roof, under the poles. So let's say two score and preferably five feet long. If we need any more we can get a few cut locally, when we see how it's going. The cross pieces I can get from the local saw mill as well.'

'What are you going to do with the overburden?'

'Pick out the big stones and build a bit of a low wharf down on one of the strands. I'll dump the rest down the old mine shaft.'

'I was going to say a lot of fresh spoil showing up on the surface would attract questions.'

'I'll dig out a false quarry by the oak grove and make it look like the stones for the strand came from there. Nobody'll think to question the difference in the size of the dig and the number of stones at the wharf.'

'Sounds alright. Drink up!' Sam waved his tankard at the squire, 'My shout!'

*

A light wind and dawn on the Breton coast brought with it the smell of wood smoke and fresh bread from the boulangerie as the Agnes tied up in port at Roscoff. The baker would have been the first to fire up his ovens, using wood split from seasoned logs, three hours before anyone else had stirred. Robert du Plessis savoured a long forgotten memory of a butter, sugar and dough pastry his mother used to bake, an early fore-runner of the kouign-aman cake that characterized that particular region and would come to define sweet, butter-based pastries long before the croissant made its debut. A coffee house located in the main street and sheltered from the sea front, served as the rendezvous for the free-traders and their Breton contacts. The squire, captain and crew jumped ship anticipating the pleasure of a smoky coffee from the little stove pots and a slab of the sweet, buttery cake.

News of the schooner's arrival must have been relayed to the 'French Connection' promptly. Gaston Lefevre turned up before the patron had time to serve all the visitors. Greetings were exchanged and the business of refreshment conducted before the business of commerce.

Gaston spoke pretty good English but, as expected, with an accent that delighted his Cornish cousins.

'I 'ave zome good Cognac for you and zome,' he hesitated, 'not so good Cognac for you.'

'What d'you mean, you old rogue?'

'Well, z'cognac comes now, zometimes in casks and zometimes in glass. In z'cask it is less zan in z' glass. Z'glass is a demijohn in wicker and straw basket but better qualeetay zan z'other. You will get more for eet.'

Robert laughed, 'How much more?'

'A quarter more.'

'And I suppose you're telling me I pay a quarter more for a bulk buy.'

'Zat iz fair!'

'No! I want to taste it first and I pay you an eighth more. No more!'

'Non M'sieu. A quarter.'

'I taste it first, then I shall see if it is worth buying.'

Both sides were used to this haggling and knew it would continue in Gaston's warehouse. As it turned out the demijohns of brandy were of significantly better quality than the usual stuff du Plessis offloaded onto the local publicans and other of his clients. There were discerning clients who would pay more. He knew he would have no trouble selling to some of the wealthy merchants and mine owners in the area.

'Tell you what, I take the two dozen quarter casks at the same as last time and pay you a sixth more for the other.'

Lefevre sat on one of the casks, 'A fifth and that's my final offer.'

Robert didn't want to appear too ready to give in, 'Show me the tobacco.'

Lefevre led the squire over to a number of hogsheads. One had been opened, resting on its side in the middle of an old, square-rigged sail.. Some of its content had been removed in such a way as to expose the remainder for consistency.

'I chose zis at random and z'leaves are good.'

Robert picked one up and rubbed it between his fingers. It had a smooth feel to it. He smelt it and dropped it back. A tobacconist in Penryn, who processed the air-cured leaf by a fermentation process, would pay good money for premium leaves.

'What are you expecting to get for this?'

Lefevre quoted a figure and it was obvious he was willing to sell partial quantities.

Du Plessis knew he could sell for double.

'Right then, at that price I can meet your figure for the demijohns. I'll take one of the hogsheads. We have a deal.'

The two shook hands.

'Now I have another request. Can you get some Breton lace before we leave?'

'I will see. I 'ave a number of ladies who make it. Let me find out. I will bring it to z'ship.'

'Good! A bientot.'

Transactions sorted out, everyone went about the remains of the day's demands. The ship, duly laden by the end of daylight hours and a bale of expensive lace part of the cargo, they were all invited back to Lefevre's for a meal.

'Before you go we drink to future trade. Zis is z'best Calvados. I get it from my fren in Honfleur.' Gaston removed the cork. The assembled group could smell the spirit as he released the rich, vapourous smell of apple brandy from the hand blown flask and filled the tiny glasses put in front of each of them.

'Is good, no?'

The assembled tribe of Celts sipped the golden liquid, chatted a few more minutes and then took leave of their host. The same breeze that brought the smell of baking to them when they arrived was still blowing in a north westerly direction and took them to the cliffs of Cornwall before daylight, as they had intended. They cruised quietly, without lights, into the estuary, the braziers at Pendennis and St Mawes castles, tended by guards long since unconcerned about French invasion, gave a cheering glow. On and up to the lower boundary of the priory, the whole group were out on deck enjoying the relief of a safe and lucrative voyage.

25

Robert du Plessis, on his earlier instruction, joined the two Redruth men just before the tunnel was due to break through above the river. He dropped the end of the rope, previously laid down outside to provide a precise measure of the distance from smoke house to river's edge.

'Do you want to hammer the last face into the water?' Paul Jenkins offered the bar and maul to the squire.

'No it's your privilege. You and Simon have done all the tunnelling. Your privilege!'

'Right. Here goes!' Paul placed the bar mid-point onto one particularly large stone, looked at the other two, paused and then gave the bar an almighty clout. With a shower of debris, not much in the way of dust, the rock disappeared into a welcome stream of daylight and tumbled down the outside face to hit the river with a satisfying splash, audible to them all through the small gap. They couldn't help giving a cheer. All three shook hands, breathing in welcome quantities of fresh oxygen as the hitherto stationary volume of stale air was replenished and forced upwards and out through the newly completed chimney in the smoke house. Robert couldn't resist knocking the remaining ballast into the river so took the bar and maul from Paul and sent stones, slate and soil cascading into the current below. They stood, silent for a moment or two. The sight of the river so close, flowing just a foot below them, was an eerie sensation, disturbing in a way. The end of a submerged branch hanging from an oak above them, oscillated to and fro in the current, metering its flow with half-second beats.

'This deserves a drink and a bonus for getting it done so quickly and with no accidents. I shall still need you to put the two bays in but that can wait a day or two. Let's get back to the house.'

*

The tunnel and bays proved their worth over four seasons. There were no cargos from late autumn to Easter. Winter storms were the main deciding factor for any free-trader but storms could blow up mid-summer or any time. The sea showed no favours, neither to the prudent nor imprudent mariner. Robert du Plessis built up a stock of goods in the bays with more perishable cargo stored in the subterranean ante room. He now made it a regular habit of going across whenever he chartered the Agnes for a run. Some of the tobacco was now being shipped from the Americas already fermented in rum. The pressed cake of the rum-soaked tobacco leaf was heady where the scent escaped through the narrow joints between the staves of the barrels.

The first window of promising weather came a week after the spring equinox. Commencement of traffic across the Channel, with some of the larger, more seaworthy square-riggers, had already begun to spawn a renewed raft of offers and requests for goods.

The stable condition afforded Cognac stored in demijohns – quite apart from the higher quality of the brandy being offered in the glass and wicker containers - inclined du Plessis to purchase less and less of the spirit in wooden casks in favour of the former. Evaporation from barrels, coupled with deterioration in taste, sometimes caused by prolonged contact with badly conditioned casks, also militated in favour of the non-reactive, glass flasks. Lefevre, unbidden, now provided him with the latter with just the odd inclusion, now and again, of a cask.

His second trip of the new season started badly. The Agnes hit fog as it approached the coast of Brittany. The rocks and submerged reefs around there were nearly as treacherous and as uncharted as those around the Western Rocks of the Isles of Scilly. Samuel Bray put down an anchor not knowing whether he was a league or less from shore. This enforced stop put them out of sequence with tide and sun and meant either delaying departure from Roscoff by a full day or taking a risk of sailing back into Falmouth at a possibly more dangerous time. They had little choice but to stick it out, wait for dawn and hope the fog was beneath a clear sky and not further compounded by a blanket of cloud preventing the sun from burning it off.

'I'll put a man up front. We'll go in on one sail and a sea anchor. As soon as he yells we drop the sail. The drogue'll slow us to a stop in a chain's length but we'll have to wait until there's enough light.'

After a wait of some forty or fifty minutes the captain decided it was light enough to spot any obstruction to the intended passage of the schooner. They hauled up the iron anchor, dropped a canvas sea anchor over the stern and got under way. The ominous sound of surf ahead of them gave no indication as to whether it was a rock or whether they were approaching the harbour wall of Roscoff. Sam gave a signal to drop the sail, waited for the various creaks and rattles of any ship underway to cease and stood with head cocked listening. The unmistakeable sounds of human activity came through the fog. A door slamming; gulls making calls they only make when land-based; a cough. They were very close to port. It had taken them almost an hour to steer through the fog.

'Alright, we're safe here. Got a fathom and a half of water below us.'

A shift in the wind and help from a still low sun, caused the bank of fog to fragment into avenues with distinct boundaries, separating pockets of the near opaque medium from the clear, navigable channels. The Agnes pulled into one of these and lined up with a town marker before the fog coalesced, again, into a visually, impenetrable barrier. They reached the quayside, tied up and made their way to the coffee house, by which time the weather had lifted and Lefevre would have a clear view of the ship. His 'spies' must have been alert because he arrived to join them before they had finished their first cups of coffee.

The usual protocols of greeting; the commerce; the hospitality dealt with during the next few hours, the Agnes's passengers and cargo disembarked later than intended. Two hours of darkness had already elapsed before they cleared the port and headed for the cliffs of Cornwall.

Twenty four hours later, crossing the imaginary line that joined Pendennis and St Mawes castles, the crew again made sure no lanterns were visible as they sailed past the town of Falmouth. There was a moon, a full moon which was a blessing and a curse. They could have done with cloud cover passing this outpost of the packet mail trade, this point of departure for the voyages to the colonies and other ports of call. They had no choice but to sail quietly up the Carrick Roads, the name given to the main thoroughfare along which the many creeks and minor rivers gave life and character to the estuary and provided further opportunity for maritime enterprise.

Du Plessis was uneasy. It was uncommonly quiet. At any time of night in a busy port there was always some traffic going on in goods and people. It was almost as if the population had been warned to stay indoors. That was it! There must be an ambush set up. It was then that he saw another, slower vessel ahead of them, a brigantine, also without candle or lantern. He recognised it as belonging to one of the other captains he sometimes used.

Unwittingly, because of the need for secrecy, another free-trader had chosen this, of all nights, to mount an operation and no one other person not in on the plan was any the wiser. Samuel Bray had spotted the craft at the same time.

'I don't like this! Something not right.'

'I'm of the same turn of mind,' du Plessis responded, 'he's genuine but I can't vouch for his care over crew. We could have an informer in our midst, of his making. He'll be pulling into Devoran, I'm pretty sure. We'll have to take a chance on this and follow him in. Pretend that's where we were making for all along. With a bit of luck, if an ambush is set up, it'll be out of the trees over by the forge, I reckon and not close to us. We'll have unloaded by then. It'll take him another ten minutes after he's passed our tunnel. Can't warn them. Might be unjustified alarm on our part but we're goin' to have to unload sharpish just in case.'

'Problem is, if they're expecting him, the same lookout that spots him will spot us.'

'I know, that's why we unload quickly and sail on up to Devoran, as if we've just returned empty and are going to load up a cargo from there in the morning. They won't register, they can't register, the delay we take unloading.'

The Agnes sailed on quietly. With eyes conditioned to the dark and moon light reflected from a practically ripple-free river, Robert du Plessis kept an eye open for natural markers, some silhouetted against the sky, others by bends and twists in the river giving warning of approach to the tunnel.

'Point Quay on your starboard. Anchor men, get ready.'

There were only one or two lights showing in the settlement at Point, across the water. Another favourite location for our free traders, Penpol, just up from the Quay, claimed its share of hideouts.

The squire gave a signal to drop anchor. They were just a few meters upstream of the tunnel entrance. That way, with a rope on the ship's boat, they could load her and let her drift in the current, with just a bit of steering, back down to the opening. It dispensed with the need for oars which, even with the most skilful handler, creaked in the wooden rowlocks. Even more beneficial, a couple of the crew could drag the little craft back against the current far faster than any oarsman could and again without the creak and splash of oars in this most silent of professions.

The whole business of loading and unloading was carried out with the speed and practised order of a crew used to working against tides, threatening storms and, of course, heightened risk of discovery by unwelcome company. The silence of their third and final transfer was interrupted by gunfire. True to misgivings, the sound came from the wharf up at Devoran. The little boat was unloaded purposefully but without haste, dragged back and tethered to the schooner's stern. To store it back on deck would be to invite questions as to why she was dripping water over the decking at that time of night. Robert du Plessis remained back at the tunnel. The presence of the squire aboard the Agnes supposedly going about its normal business of plying trade, would have been immediately suspect. The crew up-anchored and the schooner cruised innocently towards the manor house, Chy Worval, hidden from view by trees up on their right. Whatever mayhem had been enacted ahead of them, sounds of Gunfire had now ceased. They rounded the last shoulder of land jutting out into the creek. Ahead there were lanterns moving about all over a quay close to the forge. A small group of redcoats, shipped in from Bodmin, were minding a bunch of shoremen and crew, from the brig, sitting on the ground. Another group seemed to be massed around and on the boat. It looked to the crew aboard the Agnes that the platoon had allowed the vessel to unload its cargo before showing themselves. It was easy to corral the smugglers. They had nowhere to escape to other than take to the water from the tongue of land forming the quay.

In all the excitement no one on land saw the approach of the larger ship.

'Get ready to wave a lantern,' Sam spoke to one of his crew, 'I'm going to call out any time.'

The Agnes eased up to the stern of the smaller boat, 'Avast you landlubbers. Hold your fire. Friendly ship approaching.'

The mob beyond his rail turned from whatever they were engrossed in and looked with surprise at the schooner that had silently moved in on them. An officer, a young captain, moved out from a line of red coats and commanded Bray to stand off.

'What's your name and what's your business?'

'Captain Samuel Bray of the Agnes returning from Plymouth.'

This seemed to satisfy the officer, 'Right captain. Let a couple of men off to tie up but then you and your crew stay aboard until I say.' He then turned back to supervising the confiscation of the illegal cargo.

*

Dawn came early, un-delayed by a cloudless sky. A sudden ruckus broke out at the edge of the gathering. All turned to see a fusilier getting back onto his feet as the indistinct figure of one of the smugglers was seen bolting for the fringe of trees bordering the area. One of the more alert soldiers, posted further out, taking his time, drew a bead on the escaping man and let go a ball after him. The man shrieked, stumbled, recovered, put a hand down to his upper leg then carried on at a fast limp into the trees.

'Leave him,' it was the young captain, 'he won't get far. We'll catch up with him later. And if we don't find him he'll die from infection anyway with a ball that size in him.'

26

Robert du Plessis remained at the lip of the tunnel's edge, watching through the screen of branches until the schooner was out of sight. He turned, took the lantern left for him by one of the crew, from the top of a hogshead and picked his way back up through the passage to the smoke house chimney. The contraband could wait until tomorrow or the day after, before he could be bothered to get it shifted up into the lower bay. There it would be above the tidal flooding area. For now, with no spring tide imminent, it would be safe and with nothing in the cargo susceptible to damp it was doubly free from any need of further protection.

Leaving the lantern extinguished on a small ledge close to the chimney top, ready for use on his return, he clambered out onto the granite dome of the roof. Using a series of discreetly raised stones as hand holds he felt his way down to a small, stone platform, situated for its convenience, at the side of the low door to the smoke house. It was well into the approach to dawn. He opened the door and felt about on a small ledge inside until his hands located a piece of hessian. Unfolding the cloth, he took from it a flint and striking steel. With his back to the door he knelt and struck a few sparks, sufficient to show where he had laid some tinder. His eyes, now accustomed to the gloom and aided by filtered light from a sun still well below the horizon, he picked out a small wad of kapok set by the twigs. The soft, slightly oily, outer fibres flared at the first strike of flint. Kneeling lower, he blew into the tiny cluster of embers, pushing the wad under the pile of tinder with a stick as he did so. He watched with satisfaction as the pile of twigs and larger sticks soon caught. Flames licked up between an outer layer of substantial slabs of wood split from seasoned logs of oak.

Waiting until the pile was burning well, he took a brand and set fire to two more heaps. Adding lengths of green oak to these, the whole, crackling, sizzling mass began to give off the characteristic smoke that would add flavour to the hams hanging above. Before closing the door he checked that the supply of logs stacked around the walls was not too close to the fires in the middle of the floor. If any excise men turned up now, as a result of the disaster being enacted up stream, they would find a fully operational smoke house doing what it was designed to do.

Back in the priory fatigue kicked in. He went up to his bedroom, pulled off his boots and dropped onto his bed fully dressed. Well into the afternoon, he was woken by a desperate hammering on the big door. He went to the window and saw a collapsed figure or rather a pair of boots belonging to someone just out of sight who was obviously sitting, propped up against the door. One of the boots was soaked in blood. It didn't take much thinking to know this was a casualty of the encounter between excise men and free-traders. He rushed down and exited the house through a side door. The man on the front step was just hanging onto consciousness. Du Plessis looked about him knowing the revenue men would expect the wounded escapee to make for shelter of some kind. It wasn't safe to give him attention on the step of the house, even more risky to have him incapacitated inside but the man looked to be in no state to suffer further delay in treatment for his wound. The squire took a pocket knife from his jacket and cut a slash in the material where the bullet had entered. It was a serious wound but not life threatening as far as he could judge, in terms of tissue or bone damage. The musket ball was just visible. The range must have been such that the piece of lead had lost a lot of momentum by the time it had reached its target. With prompt treatment he would recover. What was worrying du Plessis was the sight of fragments of cloth embedded in the flesh, either side of a ball, now blackened by dried blood. Infection was the enemy at this point, not patrols of militia scouring the woods.

'What's your name.?'

'Roger Bennett.'

'Right Roger, you've got this far, if I get you up can you make it to that building over there?' The squire pointed to the smoke house. The man put his hand up in agreement and nodded feebly. Du Plessis managed to get him back on his feet and the two men staggered across to the back of the smoke house.

'I'm going to sit you down here out of sight and get you some water, then I'll see to your wound but not before I've hidden you. It's not safe for you to be in the house. Revenue men will search there first. They're sure to turn up.'

The squire returned with a pitcher of water and mug. The wounded man weak from blood loss, parched and dehydrated, downed two mugs of water. This revived him somewhat.

'I must swill the traces of blood from the steps before anything else, otherwise we're done for. We're then going to have to get you up on the roof here and down a secret shaft in the chimney so prepare yourself for more pain while I clean the steps.'

Du Plessis removed all trace of blood stain, then went to an outbuilding and returned with a coil of rope.

'Lift your arms.' The squire put a loop under the smuggler's arm pits and positioned the rope at his front.

'I'm going to get up and pull you to the top but you're going to have to use your hands to help me. There are some hand holds. They're difficult to spot from the ground but if you follow the line of the rope you'll see them as your head reaches them. You ready?'

'I'm ready.'

'Right! On your feet.' Du Plessis helped Bennett onto his feet and faced him towards the stonework.

The squire clambered up the side of the domed structure, dragging the rope end with him. At the top he sat with his back against the chimney. When the wounded man was ready, the two began the painful business of getting him up to the narrow shaft entrance. Bennett still had a residue of strength in his arms. Using his good leg and the handholds, the climb was easier than expected. At the top they positioned themselves down-wind of the curing smoke.

'Sit on the edge and swing your good leg over the shaft. I'll lift the other up and slide it over, you don't need to put any strain into the muscle. There are stones jutting out to put your feet on all the way down, just like the ones you can see near the top but you'll have to put some weight on that bad leg.'

Du Plessis reached down into the chimney and retrieved the lantern he'd left on the ledge earlier.

'When you reach bottom sit on the floor and wait for me to get the lantern going. But I'm going into the house first to strip an old sheet for wound dressing. I'll bring back some brandy to clean the wound with after I've removed the musket ball.'

Roger Bennett grimaced, 'Rather take my chance and wait for the surgeon.'

'We can't wait for the surgeon. I've seen wounds like this before. Need to remove the bullet soon, otherwise you could lose your leg from sepsis. If the excise men turn up when I'm in the house I'll be delayed so don't decide to show yourself because you think I've forgotten. If they turn up whilst I'm back here then both of us will have to stay put 'til they've scarpered. Big problem is, if that happens, they might post a couple of men to wait my return or to see if you turn up. They might still do that anyway, even if I'm out there. Could even insist on staying overnight.'

Bennett had no choice so argued no further, slid his hips forward and felt for the first foothold with his good leg. The squire watched him descend, painful step by painful step, until he reached the bottom, then turned and clambered down the outside with the lantern. Before fetching the sheet and brandy he checked the fires in the smoke house and put fresh logs on. Taking a piece of kindling he set fire to it and, needing light for the cellar, re-lit the lantern. Back in the house he clambered two flights of stairs to a linen room and selected a worn sheet.

Brandy was down in the cellar. Knowing the state Bennett's leg was in, he knew he needed more than the small quantity left in the smoking room decanter. Taking the sheet with him he dropped it on the same table where he'd put the lamp earlier and opened the cellar door in the hall passage alongside it. The flight of steps down into the darkness was steep. He didn't venture down there that frequently, because of this, finding the effort taxing on the return climb. Ancient cradles of wood, on which were stored hand-blown bottles of wine, were covered in dust. Alcoves, built from blood red bricks and dug into the side of the hill, contained piles of rusting weaponry. Farming implements and other rural paraphernalia, some the signature of monastic living – testified to the ecclesiastical nature of the priory.

He peered at the various racks. Eventually one attracted his attention. It was more book shelf than rack in that its timbers were flat, plain planks but instead of books it held round flasks, each seated in a circular hole. There was no need for the regime of slanting bottles so placed partly to keep corks moist, partly to allow sediments containing tannin and other lees to settle round the re-entrant cones of Bordeaux wine bottles. The liquid was already refined, free from solids, hermetically sealed with cork and sealing wax and not needing the cosseting of Grand Cru wines.

Du Plessis picked one of the flasks. It suddenly felt cold in the cellar. The bottle slipped from his hand and smashed on the slate floor. He stared in disbelief, unable to comprehend what was happening to him, unable to take in the surreal, disorientating image of the pool of spirit spreading around the lantern placed at his feet and running under the leather soles of his boots. His eyes closed. He tumbled forward unaware of any pain, any consciousness other than that of an almost comforting anaesthesia, a combination of Arctic chill and Cognac fumes.

In the chamber below the smoke house Roger Bennett began to experience the effects of shock, both mental and that induced physically by a body reacting to trauma. He could not see it but the flesh around the wound was red, swollen and beginning to nourish the colonies of bacteria inhabiting the piece of cloth embedded in his leg, underneath the musket ball. There was a cool draught blowing up through the tunnel from the river but it did little to free him from the pain and unbearable itch he was enduring from the wound. He shifted a little. There was no way he could find comfort on the hard floor.

Sometime later, he had no idea how long, he realised he had fallen asleep. His leg was throbbing now, it must have been this that woke him up. The wound had closed over and the bacteria, had they possessed minds, would have been celebrating their good fortune. Bennett was parched and in high fever. Where the hell was du Plessis? He made an effort to reach the shaft in the chimney – not to climb it but to face into the cooling draught coming up the tunnel. The move caused the most excruciating pain, immediately followed by the most exquisite relief as the suppurating wound burst open, shedding the ball and flooding his leg with a magma of yellow pus and blood. He remained like this for three or four days until he fell sideways, dehydrated, unconscious, stinking of sweat and decay.

*

A group of redcoats arrived at the priory about two hours after Bennett had and spread out around the site investigating every hiding place a fugitive might be concealed. They sought no permission. When this proved fruitless a corporal hammered on the main door. Getting no response, he tried it, it was still locked so took his men around to the side door. This time, not bothering to knock and finding it unsecured, he took his men in. He posted one man at the exit and proceeded to search all rooms and cupboards. A shout from the direction of the passage brought two of them to the still open cellar door. There was a dim glow at the bottom of the steps, the lantern was still burning. One of the two called down the steps, partly to acknowledge receipt of the call and partly for reassurance nothing was amiss with their colleague below.

'Come quick, there's a man down, could be the owner, not moving. He's still warm.'

They clattered down the stairs and found their comrade bent over the inert squire.

'Let's get him up top. Looks like his 'eart give out or stroke.'

'Wait a bit. Who's to say he wasn't 'it from behind by our wounded friend. Better check this place out first.'

Their search, of course, was to prove a waste of time. They got du Plessis up the steps and dumped him up against the panelled wall of the passage. By this time the corporal turned up and, a bit more observant than his men, spotted the worn, folded bed sheet on the side table.

'Brandy bottle smashed you say?'

'Yes corporal. Looks like he let it fall.'

The corporal had seen action in some of the skirmishes against Napoleon and had observed the use of brandy, as a wound disinfectant, when nothing else was to hand. He had an instinct for the subterfuges practised by the gentry engaged at the receiving end of free-trade.

'Our man is here somewhere. My guess, one of the outbuildings. I doubt the owner would hide him inside. It would be risking transportation for aiding a felon if discovered in his house. This one can't go far,' he said this with a brutal laugh, giving du Plessis a nudge with the toe of his boot, 'we can leave him in place whilst we search further but before we do, four of you post yourselves outside at the boundary of the main yard and outbuildings. We'll half-inch a bottle or two from down there and have a drink before we start again. You men deserve a bit of encouragement. See it as a bonus from his majesty King George, for favours rendered.'

His men guffawed at this. He was a disciplinarian but knew how to keep himself and his men alive. For that they respected him.

'You take the lantern, bring up two bottles of brandy and half a dozen of the wine. It looked like claret bottles to me. You go with him.' He addressed two of his men. 'We'll have a nip in the kitchen, sure to be some glasses there. The rest we take back to camp. Share it out with the mob. Not a word to the captain, though, or I'll have your guts for garters.'

Some thirty minutes later they resumed their search of the premises and surrounding land.

'Right, it'll be dark in an hour or so. Our quarry is hidden where we won't find him, I'll wager or we'd have found him by now so we best call it off and get back to camp.'

27

At daybreak the crew of the Agnes, still confined to ship, looked out on the haul confiscated from their unfortunate fellow smugglers.

'We'll wait at anchor until this mob departs. 'tis my belief they'll send a naval cutter to pick up this lot, men and cargo. There's probably one at anchor in Falmouth now,' Captain Bray spoke to his mate, 'I reckon they'll let you off if I say you need to negotiate trade with the merchants at Perran wharf. We're goin' to have to give truth to the lie. We need plank nails, anyway, for the shipwrights at St Marys so we might as well get 'em from the iron merchant there as Falmouth. Cheaper too.'

Samuel Bray, for a second time, leaned out over the ship's rail and addressed the redcoat captain.

'My mate needs permission to take a handful of men to pick up a consignment of plank nails from Perran Wharf. Delivery for Isles of Scilly and we don't want to be beached on the next low tide.'

The captain nodded, 'I need to check your vessel first,' he was a pragmatic man who appreciated the time constraints placed on ships' captains by tides and daylight hours but he also knew it his duty not to take any situation at face value, 'get ready to receive my sergeant at arms and three men. We'll do it now.'

Some short while later, the sergeant reported a 'clean' ship and the mate was cleared for departure with some of the crew. True to prediction, a naval cutter turned up early afternoon; loaded the contraband and stayed tied up until the corporal and his men returned. The mate arrived before nightfall, with canvas bags of nails and both ships got into mid-channel before the tide reduced the waterway to mudflats.

The following morning, having tied up in Falmouth for the night, Sam Bray called in at a number of chandleries and other stores for more items to trade on St Marys. There was a thriving boat building industry on the Isles of Scilly. It was the first port of call encountered by the ships trading from the Americas but being bereft of natural resources, most materials, pretty well everything to do with ship construction, had to be imported. Oakum - old rope used for caulking the gaps between planking - pitch and tar to seal the oakum; copper, hull-fastening pins and copper roves to clinch them with; a whole raft of sundry items like tallow for candles, sail canvas and oil to make waterproof garments, a few adze handles, a few chisels thrown in as a speculative gesture and so on, this formed the remainder of the Agnes's cargo.

He set sail mid afternoon and reckoned on arriving an hour or so before nightfall. All went well until the ship was passing Wolf Rock lighthouse. They were about eighteen nautical miles from the island port when the wind died. They weren't near rocks but the delay meant uncertainty. Currents were unpredictable and they could be becalmed for an indefinite length of time ranging from a few hours to a day or more.

The captain looked at the mate, 'Nothing for it but to hunker down and wait.'

*

The be-calming was accompanied by a drop in the mercury. Then, after about two hours, a breeze picked up. They knew they were in for a fierce blow before long. The clouds now had that ominous, intense grey that signalled the first sign of an impending electric storm.

'Right, full rig. Let's get her going for as long as the riggin'll take it.'

The sails filled out. The Agnes picked up momentum and as the wind went from force 2 to force 6 she began to scud along. With hull ballasted under a heavy cargo and wind soon gusting above force 7 she was not cresting the waves but hitting them and emerging through them rather than riding them.

'Lower the topsails and batten down the hatches.' Never was a common expression more apt. The deck was now constantly awash. With topsails lowered the mad rush of the Agnes was noticeably restrained but even in this retarded mode she still ploughed on, now rolling and pitching as well as juddering and vibrating with each thundering smack of bow wave against her timbers. This went on until an hour after dark when the lookout yelled, 'Lights ahead.'

Sam Bray strained his eyes, then caught sight of a sprinkle of lights and one slightly higher, above the rest.

'Helmsman, steer to port. We're heading for passage between The Gugh and St Marys.'

Only he wasn't. Samuel Bray had mistaken the lights of St Agnes and its lighthouse for those of Porthcressa on the south east facing beach of the big island. The ship was heading towards the rocks off the southern tip of the uninhabited island of Annet. The lookout, Thomas Trenear, was first to see foam frothing and spray flying like the cascade erupting from a firework display, as rollers hit a partially submerged reef about a cable's length ahead.

'Hard to starboard,' he yelled at the top of his lungs as he realised the captain's error.

The helmsman heaved on the ships wheel. The Agnes, responding to the sudden change of rudder, heeled over and headed for the channel between the two islands of Annet and St Agnes. But she was in a smaller channel, effectively a narrow chasm between a projecting rock and a fully submerged reef. Even in the roar of the wind and waves, the noise of her timbers being stove in and her ribs being ripped away could be heard with sickening realisation as her momentum dragged her on and over into the deeper channel on her starboard side. Little of her cargo was buoyant and as the torrent of sea water flooded her hold the schooner foundered and sank almost immediately. The crew stood no chance. They were a good two hundred yards from Annet with the south westerly gale blowing any surface flotsam away from terra firma. Those who weren't in their hammocks, riding out the storm, were in the hold keeping an eye out for shifting cargo. The two Redruth miners, who had dug the tunnel, were amongst them.

As the timbers ripped away they had just enough time to turn and see the transitory image of a black wall of water with nothing between it and them in the milliseconds it took to engulf the hold. They were crushed up against the port side of the hull, knocked unconscious along with their fellow crew members. Those in the hammocks were given a few seconds of breath before they too were flushed from their canvas cradles to twist and turn, somersault and dive in the soup of dislodged sea weed and sea water, until they too lost consciousness and drowned in the inky blackness. Thomas Trenear was taken by a wave and washed down the deck towards the main mast. The water drained enough for him to get to his feet and make a dash for the shrouds. He'd sailed the islands on a number of trips and knew from other wrecks he might stand a better chance of survival staying with the ship. He made it. Grabbing the heavy, tarred, outer rope securing the lattice of climbing cords to the top of the main mast, he swung his foot onto one of the ratlines. He made it. As he did so a large Atlantic roller swept over the ship. The netting and ropes securing a cluster of barrels, stacked on the fore deck, were torn from their anchoring points and swept down the deck.

Morning saw the masts of the Agnes projecting from the submerged carcass of the wrecked vessel. The body of the lookout man was oscillating gently to and fro in the ebb and flow of a now almost calm sea. One leg tangled in the ratlines of the shroud, his arms describing a gentle, aerobic dance from the shoulders of his ripped, linen shirt. His back bore the purple bruising and abrasions from the sickening impact of the netted barrels. Of the rest, there was no sign. Some were trapped up against various bulkheads. Others had long since, washed through the gaping hull of the schooner, caught by the tidal race that took them way out of sight of land.

The tunnel was now a secret. There was no man living who knew of its location or even the certainty of its existence. It held the body of a corpse, desiccating in the current of air flowing up through the flue, feeding the water rats that found easy access from the river. The lead ball, licked clean by some be-whiskered rodent, rested a few inches away from the leg it had been lodged in. It lay in a groove made by some piece of cargo dragged into position across the hard-packed earth at some earlier time.

28

Nat sat back against the frame of the chair scanning the accurately pencilled projections based on sketches that, over the weeks, had accumulated in his notebook. There was detail and notes sufficient to enable a shipwright to construct the craft from the information drafted on the cream cartridge paper that, until now, had remained pinned to the drawing board. He'd laid out a linear scale along the bottom.

All that remained, after proving some aspects of construction on a model, was to toss the plans to Sam Karslake and David Tresize, for them to set out the full-size lofting of the component pieces. He lifted the tee-square, drew out the pins and slid the finished design onto the oak table, satisfied with the final modifications embodying an earlier scheme. Structurally it exceeded the strength of any hull of similar proportions. He was pleased with the sleekness of the lines, the inherent sea-worthiness of the craft. The unknown quantity was the speed it could achieve with an engine unproven at sea and a propeller, as yet, waiting to be designed. But he was confident it would ride any sea that could be thrown at it from whichever point of the compass.

*

The small group, assembled at Tinners Creek on Saturday afternoon, comprised Jim Bennallack, Betty Rowe, Sam Karslake, his wife, Ralph Hooper, Jean Hooper, Mary and Bill Hawken, David Tresize, Nat and Jenny. It resembled the kind of gathering one expected to see at the launch of a new boat, where all the shipwrights and others associated with its construction would be treated to a slap-up meal or tea in celebration of its completion. This was a similar celebration, not of so momentous an event as a launch but no less exciting. It was to mark the flooding of the dam and the running of the new turbine. Nat checked the coarse, wire mesh on the entry pipe and, satisfied it would let no large debris through to the turbine, looked across at Jim Bennallack.

'Jim, your honour, wind the sluice gate down.'

Jim walked onto the narrow path along the top of the dam. The robust H frame, set in the middle, sported a well-greased helical thread that carried at its lower end a heavy, steel gate. At its top, where it passed through the solid, elm cross piece, it engaged with a lock keeper's crank-handle. Jim looked at the group standing at the side and grinned, 'Here she goes', and started winding. The little crowd cheered with mock seriousness, clapped and burst out laughing, as Jim bowed to the assembled group. They stood and watched as the water level crept up to the overflow slipway five feet above the dam's base. It didn't take long, with the three streams that were feeding it.

'Right, let's get down to the turbine house. Jenny you're going to open the turbine gate and, Mrs Hooper, you're going to throw the switch for your electricity.' Nat had briefed no one, beforehand, about their part in the ceremony marking the event. It added to the fun and lightheartedness he had intended the occasion to be remembered by. Before they could move, a stone dislodged by Jenny's foot rolled into the now, full reservoir. This was a signal to Rex. Already in an excited mood, it mattered not to him whether it was a duck or a stone: things going into water were things to be chased by dogs as far as he was concerned. The animal stopped short as the stone disappeared below the sea of twigs and leaves eddying about at the water's edge. Too late! The loose shale on the slope did not stop when he stopped. On he went and another cheer went up as the wretched animal plunged into an unscheduled bathing session. A good swimmer, he turned round, grabbed a small stick by way of compensation, paddled back to land, ever so pleased with himself and followed them down to the little, granite, turbine house.

The stop-cock for the turbine was a simple screw wheel. Jenny gave it a twist. There was a hiss and a gurgle as trapped air and water entered the blades of the Pelton wheel. A gush of water exited the outlet pipe, followed by a steadier flood as she continued to turn the wheel. The onlookers were mesmerised by the clarity and dynamic of the energy-giving jet as the glistening cascade of pure, spring water caught the sun, complementing the satisfying hum of the phosphor bronze wheel whizzing around inside the turbine casing. The four men and Jenny felt a surge of relief as the hard work they had all put in over the months was vindicated by the response of this precision-built piece of machinery.

Nat opened the little door alongside, exposing the generator and threw a lever on the switch gear.

'Right Mrs Hooper, let's go to see if your electricity is up and running.'

The crowd, now fully captured by the mood of the occasion, walked to the old miners' cottages. A trestle table outside the one occupied by the Hoopers, was covered with a damask table cloth and laden with plates of crab sandwiches, crab claws, saffron cake, a Victoria sponge, jellies, a large ham and various other good, country fare with a large enamel dish of gloriously yellow, clotted cream. Simon Hooper had been instructed to keep a watch for sparrows and other food predators.

The group squeezed into the cottage. Nat checked the small, junction-box switch high up on the wall, just inside the kitchen door. Jean Hooper stood ready and with a nod from Nat, flicked the little lever down on the bell-shaped switch. The light over the kitchen table glowed with the characteristic yellow given out by bulbs of that type. Jean beamed and walked across to Nat, plonking a great, big kiss on his cheek.

'Thank you!' After years of only using candles and paraffin lamps this was a luxury she had always dreamed of.

'Right! Before we go I'd like to thank Betty and my mother for the spread they've prepared for us outside. So let's go out and do a 'proper job' to it. Then, after, I'll show you what we've done in the foundry and the new boat house. Need to test the lights we've rigged up there as well.'

29

The following Monday Nat turned up with the finished plans. Just before crib time they sat around the tea chest.

'This is it. Final draft I hope. Before I start on the model I need your comments. If there are any snags it'll save me a lot of time if they're spotted now. I don't doubt problems'll crop up at the construction stage, they always do but I'm hoping most'll show up in the scaled-down version. In fact I might only model one or two areas where I've departed from convention.'

He unrolled the sheet of cartridge paper and put a small piece of scrap metal at each of the four corners to keep it from curling back up.

'I've done away with a tiller arm, as you can see. Gets in the bleddy way.'

'So how you goin' t'steer her then?'

'Put a rudder spindle down through, well back from the transom. Rudder'll be protected in the vee channel then. Propeller throws the jet against the rudder vane and thrusts the boat port or starboard. Won't have to worry about beaching the boat on sand or pebbles either. Shan't rip the rudder off then if she drags across a sand bank.'

'So, if you're not using a tiller what are you doing? Using a wheel?'

'Yep! Put a small ship's wheel with a motorbike chain linked to a smaller cog and drive through to a couple of bevelled gears - one on the lower end of the spindle and t'other on the shaft from the chain drive. Wheel's easier to hang onto in a rough sea, too.'

The other three men shared space and passed comment on various aspects of the design.

'The motor housing and engine, you going for diesel or petrol?'

'Diesel.'

'You're going to need a reduction gear box.'

'More than likely but won't know what's available 'til we pick an engine. Got in mind a forward and a reverse lever. Throttling up or down should provide enough variation in power for handling her in any sea, I'd hope. That's the theory anyway. Not many boats about yet with engines so not much chance of picking anybody's brains. I've left the least amount of space for the power unit and fuel tank that I think I can get away with. The design in that area is going to have to evolve with the build of the boat. Anyway, let's brew up. I'll leave it on the shelf for the day and if any of you want to look at it again, there it is.' He rolled up the drawing and tossed it on the shelf.

Seated around the tea chest the conversation turned to the staggering amount of work the foundry was attracting.

Ralph Hooper voiced his concern, 'We're going to need extra hands when you take Sam and David to build boats. Reckon we could take on an apprentice and a skilled man when we get the other furnace up and running and we'd still only be at the same strength. Less, really, when you consider the apprentice will need training.'

Nat nodded, 'It's been on my mind for a week or two now. We could, maybe, take on two apprentices. One for the boat as well. David or Sam could double across then to the foundry if things got tight time-wise, your side. There's that young lad just come up from the youth band, trombone. I've noticed he doesn't show off like one or two of them but takes note of what's goin' on. How do the two of you feel?'

Sam Karslake spoke, 'For me I'm as happy casting as shaping wood and the variety makes for a welcome change. Would suit me.'

David Tresize, occasionally uncharacteristically cheeky, turned to Ralph and Nat, 'I'll only support that idea if the band will take me on as a learner,' and laughed.

'Never knew you were interested. You serious?'

'I am. Listening to you and Ralph talking about the band's performance the day after you've had a rehearsal for a contest or one of the engagements at a local regatta, has got me interested.'

'Band's goin' to need a tenor horn player when Keith Martin moves to Devonport.' Ralph continued, 'It would be six months before you'd be any good and then you'd be on third horn whilst Jack Best moved up to solo horn.'

'That wouldn't matter.'

'We'll have a word with Cecil Brewer. The bandmaster's pretty approachable. Good musician, he'll be glad to take you on I would guess. Do you have any music at all?'

'Started piano when I was ten but the teacher went to St Austell a year later to live so I stopped when she left.'

'Had that effect on her did you?'

The others laughed.

'We'll speak to Cecil next practice. Leave it with us. In the meantime, come along to the next practice just to get a handle on what goes on.'

Tresize nodded with a look of satisfaction at the prospect.

'Right, let's get moving,' Nat got up, 'I want to sort out the saw in the stamping house. Sam, can you come and have a look, see what you think unless Ralph's got you lined up for anything.'

'No, we're waiting for that scrap to melt. Another hour or so before it'll be ready.'

'Well in that case you can both come up if you want, just to get the drift of what I'm trying to do.'

'Let young David go, I'd better stay and keep a watch on things here just in case.'

*

'I've dismantled the cam and drive system for the old stamping machinery. There's enough power from the big wheel to drive a circular saw but we need to step up the revs. That'll be easy enough if we use those two old, cast-steel gears,' Nat put a foot on the larger of the two wheels, 'just reverse their positions and get an arbor made up to take the saw blade. Should do the job but we'll need to put a raised concrete bed to take the new bronze bearings unless we can put a heavy wood platform to take 'em. Sam, can you give me a hand, now, on that?'

Sam took it all in, 'So you need the two of us to support the weight whilst you ease 'em off?'

'Right!'

'Let's get on with it then.'

The three men set about detaching the heavy, steel gears. As they were engaged on the task Nat, in between the tapping and easing of the wheels off their shafts, discussed the logistics of aligning and setting up the drive for the huge, circular-saw blade.

'How easy d'you think it'll be to have a band saw rigged up about there, as well,' Nat pointed to an area adjacent to the proposed site of the circular saw.'

'I dunno,' Sam shook his head, 'easy enough to rig up but it's a bit late, maybe, to say it but are you going to get enough power for the circular saw on its own even? I know you won't run both together. The band saw won't need as much power as the circular but some mills have had to put in a steam engine to drive their big saws.'

'Yeah, I've looked at that. Had a chat with Dave Williams over at the timber yard. His wheel wasn't taking as much head and volume of water as ours, about a third less. He said it coped well with balks of timber up to certain thickness but the saw then jammed above that. So we know we can cut above that by about another third.'

'Fair enough. You can easily gear up a rig with a blade tensioner. But then, you know that.'

'What I was thinking. Just wanted your take on it.'

'If you've got a bit of power to spare,' David Tresize broke in, 'you've got enough room to rig up a feed system to push the logs onto the saw. As long as you've got 'em loaded on fairly free-running rollers, you won't be taking much power from your blade.'

'Good idea and as it's come from you you're the best person to design one. Tracking, feed mechanism, rollers, the lot. Once we've got it running we can cut the lumber for the cradle supports we'll use for the boat in the adit.'

David Tresize looked pleased. The youngest member of the work force, he valued the recognition and trust from the older ones. Emboldened by the encouragement, he continued, 'You could increase the power from the waterwheel by adding another bolted to it, alongside. You've got spare water being diverted that could be put through a new race. You could dig out the existing one to double the width.'

Nat nodded, 'It's a possibility. I'll give it some thought.'

The three men surveyed the dismantled bits and pieces of machinery for a short while, taking in the consequences of their work, visualising, each in their own way, their perception of the different suggestions just voiced.

*

The various modifications, being straightforward in concept, were easily introduced over the next few months. Doubling up the waterwheel took most of the effort. The steel components, for fixing the new twin to the existing wheel, were cast on the spot. David Tresize, having gained a reputation for lateral thinking, had been tasked with an additional job of designing a furnace blower. It was powered from the belt and pulley system already upgraded for the additional machinery they had put in place in the foundry. This enabled them to work at the higher temperatures melting steel demanded.

The day came when the first, massive piece of oak was laid on rollers and passed through the shiny, new, circular-saw. The hum of rotating machinery and the high-pitched note generated by metal shearing its way through wood gave a satisfying buzz to the old stamping house. There were smiles all round as the single log parted into two with the smell of green oak permeating the air as sap and other fragrant oils were liberated from the unseasoned timber.

'Bleddy hell! No!'

The other three turned to see what had alarmed Ralph Hooper. In the large, open doorway stood a figure whose features were rendered indistinct against the background glare of bright sunlight. But the profile was unmistakeable and familiar to the men assembled around the still spinning saw. So too was the outline of a twelve bore, double-barrelled shotgun unmistakeable, pointing diagonally across its owner's body, signalling an ominous and threatening intent. An inebriated Jake Lewis took a few, unsteady steps into the stamping house.

Without a word and gesturing to the group to move to the side in the clear space on the main floor, with slurred speech he pointed the gun at Sam Karslake as he did so, 'You, Mr Karslake, are going to apologise to me aren't you for what you did to me? And you Mr Hawken and you Mr Hooper I believe your name is, are going to enjoy the pleasure of the pig sty where you put me once. But first I'm going to teach you a lesson.' He addressed his remarks again to Sam Karslake as he held the shot gun with one hand and slid a riding crop out of his belt with the other. The men aware Lewis was beyond any sense or reason and dangerously unstable, kept quiet.

David Tresize, still at the saw bench, measured his chances of distracting the swaying Lewis. He had been in the process of lifting the lighter plank away from the saw as this whole debacle was unfolding. Having seen the odd log catch and mount an up-cutting blade with devastating results, he guessed any one of the other three would understand the chance he was offering them if he could somehow spook Jake Lewis. Lewis took a few steps towards Sam. Anticipating any possible threat lay with the three men, he gave less attention to the younger man.

Waiting for the gunman to take another unsteady step David, still holding the severed plank, gave it a quick twist and flicked it onto the teeth of the rotating saw. At the same time he dived to the side out of the line of fire, protected by the saw bench. Jagged teeth engaged with the green timber. The piece of planking, caught by the spinning blade, lifted and flailed through the air faster and higher than any man could have thrown it. Jake Lewis turned his head and, startled by the initial noise, inadvertently pulled on one of the two triggers as he ducked the oaken missile. Nothing happened. This was a time when shooters could recharge their own cartridges with cordite, shot and a card disc using a little re-crimping tool. Somewhere in this process Jake had either neglected to use a dry cordite supply or the percussion cap in the end was dud. Sam Karslake took his chance and leaped on their assailant. Both fell to the floor. Jake Lewis, still holding the shotgun, finger still inside the trigger guard, pulled the other trigger as his face hit the hard surface of the stamping house floor. This time there was an almighty bang, the noise accentuated by the confines of the granite walls. With the muzzle of the gun poking into what had been the underside of his jaw, the outcome was spectacular, almost a piece of art.

The four men, slightly deafened by the detonation, were shocked by the appalling sight on the floor. Jake

Lewis, still stretched across the top of his gun, lay in a pool of blood, spreading like a huge, red halo around his head. His face and the top front of his skull were missing. There were bits of bone fragment and brain scattered in a narrow splash of red that gave the bizarre impression of a plume from a decorative piece of headgear, fashioned for a carnival.

'Don't move him. We can't do anything. He's obviously dead,' Ralph Hooper spoke, 'leave him exactly as he is. It'll be obvious to the police he's the cause of his own death. Otherwise there'll be doubts as to exactly what happened if we turn him over.'

The others agreed.

'Let's brew up a cup of tea before we go for the law,' again it was Ralph who spoke, 'I'll ask Jean to cycle over to Penryn, for the sergeant, whilst we're drinking it. Best thing for shock.'

*

There was an inquest but no repercussion. Victor Lewis sold his yard a few months later and settled for the life of a recluse. Irene Lewis found a discreet way of getting gin delivered and settled for a daily, alcohol-infused existence. The new owner was not interested in boat-building. He wanted to demolish the premises to use the site for a grand, river-front home with a yacht mooring. Nat was quick to take advantage of the situation. The owner was glad to have tools and equipment taken off his hands, tools and equipment Victor Lewis had left in situ, unable to sell through other channels. At a knock-down price the arrangement suited buyer and seller.

Activity at the Creek continued to grow and began to take on the character of a small but prosperous outpost of Falmouth as more and more boat-builders and other peripheral enterprises, got to hear of the design and manufacturing skills of the foundry. The incident was not forgotten, how could it be? But life went on as ever and the memory just receded as memories do, into an infrequent comment here or there as the months went by.

30

The birth of a son was no unexpected cause for celebration. The Hawken and Bennallack families were joined by the Creek employees, a few bandsmen and the lifeboat crew when the baptism was performed in the little church adjacent to Tregennza. Robert Hawken was the first boy to be born at Trelogan in fifty years. Amongst the many Christening gifts was a little wooden, boat-shaped trolley from the crew, painted in lifeboat white, red and blue. At the reception, in the big house, Andrew Nancarrow, still Coxswain of the lifeboat, found time to have a quiet word with Nat.

'We're missin' you at the boathouse. Anymore progress on your gettin' a nag to ride down when the maroons are fired?'

'Thought about that. Reckon my best bet is a motorbike. Could get there quicker even than some of the Falmouth mob. If I had to saddle up a horse every time – which I can do now in less than a minute for Jenny – I'd still be fifteen or twenty minutes getting there, at the earliest, depending on whether it's dark or daylight and raining and, to tell you the truth, I'm not really comfortable on a horse.'

'Well, we still want you on board boy. Now isn't the time to push it but it's good to know you're still with us. Let's go and whet the baby's head.'

*

The increasing number of orders prompted further discussion about the earlier recognition for increasing manpower. Two apprentices were taken on – one for the foundry and one for the boat-building, although both were regarded as interchangeable to begin with. Now that there was an adequate pool of labour, Nat found time to pursue his research into boat design and develop the boat building facility in the adit. With Ralph Hooper a shareholder, he could leave day to day running of the foundry in his hands.

Nat rigged up a small, mobile platform with a couple of wheels so that he could shift it, unaided, around the cavern walls in the inner depths of the mine. He could now reach any part of the roof space and rock face. With a few tools and the benefit of a roaming lamp on a generous length of cable, he fixed a number of lamp brackets, marking out their locations first with a piece of chalk. Lighting the cavern proved more effective than anticipated. Shiny flecks of mica, embedded in the grey granite, reflected the light from these lamps, giving it a silvery glow, not unlike the reflection projected by the moon off the bay on a clear night. A main concern was to secure the premises. He and the other carpenters - for, effectively, that is what the shipwrights were - soon cobbled together a pair of doors to the adit. A level yard in front of the doors provided a zone for unloading materials and equipment used for prosecuting the business of boatbuilding but equally as important: preparing any vessel for its journey to water once it had left the shelter of the mine gallery.

He completed the model for the lifeboat but decided to build a standard, Falmouth, working boat first - a single-masted crabber - just to try out the premises and give the apprentices experience of conventional working practices and construction. Sam Karslake and David Tresize set about 'furnishing' the premises with a few bits and pieces scavenged from here and there. The Turtle stove from the old boat yard was one of the items that Nat had purchased from the new owner. This saved the need to trek across to the foundry to make a brew-up in wet weather. Always there were off-cuts of wood to burn and pieces of kindling from dead branches to start a blaze with. The practice of burning off colonies of live gorse gave local people a ready supply of smutties - bare, blackened, gorse stems - as they were referred to in local dialect. There were supplies of these to be had close by, the sooted stems giving the fuel source its name.

The new crabber took shape. Jenny Hawken was now a frequent visitor to the Creek – with or without young Robert. She always found something to do, whether visiting Jean Hooper at the cottage, bringing a basket of buns to the men or, being the outdoor girl that she was, clearing a few brambles or other growth around the site with a hook. The little boy would sit amongst wood shavings and put them to his nose enjoying the scent of pine or oak. After his first birthday he would point to the freshly built hull knowing his mother would lift him in to sit on the seat at the tiller end of the boat. Caulked and painted, the day came when the craft was ready for her journey down to the creek. She was lowered gently across log rollers on the floor of the mine level and coaxed out onto the flat area fronting the premises.

The track down had been cleared long since but all were eager to try the stream as a transport channel. It was too shallow for sailing the vessel on but cleared of large rocks, stones, dredged in places and newly widened, it would float a boat of that size as long as it was carrying no one or no ballast. Stripped of her mast and other non essential equipment and supported either side with a man or two and a few rope lines, the vessel could be guided down, it was hoped, without fear of holing her timbers. This phase of any boat's life always aroused excitement: its launch into the hostile medium of salt water. But in this particular case an initial baptism in the less buoyant medium of fresh water. It was like gambling, almost, in terms of uncertainty of outcome, except no money would change hands and no horse would fall at a fence.

There were enough of them on that day to guide the boat along a short stretch of track to the edge of the stream. The bed of the stream at this point, locally deepened and widened, provided something of a docking area. If any unexpected, in fact unlikely problem of buoyancy manifested itself, she could be hauled back out of the water and modified more easily on site there than down at the creek's edge.

A few lengths of four-by-four launching stanchions were placed flat down the bank and the boat rolled up alongside. With two or three steadying her, two others set about using long poles and levered the hull across the rollers. The tricky bit came with the transfer from roller to stanchion. The gang rested.

'Ready?' Nat looked around the group as a hint of restlessness and desire to get moving began to set in.

They nodded.

'Right. Let's go.'

Two ropes, passing over the top and under the hull, were held at both loose ends by pairs of men above the short, shallow slope to the stream. Jim Bennallack and Bill Hawken, press-ganged into helping, were stationed one at the stern the other the bow to keep her upright. Two others again took up poles and, against the steadying tension maintained in the ropes, eased the hull off the ends of the rollers onto the launch planks. They dropped the poles swiftly and dashed to the assistance of the rope holders. The boat slid easily, by stages, down to the stream. Before they actually committed the keel to water they all looked at each other, grinned nervously and finally let the newly painted hull slip into the narrow, artificially created dock. A cheer went up as the shiny, black-painted timbers plunged into the pool. She created a mini tsunami, submerged her waterline planking a few inches and, with a slight roll, righted herself and sat tethered, gently oscillating in the current. There were no anxieties about her seaworthiness. She rode the element like a duck.

'Let's put the boy in.' This was Sam Karslake to Jenny Hawken, who was watching the whole thing. Nat agreed when Jenny nodded her head in agreement. Sam stood calf deep in waders and took the excited little boy from her and placed him where he'd sat many times in the boat house. It made little difference to the buoyancy.

'I'll hang onto him. He'll be right.'

Nat sized up the situation, 'Right, let's take her down. Two either side in the stream and two holding the stern rope. Let's go.'

The short journey down to the creek justified the effort put into clearing the bed of the stream. In fact stream was too modest a word now. Since its dredging, the waterway would be better described as a small river rather than a stream. In the shallows, by the reconstructed jetty, the boat was tied up by the side of a short, newly constructed ladder. Robert was handed back to his mother. The men involved in her making clambered down into the pristine hull and gave her a rocking. The two apprentices, congratulated on their contribution, joined them. Her mast, already laid out on the jetty, together with the jib boom, was waiting to be fixed in place, with sails, rigging and other gear alongside. This was speedily done. Nat took the tiller, invited Jenny on board with Robert and took the new craft out from the creek into the wider tributary. She sailed like a dream, cutting through the water with hardly a sound. Back at the jetty the two apprentices, itching to try out their handiwork, jumped into the boat and gave the craft its second outing.

*

Again, yet another celebration. It was decided to name her The Jenny Bee. Jenny had made herself so popular and busy at the site that one of the men suggested the boat be named after her with a 'busy-bee' connection to the B for Bennallack. So it became.

31

Now that the creek had one boat under its belt, so to speak, Nat felt equipped to press ahead with his long and patiently held dream to build the lifeboat. The complications introduced by a re-entrant keel were sorted out at the model stage. The bulbous superstructure - the main structure added to ensure self-righting should the boat roll over - looked odd on the plans. It resembled a truncated tunnel grafted onto the main deck, the prow end of it tapering into the deck timbers. He felt uneasy about it. The model demonstrated the principle alright in a bath tub but baths don't have waves and aren't subject to force eight gales. As long as the boat's centre of gravity was well below the centre of buoyancy he knew she'd stay upright. But he also knew that the centre of gravity and centre of buoyancy in model and full sized craft could not be accurately replicated. A certain amount of balance between model and reality could be achieved by tweaking ballast arrangements within the hull and seating the engine as close to the keel as space would allow. He was prepared to press ahead, to make adjustments after it was built. But this could only be achieved by repositioning fuel tanks, engine and whatever means of stability control he designed into the water ballast system - if, in fact, he needed a water system at all.

Little pieces of metal, in the model, represented the engine and fuel tank. He was beginning to think scaled-up metal weights, along the full sized keel, would also suffice as ballast. They could be bolted down, whereas stones and bricks - often used in providing stability - would migrate in the event of the hull turning upside down, even when roughly confined by a false lower deck. The problems associated with on-board water tanks were well known. But they were still being used because, when new, they functioned adequately. Difficulties arose when their caulked, timber reservoirs began to warp . He took a gamble and rejected any further consideration of a water-based system. The decision lifted a whole load off his mind. He would start to lay the keel next week.

There were now a few reliable diesel engines beginning to appear in the odd fishing boat and craft of similar size. One of the bandsmen, Tom Hicks, the flugel horn player, worked in the docks on admiralty and other government contracts.

'I hear you're looking out for an engine.'

'Yeah! Need it to equip a new lifeboat I'm building.'

'Well, if you can spare an hour or so, I'll have a word with the gaffer. We're working on a couple of small cutters for the revenue people. In fact, we've built one. She's about ready for full sea trials. I reckon he won't mind you comin' to have a look at what we're doing. They're both equipped with a Larsson diesel.'

'I've heard about them. One or two Newlyn boats use 'em. Pretty forgiving in rough seas I'm told.'

'Yes. They can take the higher revs when the prop is free of the water. Got a larger than normal flywheel that absorbs the extra energy when she lifts out. More importantly, prevents cut-out when she's idling. Of course means she's slower to respond to throttle but then there's always a trade-off.'

'That could be a problem. Need fast response in tricky situations.'

'Well, maybe, not that slow. It's all relative. When you think how clumsy a boat is with oars you're still at an advantage. But you could get a smaller flywheel fitted or drill out surplus metal from the existing wheel.'

'True, that would be easy enough. Look, yes, I'll take you up on that. Better still what's the chance of seeing the completed job?'

'Well, the gaffer would support anything to do with rescue work. Leave it with me. I'm pretty sure he'll welcome a visit.'

*

'This is our lifeboat builder, Nat Hawken.' Tom Hicks introduced his fellow bandsman to Ted Mennear.

'So you want to have a look at our cutters, hey?'

'Yes, I'd be interested to see how you're fitting the power unit and steering. Even more so, get a feel for the way she handles, the one you've got afloat, if that's possible.'

'No problem. Glad to give you a run since Tom tells me you crew on the lifeboat.'

'Can I drop this satchel somewhere?'

'I'll put it in the boathouse. You can pick it up after.'

The three men made their way to a floating walkway at the side of one of the inner pools. A small, robust looking craft was tethered to a couple of rings set in the stonework above. Tom loosened the lines, coiled them and tossed the loops down onto the decking.

'Jump in Nat.'

Nat jumped down onto the deck. The craft must have been about thirty five to forty feet long with a beam of about nine feet. Didn't rock much as he landed. A cockpit area sported a wheel offset from a central door to a cabin that, as far as he could make out, would take about four or five people and which led to further space below deck up for'ard. The stern area featured a narrow quarterdeck. Below this, Nat was soon to discover, was where the engine was located. Tom joined the two men and opened up a door set in the facing partition sealing the aft deck from the cockpit. He reached in and retrieved a lantern hanging from the under-decking. Door was probably too generous a word to describe this access to the engine compartment. It was more a kind of flap that hung from a cross-coaming and resembled an enlarged dog door.

'There's the engine compartment. I'll fire up the lamp, then you can crawl in and check it all out in there.'

Nat waited until the flame was burning and the wick adjusted. There was just enough room to crawl along both sides of the motor. He noted the compactness of the unit and was pleased with the means of bolting the engine to the various floor pieces supported by the keel. A rod and lever system operated forward and reverse with a gimbal coupling taking power to the bronze screw. It would suit his purposes fine as a power plant for the lifeboat. He crawled out satisfied with what he had seen.

'Right, let's give her a spin.'

The ignition system, fed by a sealed, acid battery, powered up a glow point in the cylinder head. After quarter of a minute Ted Mennear judged the point to be ready for the ignition cycle and nodded to Tom Hicks to give the engine a few turns with the starting handle. The engine kicked in with a satisfying sequence of detonations and settled to idling speed.

'We'll take her out into the mouth of the estuary. You can take over the wheel and throttle there.

There was a fresh breeze blowing up the Carrick Roads. The cutter rode the choppy surface leaving a vee trail of foam in its wake. Nat could feel a light vibration through his feet from the engine and was encouraged by the smoothness of its power delivery. Out beyond Pendennis Head Ted handed control to his visitor.

'Just take her up to two thirds throttle travel and head towards St Anthony Head.'

The engine responded much quicker than he expected. It surprised him. The bow lifted about seven or eight degrees; the noise from the motor was not excessive but this speed was not something he was accustomed to. The boat must have been running at eleven or twelve knots so he guessed at full throttle it would be a fifteen to eighteen.

'Right, turn her broadside onto the swell and do a full circle with a port first and then a starboard turn.'

The craft sliced through peaks and troughs, riding first with a left or right roll down each wave face then correcting as it started its ascent up a fresh wave front. True to form, at points where the propeller broke free into atmosphere, the engine did not over-rev. The cyclical nature of the wave patterns allowed the stern to re-engage with water before the screw had time to race. Nat was impressed with the set up, turned her round towards the port entrance and handed the wheel back to Ted Mennear.

'Impressive piece of kit. Thanks for giving me the chance of a run. I reckon with the size of hull I'm looking at this engine will more than suit the bill.'

'I thought it would. When Tom here told me about your intentions, I guessed your lifeboat would be just right for the engine we've got here. Reliable; good workhorse; good all rounder and easy to service.'

They pulled up to the mooring site. Nat was invited in to the adjacent boat house where the second cutter was being built. The engine was not yet installed but rested on a rough, wooden frame waiting for the necessary bits and pieces to convert it to a marine environment. Nat took his notebook from the satchel he'd dropped off earlier. With a rule borrowed from Ted he set about sketching the locations and measurements of the engine's anchoring points, its overall dimensions, adding a few other peripheral sketch details and pertinent notes. Nat picked up a three-bladed propeller that was waiting on a nearby bench.

'This for that engine?'

'Yes. But I reckon another inch or so on the diameter would slow the revs down a bit but at the same time increase the thrust and lower fuel consumption. That's why I said don't take her beyond two thirds throttle. Blades tend to cavitate at full engine speed if they've been poorly matched with the engine. You can sense it; the noise gives it away. That's something you've obviously thought about I would guess, fuel consumption I'm referring to. If you're out hunting for a casualty, range and endurance is crucial for a lifeboat.'

Nat nodded, 'Propeller design and casting is something we want to go for at the foundry. Everything is trial and error at the moment but there's going to be a market for good propellers and also low friction, leak-free, exit bearings. Question of satisfactory lubrication. Especially the design of shaft seals and the housing they're seated in.'

'Any significant advances you've come across?'

'Some boat builders are fitting little cup reservoirs to phosphor bronze bearings, with a rubber ring-seal both sides of the oil grooves. We'll need to fit sprung lids that stay in place if the boat turns over, otherwise the cups will spew oil everywhere.'

'I can see the problem but an easy one to address. It's propeller blading, that's the key to performance. I wish you luck. I shall be interested to know how you're getting on so drop in from time to time, will be glad to hear how you're progressing.'

'Thanks again for the run. The engine's got plenty of poke with it; really impressed.'

'Pleasure.'

'Well, you've work to get on with so won't take up anymore of your time. I'll definitely look in when I've got anything worth reporting on.'

They all shook hands and Tom showed Nat to the door.

32

Jim Bennallack decided it was time to inform his daughter and son in law that Betty had accepted his proposal of marriage and that they would be taking up residence at The Priory. He made his way through the passage to the east wing of Trelogan and knocked on the door to their living room.

'Come on through.' Nat and Jenny were familiar with the signature knock announcing his wish to enter their wing of the big house. He respected their privacy and they never found him intrusive. Young Robert always pleased with an impromptu visit from his grandfather, got to the door as it opened. Jim took his hand and led him back into the room.

'Brandy?' Nat, standing, voiced an offering that he knew would be accepted.

'Yes, that's if you will join me.'

Nat poured a splash of the spirit into a couple of glasses. Jenny declined when Nat turned to her, inclining his head by way of invitation. Jim settled down in one of the leather armchairs, sniffed the vapours from the amber vortex he'd generated in the thin, glass globe and continued warming its contents in the palm of his hand, releasing yet more of the heady vapour.

He took a sip, 'Betty and I are tying the knot. No surprise to you I'm sure. Decided to move to Tregennza farm soon. The few alterations and improvements we've been making to The Priory are nearly complete. I'm guessing you're happy to stay here, take over the whole house? There is room at Tregennza but can't see you wanting to move.'

'Lovely, Dad. I am so pleased.' Nat shook hands and expressed his congratulations with a wide grin as Jenny got up to hug her father.

'Let me call Betty. I'm surprised you didn't bring her.'

'She expected you to say that. Give her a call. She's within hearing distance.'

Betty didn't take long to respond and came in smiling. Jenny took her hands, gave them a squeeze then both hugged each other, giving expression to years of a close relationship that no words could express as sincerely. She sat on the arm of Jim's chair and, like Jenny, declined the offer of cognac. 'This is lovely news. I'm so pleased,' Jenny, again, repeated her pleasure as she sat back on the sofa by Nat.

'Well, in answer to that, staying here,' Nat gave his glass the briefest of waves to the walls, 'makes for a more convenient access to Tinners Creek than Tregennza but the decision is one to share with Jenny.'

'I like both places but growing up here, it's part of me. And closer access to the foundry and boat house for Nat makes it the sensible choice.'

'I thought you'd say that.'

'What do you feel, Betty?'

'No feelings either way. As long as I can come over and see you all, from time to time and you come to us, I'm happy.'

'What you mean is,' Jenny laughed as she said it, 'look after and spoil Robert from time to time.'

They all laughed.

'That settles it then. We're all clear and I guess the coach house will be more and more useful now that business is expanding.'

'Well, I must admit there is a need to store documents and deal with a lot of the commercial activity, as opposed to the manufacturing activity, away from the foundry and boat house. And, particularly, I still need somewhere private to pursue ideas and put them down on paper.'

'I'll empty the coach house. Need to fill the library I've created at Tregennza. Lots of book shelves devoid of books. But since some are useful to you I think we should let those stay. I can always come over to consult. You choose those you can make use of.'

'It's still your property. I'm grateful for what you've given me and Jenny, as it is but I need to start building my own set of reference books as well. There is a handful of books that I do find useful but I think it a bit unfair to rob you of any from your collection. One thing I would like is to continue your practice of holding talks here, like you've done in the past, if you don't intend to carry on with it. Or maybe you might still consider organizing them from Tregennza and coming over when they're scheduled.'

'Do you think you'll have time for that and run the foundry and the boats?' Jenny looked at Nat.

'Well, I'm wondering if Jim might be glad to keep contact with The Royal Cornwall Polytechnic and his like-minded friends. It could work very well and he and Betty could stay the night here when it's on.'

Betty beamed, 'That's a good idea. Get him out of my hair for a few hours.'

Jim put on a mock frown, 'See, she can't wait to get rid of me and we're not even married yet. Anyway, joking aside, it could be a good idea. Let's see how it goes. On a different tack, I know you're busy this end but if you can spare the odd hour at a weekend, occasionally, there's a number of jobs I could do with you giving me a hand. Nothing particularly difficult. The old smoke house is almost disappearing under a pile of ivy. Need someone who can climb up on top to strip away the creeper. I've bought a couple of breeding porkers and want to start putting a few hams in to smoke when the piggery's up and running.'

'We could all come over. Robert will love to see the pigs.' Jenny remarked.

'Fine! Settled then.'

'Let's make it next Saturday afternoon. That suit you?'

'Ideal.'

*

Jim opened the door of the smoke house, 'Don't know the last time this was ever used as a smokery.'

The interior had long since been cleared of ash and partially burned logs. It contained a few pieces of household junk, gardening implements and a tray of shrivelled apples on an old bench. He selected a long-handled hook and a pair of secateurs lying on the same bench.

'Not sure how useful the hook will be but the secateurs will do a good job at the chimney, if you can force the blade under the main creepers. Let's strip away from the base here, first.'

The green netting of ivy gave off an unpleasant odour as sap was released from the cuts. The two men cut and stripped away swathes of the clinging, liana-like strings, both starting at different sides of the structure.

'Jim, have a look at this, there's a set of foot and hand-holds set in the stones here.'

Jim came over, 'Bit unusual for a building like this. Unnecessary, almost, I'd say. Although a ladder won't sit very well against a curved surface so maybe not such a bad idea.'

'Makes the job of getting up there easier.'

They continued stripping away the growth until the lower part of the dome-like structure was clear and the mix of granite and slate stonework was exposed.

'Warm work. Let's go in for a pot of tea. We can finish off the top after.'

Tea was welcome. Outside, later, Betty and Jenny came to see the results of the effort Jim and Nat had put in. Robert dropped the teddy bear he'd brought with him and discovered that pulling on one end of a length of creeper he could also drag a larger pile entangled with it, across the hardened surface of the yard. It turned into a full time game when his mother stuck the teddy bear he'd dropped on top of the debris. Eventually, tiring of the activity, he pulled the bear off and asked to be picked up by his grandfather.

'Right! Seems like a good time to start on the rest.'

Nat stuck the secateurs into his belt and climbed up the side of the smoke house. It didn't take him long to rip away the ivy at the junction where the chimney exited the summit of the dome. This exposed the remaining footholds and allowed him to reach up to the lip of the stack. The ivy, bushy at this point, screened the open duct. He cut and pulled, cut and pulled, placing the secateurs on the lip of the flue each time he removed a bundle of creeper. He had practically cleared the growth from the top when one length of liana dislodged the cutter from the lip. He heard it hit bottom.

'Jim can you go into the smokery and get me the secateurs? I've knocked them off the edge.'

Jim came out after a short time, 'They're not in here. Not stuck on a ledge anywhere?'

Nat bent over the open end and peered into the flue. He cleared away the remaining ivy and looked down again to see if the tool had lodged on any ledge. There was a distinct whiff of river blowing up through, which was odd. His eyes, now becoming accustomed to the level of light in the shaft, discovered there were two channels, one soot-grimed the other clean. He leaned further into the gap and picked out the granite stones jutting out at regular intervals down into the larger of the two holes. There was something white at the bottom.

'Jim, there are two flues. One of them is clean and big enough to climb. Steps, look like steps anyway, all the way down as far as I can make out. Can smell the river. Reckon we've found our tunnel.'

'Let me come up and have a look,' Jim handed Robert over to Betty.

Jim was fit for his age and soon reached the top, 'You're right. No other explanation. Let's get a lamp and go down. There's a paraffin lantern in the smokery, you nip down and get it. Get a length of rope. We'll tie it to the handle then one of us can lower it to the other at the bottom.'

Nat slid rather than climbed down to ground level. He soon got the lamp burning, tied a line to it and passed it up to Jim.

'I'll climb down first, then watch you down.'

Nat swung his legs over the edge, let his feet contact one of the protruding stones and turned round to start his climb down. The vent had been slightly tilted to ease the transfer of contraband with the minimum of delay. Reaching the last few steps, Nat leaned out until his back was pressed against the opposite wall. He could now look down between his legs for a closer view of the floor. The unmistakeable image of a partially gnawed scalp, exposing the snow-white gleam of a cranium with its skull still attached to its vertebrate, above a still intact rib cage, left him not shocked but disturbed. He stepped away from the skeleton down onto the hard-packed floor.

'Send her down.'

Jim let the rope slide smoothly through his hands as he guided the lamp, as best he could, without allowing it to bang against the protrusions and sides of the vent. Nat took it, waved it about then placed it on one of a number of half-casks close by.

'You ready?'

'Ready.'

'Right, it's easy. Just watch it the last bit. There's a skeleton sitting propped up against the base of the vent. I'll guide your feet when you reach it.'

Down below, Jim looked about him then turned his attention to the sad little scene in front of him, 'This is our tunnel alright. That poor devil must have copped a bullet. Look at the staining around the hole.' Jim indicated the dark patch of clothing on the man's thigh.

'Don't know what we're going to do about him but let's have a good look at what we've got here before we go back up.'

The two men checked out the length of the passage from chimney to river's edge. The tunnel was still in good fettle. Little evidence of roof debris on the wooden sealing plates of the casks in the bays, attested to the soundness of the roof.

Jim put his foot on one of the flasks, 'This is cognac. Should still be drinkable. The sealing wax on the corks is intact. Let's hope the corks haven't tainted it.'

Nat tapped one of the tobacco casks with his fist. It gave off a dull, solid thud.

'What d'you reckon? Tobacco?'

'My guess,' he bent down close and smelt the timbers, 'yes, definitely. Let's get back. The women will be wondering what's happening. We'll bring a chisel down later and broach one to see what sort of state it's in. But judging from the smell I reckon it's been soaked in enough rum to keep for a century.'

The two men made their way back through the newly discovered passage.

'What do we do about the skeleton. Going to be a problem. Can't really inform the coroner until we've shifted the merchandise, because I don't intend to let it be confiscated by the customs people. It's pretty likely he's a local man. Possible some of his descendants know of his disappearance. It would be the stuff of legend, almost, by this time but it would clear up a mystery as far as they might be concerned.'

'Well, he's lain there nearly a century I'll be bound. A few more days won't hurt him, unless we say nothing and just burn the bones or toss them in the river. It's your land but it would be nice to keep this tunnel a secret, a piece of folklore as it's always been.'

'You're right; don't have to make up our minds now. Let's get back out.'

*

Sometime later, inside The Priory, the group discussed the discovery.

'I agree with you and Dad, we keep this a secret until we've moved all the goods but I'd love to see it before we do that. What do you think Betty?'

'No point in letting the Crown have any of it. The skeleton is in the way, you say. Could he be moved then put back in place once you've emptied the tunnel, then the authorities informed? It would be nice for his descendants, if he's got any, to know where he ended up. There would be an account somewhere, no doubt, of a missing man. Doesn't look like a murder between rivals, more a case of someone fleeing the revenue men I would guess.'

Jim leaned back in his chair, 'I'm inclined to leave the merchandise in place for the time being anyway, until we've thought this through properly. It's as well left there as moved into the house. If we clear it and then notify the authorities they might suspect that we also discovered and cleared a cargo of contraband and then start sniffing around, in which case they might ask to inspect the cellar.'

'I don't think it would occur to Customs that there was abandoned contraband here. Moving stuff to the cellar should be safe enough.'

Jim looked at Jenny, paused, folded his arms across his chest and nodded agreement, 'Maybe you're right. We'll stick it in the cellar. Could move some back here after if it gets too chock a block down there.'

Nat looked at the rest seated round the table, 'Jim, it's your tunnel. Let's leave it for now and see if we can find out anything from newspapers. Trouble is we don't know the likely date around the time it happened.'

'That might not be too difficult,' the others looked at Betty, 'according to folklore, du Plessis, the owner way back, was discovered dead in his cellar under suspicious circumstances. It'll be worth looking at records around the time his successor took over the Priory. We can check the date on the deeds, that'll give us a bit of a lead. Jenny and I can go to the newspaper records and the county assize office to search.'

'Good point! Mind you if we're going to declare the discovery we might as well let the authorities do the work.'

33

There were still channels of opportunity for the enterprising smuggler. Back in the tunnel Jim placed an empty brandy decanter on one of the casks and set the lantern alongside it. He and Nat then broached one of the tobacco casks. The air-cured leaves had been layered and individually treated to a spray of a water, molasses and rum solution, then allowed to ferment under the pressure of the circular, wooden top. The cake, for that effectively was what it was, gave off a pleasant, heady aroma not foreign to that encountered in some distilleries. Jim took a clasp knife from his jacket, carved a few incisions in the dense layers and dug out a small plug of the sweet-smelling cake. He cut a small piece from the same and popped it into his mouth.

Chewing, he handed knife and plug to Nat, 'Try a quid of this. Haven't indulged myself for years. Go on, give it a go. It's in prime condition. We can offload this in Falmouth, Truro, Redruth and Camborne. I know plenty of takers who will be glad to have a share of the loot, specially the miners.'

Nat cut himself a small mouthful. He'd never tried chewing tobacco and found the initial texture not unlike biting into a wodge of what he imagined compressed figs would feel like.

'Not unpleasant. Can see why the miners like to chew the stuff.'

They chewed for a short while then spat the contents against the loose wall of the tunnel.

'What are you going to do about the demijohns?'

'Keep them. Too good to sell even at the price it commands today. You enjoy a snort yourself anyway.'

'I do. Not my property but I was hoping you'd say that.'

'Well let's get on with sampling some of it. Give me a hand. We'll lift this one onto that lump of slate there. Easier to pour if we get one on each side.'

It took a few minutes to chip away the brittle sealing wax. The cork was in sound condition. Not yet at the stage of crumbling.

'You lever it out. I think you'll be a bit more careful than I will.'

Nat found the stopper resistant to his efforts, 'We need a piece of rope. I'll nip out and get one from the smoke house.'

He soon returned and dropped a hitch of the thin hemp round the grip of the cork. With the two ends lined up away from each other he instructed Jim to hold his end whilst he proceeded to pull the other. The cork started to rotate.

'Little trick I learnt in The Americas.'

Their senses were hit with the unmistakeable scent of brandy. Not like the harsher smell of young, un-aged Cognacs, these gave off the rich notes of a mellow spirit aged in carefully selected woods.

'Nat, you tip whilst I hold the decanter under the lip of the flask.'

The clear, amber liquid flooded into the decanter. None spilt.

'Let's take a sip here in the tunnel. No glasses. Seems appropriate somehow.'

They both took a very modest swig from the decanter.

'How many of these are there?'

'Four.'

'How much d'you reckon's in them?'

'About sixty to sixty five litres.'

'What's that in pints?'

'About hundred and twenty, hundred and thirty, give or take.'

Nat did a bit of crude, mental arithmetic.

'That's a hundred bottles a flask. You'll never get through that.'

'No, 'spose you're right. Got carried away. Can afford to let three flasks go, easily. Two anyway, to start with. One maybe. Keep the rest as investment. Let's see how it goes.'

'Hell of a lot of bottles you'll need to bring in unless you sell in gallon jars.'

'No problem. I know the Dean of Truro cathedral. He'll take a gallon and the Bishop likes a tipple too, I gather so that's two gallons. There's a few others I can trust at The Royal Cornwall Poly who'll take a ration or two of tobacco and brandy. Anyway, we'll have to shift it all out of the way before we let the police get a coroner to yon skeleton. That'll take a couple of weeks. I don't intend to bust my gut shifting it. All in good time.'

A voice shouted down the chimney, 'I'm coming down.'

Jenny soon appeared at the foot of the shaft, she looked around, 'It's bigger than I expected. It would be a good place to store the cheese you intend to make, that's if you could stop the rats from eating it.'

The other two grinned, 'What gave you that idea.'

'Well, it would be. Cool and dark. Anyway I've come to see what's down here.'

Her nose picked up the traces of cognac and her eyes, now accustomed to the light level provided by the lantern, spotted the decanter alongside it.

'So that's what you've been doing down here. I might have guessed.'

'Have a swig. It's good stuff. Haven't tasted spirit like this in a long while.' Jim held the decanter in front of her. She took it, put it to her nose and breathed in the fumes as she gave the flask a bit of a swirl.

'Does smell clean,' took a small sip, 'good stuff, smooth as silk.' She gave back the decanter and picked up the lantern to have a closer look at the skeleton.

'I see what you mean about the likelihood of a clash with the revenue,' she commented as she bent down to take a closer look at the dark stain around the hole in his breeches. 'Would he bear being moved about or is he going to fall apart if you shift him?'

'Don't know,' Jim answered, 'it'll be safer and easier to leave him where he is until the law has had a look at him. We could probably do with a hand from you when we start moving the cargo. Let's take you down to the river opening. You can see how much there is to shift then.'

Nat chimed in, 'Judging by the number of casks and demijohns down here, untouched, I reckon something must have happened they weren't expecting. Otherwise this would have been cleared of contraband long ago. It looks like the whole cargo was unloaded and something spooked them but what I can't understand is why it was forgotten, because it must have been. Nobody would let this lot lie rotting so to speak. There would have been at least a whole ship's crew and, more than likely, shore men who would have been involved in shipping it. Mystery! Anyway, let's give you a tour.' Nat took the lantern from Jenny and guided her onto the slope down from the antechamber.

She found the passage towards the river a touch surreal, maybe eerie was a better description. The rectangle at the far end framed the unmistakeable presence of water as the ripples reflected the dynamic of sun and shadow ceaselessly picking out the eddies and whorls caused by the branches bobbing up and down in the flow. They stopped at the two bays en route. Jenny counted the casks in each. As they got closer the sound of the river was much quieter than she expected. What she did experience was the strong smell of seaweed. At the lip of the opening a pile of damp, congealed weed, left by a spring tide, gave off the characteristic iodine smell that kelp and blisterweed produce when decomposing.

'It might be easier to roll the casks back down here onto a boat and off-load them at the end of the track from The Priory. Easier than trying to lift them up through the chimney shaft.'

'You might be right. I don't much like the idea of getting those glass demijohns up through that flue. They're heavier than the tobacco casks. The handles either side, though, make it easy to hitch a sling to so it might not be as bad as you think. Once we've tried one we'll have a better idea of how to go about it. Seen all you want to see?'

'Yes. We'll have to think of a use for this tunnel. It's too good a space to waste.'

*

The removal of the cargo from the tunnel took a couple of weekends to achieve. Cellars in The Priory were big enough to store the contraband, just. Jim was in no hurry to find takers but set about filling a few bottles for himself and Nat. Caps, with toggled levers, the standard means of securing the liquid, were readily come by from wine and cognac shippers. Eventually a few were dispersed amongst favoured clientele and further orders generated, discretely, by word of mouth. The tunnel cleared, it was now safe to contact the law.

A coroner was despatched to examine the corpse. Local newspaper records were consulted. It was suspected that 'their man' was the one who had been wounded and escaped at about the same time as a report of a Falmouth schooner, wrecked off the Isles of Scilly, appeared in the same weekly newspaper almost a century earlier. The news of the skeleton's identity cleared up a mystery for one local family. But there was no benefit to them other than the certainty of knowing he had been spared the ignominy of the hangman's noose or transportation to the colonies.

34

Nat now set about acquiring timber for his lifeboat. He favoured oak. Its main drawback, weight; its main advantage, strength. There were some splendid trees about Trelogan, the creek and around The Priory at Tregennza. Their bifurcated trunks and angled branches provided the curved ribs, stem and stern knees and other pieces that required the strength afforded by grain running in the right directions in one single element. He engaged sawyers to fell these oaks. Some he dragged to the river and floated to Tinners Creek. Others: paid local farmers for the services of shire horses and chains to tow the logs to the old stamping house for rip sawing. The logs at the creek he dragged up the bed of the stream by the winch acquired from his uncle's old boatyard.

Putting down the keel was a symbolic act. Though not a particularly religious man, Nat felt an overwhelming sense of occasion, akin to baptism, when he stood looking down at the newly-shaped spine of timber that would define the boat's character.

The slow, exacting process of measuring, marking out, cutting, aligning and fixing the parts of the assembly was accompanied by occasional visits from curious members of the lifeboat crew. Their observations and suggestions were welcomed by Nat. Overall, his original hull design remained unchanged but he allowed a measure of flexibility in the ongoing build of the superstructure to accommodate further improvements in design or modifications to form, as these suggested themselves.

The one area he was troubled by was the effect of a capsize on the propulsion system. He needed both to keep out sea water but simultaneously to allow air to flow from the outside into the engine compartment and exhaust gases to be funnelled out from the engine. The fuel had to be fed by gravity yet remain constant in delivery in any mode of pitch and toss, roll and swing. Ventilation would need to be guarded by some kind of flap or gravity-operated shutter or levered float that sealed air entry when awash with heavy deck swell. These were details he was hoping to finalise closer to completion. The whole problem was one that continually exercised his design skills. This was real design. Not the inflated image of 'style' that masqueraded as 'design' but totally lacking in substance. This was design in the true sense where function, performance and durability were essential features and not cosmetic, superficial externals where art masqueraded as engineering.

Young Robert was an increasingly frequent visitor. Nat rigged up a temporary gate that allowed the little boy to roam about the boat shop at will. It wasn't unusual for a young boy to be brought into such a workplace by a father or uncle. After being scolded a few times for touching things he shouldn't have meddled with, he soon developed a disciplined respect for his environment and became popular with both men and apprentices. The form and smells associated with the architecture and crafting of wooden boats, the sounds of tools sculpting shapes by artisans totally focused on their tasks, was gradually infusing his young mind. Immersed in this atmosphere, subconsciously he was developing the kind of curiosity that would lead him to question origins, sequence and structure as he encountered new forms, new experiences in later years. But for now he was content to collect and play with small pieces of off-cuts, little building blocks of irregular shape that the men tossed to him.

'That boy's goin' to be a natural,' Sam Karslake nodded in Robert's direction as he assisted Nat with the placing of a batten.

'He's lucky to be able to spend time with us. I wouldn't allow him in here if he was a liability. We're lucky to have Betty take a turn to look after him when Jenny's dealing with the paperwork. Mrs Hooper seems to have taken a shine to him too. Just have to watch he doesn't get spoiled.'

'Don't worry, I'd kick his ass if he tampered with anything he shouldn't. But he won't. Knows the bounds. Knows the other men won't take any interference either.'

*

As the weeks passed the hull took shape. The refuge area, containing the engine compartment, would, eventually, be sealed front and back, port and starboard to provide a self-righting, buoyancy zone. Access would be through a robust, heavily wave-resistant door; the design and exact positioning yet to be finalised.

A raised prow provided a deflector for all but the more monstrous waves and give further, closed storage for a sea anchor and towing gear.

The propulsion system - propeller, propeller shaft, reversal mechanism and bearings - was made from in-house castings or machined from bought-in raw materials in the now, well-equipped, machine shop. An inverted box, fastened by four quick-release clips, protected the engine. Where to put the fuel tank? This was an issue needing careful consideration. Too far into the compartment and there would be a long fuel line posing the problem of where to site the copper feed pipe. Outside on deck and the ease of refuelling would be countered by the problem of fixing it securely against rogue waves. An exterior location also meant risk of salt water ingress, minute though the breather hole in the cap might be. It aroused some discussion during one of the morning breaks.

'It's a real bugger that,' Sam shook his head, leaned forward, pulled the notebook towards him and pointed to the elevation showing the wheel mounting location, 'why don't we offset the helmsman's wheel to port and have the access door still pretty well central on the stern face of the compartment? Fuel tank could then be stowed in a hanging cradle high up on the starboard wall, just to the right of entry. Then run a pipe along the top beam directly down to the engine.'

Nat, along with the rest of the group, considered this in a short period of silence, searching for snags but finding none. 'That would work Sam. Ralph, d'you reckon we could knock up a tank that would fit in the roof area, like so?' Nat quickly roughed out his proposal on a page of his notebook, a page already marked with thumbnail sketches outlining other, unrelated ideas.

Ralph turned the book around and nodded almost as soon as his eyes took in the sketch. After a further pause he pushed the book back, 'You'll need to get a standard filler pipe and cap to solder into the reservoir. Apart from that we can make everything here. It still leaves the matter of where the engine exhaust exits your compartment unless you run it out through the deck somewhere. It's going to be a bugger wave-proofing the hot pipe. We'll have to put a U invert at the end, I reckon, like the air intake, to prevent swamping.'

'I don't want the end exposed to atmosphere. So that means we'll need to vent to some kind of chamber.'

'You could lag the pipe where it leaves the engine and take it through aft to exhaust into the sealed, secondary, buoyancy zone,' David Tresize chimed in, 'put a double flap gravity lever and float on the end of a U vent, then out from there to open deck.'

Nat sat motionless a few seconds considering the latter suggestion, one he had earlier pondered. There seemed to be good reasons to follow this solution but he couldn't recall why he had not pursued it at the time. Maybe it was a lack of any obvious difficulty factoring in this aspect of the construction. It seemed too straightforward. He appreciated simplicity over complexity but one could mask the other. Then it hit him.

'It'll work well as far as keeping the engine running but relies on the buoyancy zone being totally air tight below decks, as we need it to be.'

The others looked at him, 'But if the caulking has the faintest gap it isn't air tight and if isn't airtight it isn't exhaust tight, which means gases leaking into the refuge zone will affect anybody in there. But we could run the pipe through it and into a muffler inside the transom, then push a pipe from that through to atmosphere. Any sea getting in could collect in a sump combined in the muffler. It'll make it quieter too. Right? That's sorted that then!'

35

With the hull now decked-over, the motor installed, the refuge area completed, Nat paid attention to the propeller. Over a short period of time prop design had improved exponentially with the growing use of diesel and steam-propulsion in smaller vessels. In parallel with this, techniques at the foundry benefited from advances in metallurgical knowledge that filtered across from various establishments, locally and nationally. Cornwall still maintained a healthy stock of engineering entrepreneurs and scientists. Its traditions of experimentation and openness to innovation had kept it in the running. With networks through to admiralty contracts at The Royal Naval Dockyard, Devonport, Nat was able to access a host of naval architects and marine designers. Having recently bought the motorbike he'd promised himself, the occasional journey to Devonport took about an hour and a half.

The latest performance trials of two-, three-, four- and five- bladed propellers were available to trusted contractors. Nat was quick to latch onto this. One of the apprentices, Robin Sanders, was showing an aptitude for solving minor snags arising during prototype development. Nat encouraged him to enrol on a mechanics and technical drawing course run during the evenings at the Royal Cornwall Polytechnic in Falmouth and took him on one of his visits to Devonport as a pillion passenger. Two minds were always better than one in retaining detail.

The lad, of his own volition, had signed on for an additional evening course in differential and integral calculus. With this mathematical facility, Nat was able to employ him in marking out the complex, three-dimensional surfaces that gave form to the wooden patterns used for casting experimental blades.

These propellers found homes at a number of boatyards in the area. To select one suited for the new lifeboat, Nat relied on feedback from those yards to which he'd sold props. It soon transpired that an in-house designed, five bladed screw in spiral form, afforded some guarantee of performance. The design was unique in that it comprised five separate blades fixed onto the shaft, each on a separate sleeve to avoid the complexity of an integral, five-bladed casting. Performance was thus readily maintained due to ease of removal and replacement of damaged blades. Production costs were also proportionately lower. As a consequence the foundry found a ready market for their five-bladed screws and the departure from admiralty specifications led to a unique product excluded by patent to other manufacturers.

Any increase in performance meant an increased range from an existing fuel supply, meaning greater cover in a search and rescue capacity. As a consequence of such discoveries, the Creek foundry soon acquired a reputation for quality products and sound workmanship.

'We ought to consider adding another furnace,' Ralph spoke to Nat at the end of one particularly busy day, 'there's no room inside here but we could build on one end or to the side, just clear of the small wheel and add a few other facilities, a fettling bay and more storage area for all these patterns. Alternatively a smaller side building just for patterns, moulding sand and mould boxes, would free up space in here and we put a new furnace there.'

Nat nodded, 'Agree! Admiralty's getting nervous about the Kaiser's ambitions and putting out more contracts. I think we'll also need to add another turbine, a bigger one. Means increasing the height of the dam to get another five or six foot head of water or putting a secondary one way up and have a longer pipe down from it. Would need to divert more of the stream into the dams but that won't be hard to do. We could do with being able to cast two or three foot diameter props. Some of these new naval corvettes are greedy for power. Anyway, I'll leave that in your hands. I need to get this boat off the chocks and into the water.'

Fully rigged out, as far as the essentials of seaworthiness were concerned, Nat gave the boat a livery of what were becoming well-recognised as RNLI colours. She was a smart craft. She looked good. Her lines seemed to have a balance about them that inspired a certain pride and confidence. The set of rollers used to run the Jenny Bee out of the adit were put in place for a second time. The side stays, propping up the rescue craft, were removed and all hands, with the assistance of two or three lifeboat crew called in especially, were lined up both sides to assist in getting her off the chocks onto the rollers. She would rest a few days outside the mine whilst minor additions to exterior and interior were made. She hadn't got a name yet. Nat was going to put her through a few trials before even considering the formalities of celebrating an official naming.

Again, once the craft had been given a thorough inspection, outside in daylight, Nat set about organising the journey down to the waters in the creek but first gave the vessel a buoyancy check in the pool the Jenny Bee had been floated in. There was little or no noticeable list as all of the men present stepped aboard to get the feel of her. This augured well for a stable platform in rough waters. There were one or two tweaks to the ballast needed which raised the inclination of the keel, guaranteeing the bow a better angle of attack into head-on seas, giving her lower drag and higher speed. The engine was tested with the boat tethered to a large spring balance attached to the trunk of a substantial elm tree. The thrust recorded on the violently oscillating dial, guaranteed reserves of power well in excess of a boat powered by ten or a dozen oars. Nat was pleased that the time invested in propeller design was justified by this result.

The two apprentices had been given a project to design and make a wheeled cradle for transporting future, newly-built craft down to the creek - those too big to be floated down the stream. It would also serve to bring boats up that needed repairs. In parallel with that Nat had rigged up a pair of rails, alongside the stream, for this trolley to run on. All this took time but the foundry and boat building wings benefited from the enhanced facility.

Getting the boat down to the creek was a relatively simple exercise, once loaded onto the launch cradle. The winch cable used for dragging logs up was uncoupled, attached to the trolley and the whole set-up eased down the rails with little effort on any one's part.

The boat was to prove itself sooner than Nat had planned, before even the low-key, launch ceremony was performed. It hadn't been in the waters of the creek for more than ten minutes when the detonation of a maroon was heard calling out the replacement, pulling lifeboat. The relatively sheltered offshoots along the river gave no indication of the conditions out in the bay. The men on the boat looked at each other. They were simultaneously thinking the same thing.

Sam grinned, 'What d'you think? Shall we give it a go?'

Nat looked down the river then at the mixed bunch on the boat. It took him only a brief moment to take in the ripples further out beyond the mouth of the creek. Ripples stirred up by a fairly stiff breeze blowing up the estuary.

'That's what she's built for. Robin run back and fetch the can of diesel. We'll fill her and take her down to see what's up. I'll nip up to the cavern and grab a coil or two of rope.'

The adrenalin buzz reinforced by the lower key excitement of the launch into the creek, affected them all.

Fuelled up, Nat turned to the two apprentices, 'We'll take you down with us. Don't want you to miss the first run out but will have to put you off at the quay. You haven't got parental permission and both under seventeen anyway.'

They nodded, understanding the situation but pleased their employer gave recognition to the work they had put in on the boat's construction.

'There's nothing in the furnaces at the moment, is there?' Nat spoke to Ralph.

'No. Just some castings cooling down in moulds.'

'I'm thinking you don't want to miss out.'

'Too bleddy right.'

'Let's get on with it then.'

David Tresize cast off the two lines securing the boat and jumped across to a gap between the rails on the side deck. Nat signalled to Sam Karslake inside the refuge area. The latter gave a few turns on the crank handle and the engine fired up with a steady note. The makeshift crew, mentally refreshed by the contrast with the mundane activities at Tinners Creek and the prospect of an excursion to a potentially dangerous shout, allowed all their senses to absorb the first motions of the boat, the throb of the engine through their feet and the changing sound of the various propulsion noises as the craft picked up speed.

Nat headed out from the creek towards the main watercourse. A few experimental, light flicks to the right and left on the wheel let him get his first feel of her response to rudder control. There was little drift. The boat changed course sharply without too much rotation about some non-existent axis through her mid-ships. Out in the more open expanse of the river she cut easily through the still relatively small waves whipped up by what little wind was getting through to this more sheltered reach of the river. The bow was parting the water with a clean cut. The big test would come encountering open sea. Nat slowly increased the travel of the throttle lever up to maximum. The boat's keel lifted a few degrees as the propeller churned up the muddy water, giving it a dressing of air and lighter coloured bubbles. Satisfied thus far, Nat reduced speed, marginally back to what he guessed was about fifteen knots and handed the wheel to each of the group in turn as they headed down the river to the port. Each of the men and the two apprentices were unanimous in their opinions, enthusiastic in their appraisal of the craft.

36

The boat's passage up to the lifeboat slipway was the occasion for every gull close by to take to the air from whatever perch - be it tall-ships rigging, roof top or quayside - with the usual scream of protest. Motorised vessels were still uncommon and mariners engaged in whatever activity stopped what they were doing to observe this new craft as it approached the lifeboat house. Andrew Nancarrow turned from supervising the launch procedure. He moved down the slipway as he recognised Nat Hawken and it became obvious the new boat was going to draw up alongside.

'Hell, I was expecting your motorbike any time and wondering where you'd got to.'

'We just got her into Tinners Creek when the maroons went off. What's the score?'

'Experimental submarine down here on her way back to Plymouth. Was on exercise in Mounts Bay. Dual propulsion system: steam on surface, battery when submerged. Blew her boilers and diesel fired not coal. Managed to limp into the bay here on what's left of her batteries. Blast ruptured her rear ballast tanks off Helford. Half of her sticking up out the water whilst her stern's resting on the sea bed.'

'Crew alright?'

'Don't know. We only know she's there because one of the gigs raced in from a contract to alert us. My guess is the engineers will be injured.'

'Right. I'll get these two boys off and go out to her while you're launching your boat. Sky's looking a bit wild. Toss over a couple of cork jackets just in case we need to give some extra cover. Where is she?'

'You can't miss her. She's in close to Swanpool.'

The two apprentices and Ralph Hooper were dropped off and an extra couple of volunteers from the lifeboat house jumped aboard with spare cork jackets. Nat wasted no further time. He took off from the slipway edge and sped towards Pendennis Point. As soon as they rounded the Point they could see the sub was in real trouble. The top of her conning tower was just clear of the water. Her crew or those who were able-bodied, were outside clinging to the sloping exterior of the unsubmerged part of the hull. Nat drew up and held as steady as he could alongside. Sam and David Tresize were persuaded to put on the cork buoyancy aids and got ready to grab each one of the crew as they were instructed to jump.

'How many left inside?'

'The Commander and three others.' A lieutenant, the last to cross over, answered Nat.

'I take it the Commander is not injured.'

'He was in the tower when it happened. The engineer and the two others were scalded. One's unconscious.'

'Is it going to be difficult getting them out?'

'We've got two of them on stretchers below the tower. No point in getting 'em any further because nowhere they could be put here, outside.'

'You can see the way this sea is building up,' Nat gestured to the lieutenant, 'it'll only need one good swell and that thing'll be swamped. I'm going to take a rope down and we'll see how we go about pulling them out but I better take a look first. In fact, you can toss a rope down when I'm ready. I don't need to climb all the way back out again for it. Falmouth lifeboat is on its way,' Nat turned towards the Point, 'in fact she's just rounded the head, now. I can then tell the coxswain what it's like down there if I've had a look.'

'I'll go down with you.'

'Right, let's get back across then.'

Sam Karslake took over from Nat and steadied the boat. When the swell eased, momentarily, Nat and the lieutenant jumped across. The ladder up to the top of the conning tower was wet and slippery. With each wave surge the submarine, grounded on its rudder, swayed back and forth throwing spray up into the faces of the two men but they reached the lip of the tower without incident. The ladder down into the hull was inclined inwards. They would have to hang outwards and rely on the strength of their arms, rather than their legs, in making the descent.

'No point in us both going down,' Nat spoke to the naval officer, 'I'll take a quick look and call up if I need your advice.' He swung over the front edge of the tower and twisted round until he could hold the steel apron above the hatch. The descent was less difficult than he expected. The ladder rail and rungs were dry. Down below, Nat caught the whiff of lubricating oil and air contaminated by steam-infused diesel. Spilt battery acid gave off a more foreign odour, a kind of vaporous, metallic snuff.

'Commander, I'm Nathaniel Hawken,' Nat turned and held out his free hand as he hung onto the rail, 'Falmouth lifeboat is close-to ready to give assistance.'

'Glad to see you. Commander Trevor Bailey.' The older man introduced himself and shook Nat's hand.

Two of the three injured naval men were in a poor way. The engineer, least affected, had been side-on, further away from the boiler when it ruptured and so had one good hand free from burns. But he was in no way able to climb, unassisted, the backward-sloping ladder out of the hull. Nat sized up the scene in what little light was penetrating the conning tower shaft.

'This swell's getting higher. Won't be long before it'll ride in over the hatch. I'm going to shout up for a rope. We should be able to haul the stretchers out a lot more easily with the sub sloping than if it had been afloat and level. Can we strap the two men in so they won't slip off?'

'There are webbing belts attached to each side that can act as stays. Too dim for you to see. We've left them unsecured in case we flooded. I'll strap them in while you're getting the rope.'

Nat wasted no more time and climbed close enough to make himself heard to the lieutenant.

A rope was despatched and, by this time, Falmouth lifeboat was alongside, separated from Nat's boat by the hull of the submarine. Andrew Nancarrow jumped across but removed his cork jacket before climbing down the tower. Men had drowned when trapped against the ceilings of flooding bulkheads, too buoyant to struggle free. The two Falmouth men, with the assistance of Commander Bailey, set about manoeuvring the unconscious submariner into position. The steel tube rose then fell a few feet as a particularly large wave rocked and twisted the hull on its pivotal point.

'Hold on!' Andrew Nancarrow didn't need to give warning. It was just the kind of reflex response anyone would utter in the circumstances. A shower of water cascaded into the hold and drenched the men. It was getting crucial. With the stretcher more or less vertical below the hatch, the coxswain, who had now taken control, shouted instructions to the two lifeboat men and the lieutenant to start hauling. Nat and Trevor Bailey steadied the unconscious man and lined him up with the overhead hatchway, as he spun freely on the rope's end. Once lined up and with a bit of further coaxing, the stretcher arrived at the top and was balanced across the apron of the tower ready to be received by the lifeboat.

Dick Trenarren, the second cox, looked at Sam Karslake and shouted across, 'This man's going to be more comfortable and safer on your boat than resting along our benches.'

Sam nodded agreement. The lifeboat crew quickly transferred the stretcher across to Nat's boat. The second stretcher was similarly despatched.

Commander Bailey turned to the coxswain, 'We're going to have to free up that last stretcher for the engineer. He's in no fit state to help himself up with only one useful hand to his name.'

'What I was thinking but we need to get a move on. Don't like this sea.'

Andrew Nancarrow shouted instructions to the faces looking down, 'Send back that last stretcher.'

There was no need to add any term of urgency. His voice conveyed his concern, the same concern felt by the crew. It took just a few seconds to remove the mariner from the second stretcher and lay him along the side deck. The freed up stretcher was dropped down the tower. The engineer was in too much pain to care about the means of getting him out. He allowed Nat and Andrew to strap him in as he stood erect with the stretcher held vertically up against his back.

Again, this time with three submarine ratings relieving the original three men, the man was pulled up through the tower. The hull gave a lurch. With space for purchasing foot-holds a premium at the best of times, one of the ratings let go the rope and fell off the sloping conning tower into the water. The other two managed to hold onto their stretcher case and were able to prop him up diagonally across the sparse decking in the well of the tower. A second wave, bigger than the first, slopped over into the hatch. The injured engineer was the only person to benefit from the dousing. The cold, salty water gave some relief to the burning pain that had penetrated the flesh below his seared and blistered skin, reviving him somewhat. Below, the water had drained down into the rear engine compartment. There must have been some other leak, apart from that filling the damaged ballast tanks, because water was now visibly creeping up the interior deck from the direction of the engine room.

'Get moving up there,' Andrew Nancarrow bellowed to the outside, 'she's taking on water,' and, to himself, 'if we get a few more like that, she'll bleddy scuttle.'

The rating falling off the submarine had taken the attention of everyone outside. It took a while for them to realise his plight was secondary to the danger now facing the three below. There was a mad scramble with people clinging to what holds they could, frantically attempting to get back up to lift the engineer out from the cramped oval of the tower. They got him up, over and down in record time.

Down below, the Commander insisted he should be last to leave his vessel and ordered the two Falmouth men to get out. Andrew Nancarrow ordered Nat to go first. Nat reached the top, closely followed by the coxswain. Turning to give him a hand, he was knocked backward by a heavy surfing wave breaking across the little platform. For a brief period the whole aperture was inundated. Fortunately his shoulders took most of the impact but the submarine was now unstable, hovering like some raptor, uncertain whether to soar or dive to some wretched prey it had spotted below.

Andrew was flushed down the shaft onto the shoulders of Commander Bailey. Fortunately, Trevor Bailey, a man toughened by service in various of his majesty's ships, had both hands on the ladder when it happened and managed to keep a hold on the rungs he was gripping. The deluge of water by-passed them both and flooded down to meet that bubbling up from below.

The Commander recovered his balance quickly as Nancarrow secured a fresh hold on the ladder, 'Anchor your arm through the rungs, quick. If you let go again we've had it.' Nancarrow didn't need to be told.

A repetition of the previous scenario would have seen both men flushed down into the rear compartments of the sub. Nat heard all of this and was relieved to see Andy respond. A second wave took the submarine. This time, true to prediction, the craft inundated. Nat was swept off the steel decking into the open water. Twin downward surges of water sucked onto the exterior decking as the sinking submarine displaced the water immediately below its hull, simultaneously pulling both boats across the foaming gap. For those in the two boats the situation was surreal. The relatively clear water of the bay, in spite of the choppy surface, permitted them to watch the craft as it dropped, gracefully, onto the sand below. Nat was pulled down by the same undertow but had taken a good lungful of air before submerging. He surfaced close to his own boat not far from the conning tower, which was only a few feet below the surface.

Glops of filthy foam and debris erupted from the hatchway in a mixture of air and sea water. The noise was unlike anything replicated on land. There was no sign of the two men below. A further fountain of poisonous water emerged from the hull. This time a head surfaced with it, followed by a second. The relief of those watching was expressed by a spontaneous release of breath from lungs locked in tension with the prospect of a double tragedy. Bailey, Hawken and Nancarrow struck out for the nearest of the two boats, the newly constructed lifeboat as it happened.

Sam Karslake and two other men helped the three aboard, 'Close shave, we thought you were done for.'

'So did we! Let's get back to dry land.' Andrew Nancarrow bruised and shaken was beginning to shiver with cold.

Nat, having experienced less of an ordeal, took in the spread of men in both boats, 'We'll hitch the lifeboat to the stern and give her a tow. You happy about that?' It was his boat but he still deferred to the Coxswain. The latter nodded.

Nat let Dave Trenarren take charge of the hitching of the two vessels together, as he manoeuvred the boat into position. Slowly he took up the slack. The tow ropes, both from Andrew's boat and those he had brought, were twisted into a triple cable. As the tension increased, the cable's girth narrowed and water was squeezed from the hemp fibres. The taut line was going to be more than adequate for its job back to port. Nat sized up every head-on wave likely to give trouble, easing back on the throttle and then increasing power again as each potential threat was managed.

The new boat made easy work of the journey back. An excited crowd of people, some of whom had been observing earlier from the cliff above Swanpool, were waiting to watch proceedings back at the boat house. The injured men were transferred to a horse-drawn carriage and taken to the small hospital above the town. Both apprentices had been amongst those in the crowd at Swanpool and were pleased to jump aboard again to assist. Nat suggested, since both lived in the town, that they could leave but each one wanted to take the return trip back to Tinners Creek. His immediate concern, though, was to get out of wet clothes. There were items of gear in the boat house. Ill-fitting oilskins, bib overalls, jackets that, at least, would bring to an end the uncontrollable shivering. Suitably garbed, he returned to the boat.

Back at the creek, Nat floated the vessel onto the submerged cradle and let the rest of the crew take turns to winch it out of the water. At the top he gave it a cursory inspection, meaning to give it a more thorough going-over the next day, since it was getting dark under the trees. Everyone trekked back up to the foundry, collected the belongings of their daily visit to work and left for their homes tired but fulfilled.

37

The premature trial of the new boat was to be followed, soon after, by an official naming ceremony. Because of Robert's fascination with all things happening at the boat yard, Nat decided to call the vessel Robert Ben-Hawk. There was going to be a bit of a dilemma in his mind over the existence of two lifeboats. Although the cost had been covered by the lucrative business being generated by the foundry, the men working on it had put in more than just the paid hours to produce it. He knew they had invested as much pride in its creation as they had skill. It was this that led him to discuss, with Jenny, rewarding his team of artisans at the same time as discussing preparations for an official naming ceremony. The issue of where to keep the new boat – that's if the crew decided they would accept it – also exercised his mind.

'Why don't you get The Falmouth Packet to run a public subscription feature?'

Nat, who was warming a glass of the 'tunnel brandy', as they had taken to naming it, knew the editor would support the suggestion. He always gave good cover to lifeboat news as did the editors of The West Briton, The Western Morning News, The Cornish Guardian and The Cornishman.

'Good idea! We made a friend for life rescuing the proprietor when his yacht foundered in a storm couple'a years back. He'll jump at the chance to help. Getting a site for a launch house will be tricky, though. That's the difficult one. There's a bit of space either side and at the back of the present shed. It's only used to store outside stuff. Some of that could be kept inside anyway. But there's something to be said for knocking it down and building a wider job that'll take two boats, side by side, with an upstairs for other gear.'

Jenny nodded, 'How would you go about rewarding the men at the creek? Give them money or what?'

'Dunno! I was thinking, maybe we could take them to Bentons, the outfitters, get them to choose a suit each for the naming and give them a cash bonus as well. The apprentices always appreciate a bit of extra cash and I know the men see me more as one of them than as 'the gaffer and won't feel patronised.'

'That's settled that then. Dad says we can use The Priory for a reception, that's if you want to, as it's a bit nearer than Trelogan. I take it you're thinking of the actual naming happening in Falmouth rather than Tinners Creek?'

'Customs House Quay. Plenty of space and those who come along just to see the jolly have got The Chisel & Adze on site.'

Jenny poured herself a small brandy. Never one to crave alcohol, she felt, nonetheless, moved to mark these proposals with a salutary drink.

'How are the crew reacting to the boat?'

'No outwardly hostile comments. If they don't like a thing they say so. That's how it's got to be when you're dealing with other people's lives as well as, more importantly, risking your own, particularly when other people's stupidity is the reason for a call-out. My gut feeling is they want to give her a try. The two who came back with us, after the Swanpool incident, were full of enthusiasm. What I really want to do is take her out in a real storm but I'll need at least four or five crew with me so they can form a judgement. I don't want, deliberately, to tip her upside down but I want to find out what she'll do if it does happen.'

'You'll need to have the pulling boat with you if you're going to try that.'

'I know but there's a limit to what the puller'll take. If it's bad for the new one it'll be worse for the puller. Shall have to wait for the right chance.'

At the next meeting, of the volunteer crew, Nat broached the subject of adopting the new lifeboat as part of the search and rescue service offered by the Port of Falmouth. There were no dissenters.

Andrew Nancarrow had long considered the inadequacies of the boathouse and was enthusiastic about Nat's radical proposals for improving the premises. The idea of some kind of appeal to coincide with the official naming and adoption of the Robert Ben-Hawk, also met with the approval of the crew. With this support Nat went ahead with contacting the various editors of the newspapers well known to readers in the South West, giving details of time and date of the naming ceremony, together with an appeal for subscriptions.

*

Crowds of well-wishers filled the quay below the Customs House. The naming of the Robert Ben-Hawk was carried out by the owner of a local brewery who, in response to the newspaper appeal, made a substantial donation to the new boathouse fund. Afterwards, up at Tregennza, a private function - in the form of a lunch for the volunteer crewmen, the skilled workmen who built the Ben-Hawk, their families and those supporting the naming ceremony - celebrated the more personal character of lifeboat crews committed to the safety and well-being of others at sea.

38

Matthew Bennett, the master of the brigantine, White Goose, watched as the last shovel of China clay was tossed down the chutes into his hold. Teams of horse-drawn carts had been lining up all morning with loads of powdery, kaolin briquettes - decomposed mica that, weeks earlier, had been washed out of the granite matrix it had formed in. Allowed to accumulate in settling tanks the mica had been transformed from a slurry, six inches deep on the kiln floor of a 'dry', as they were named, into cakes roughly ten inches square. Baked solid, the cakes gave off a white dust as they were broken and tossed into bays below the kiln. The clay workers were to suffer as much from this white killer as the coal miners were of the black dust they inhaled below ground.

These kilns, some forty yards or more long, provided an unintended playground for the local boys. They knew the clay workers would knock off at five of a summer's evening. This was a time to enjoy the pleasure of running up and down, stripped bollock-naked, on the warm, solidified cake. It was their interpretation and version of Greek Olympia but trespass did not limit itself to 'Greek Games'. On a Saturday morning, when the kiln workers were due to take their crib in the firing area below the hot, bubbling sludge, the boys would nip in, piss on the furnace doors and scarper. It was a matter of boastful banter as to who could piss the highest and create the longest dribble of 'eau de parfum' bubbling and steaming its way to the floor. The master of the White Goose grinned to himself at the image, clear, still in his mind, of the slick of steaming urine running down the rusted cast steel of the furnace door. He had been one of those boys 'perfuming' the air around the furnace doors but his mind soon returned to the business in hand. There was an ominous shade of grey appearing in the clouds building up towards the south west. He was trapped in the small dock behind the lock gates. High tide was three hours away and the dock gates wouldn't be opened for at least another two. His ultimate destination was a small port on the south east coast of Ireland.

The trip from Charlestown, a small China clay port in St Austell Bay, would take him a day and a half. He needed to pull up to the end of the narrow, wet dock to allow one of the two remaining schooners - the vessels were three abreast - to take its place below the chutes, ready to receive its cargo from the queue of carts. The other had already filled up with clay and would be bound for Liverpool. Bennett secured the hatches over his consignment and got his sails ready to hoist, not happy with the disquieting signs further west.

By the time the gates were opened it had begun to squall. Rain made the white dust that had settled on the deck, slippery. The crew had to watch their footing. They were used to wave-swept decks but this fine coating of cream was treacherous, even without the added pitching and rolling they would experience once leaving the relative calm of the outer harbour.

There were four of them on the vessel. Once beyond Dodman Point they began to encounter a build up of heavy seas and strong gusts. Matthew wasn't particularly concerned, the boat had been in worse and he considered a run to the harbours at Penzance or Newlyn would present no problem for the White Goose if he needed to shelter there. He gave an instruction to drop the topsails. Off to the right he could see Nare Point above Polnare Cove. A group of residents, staying at The Nare Hotel, were visible on the veranda watching the storm-swept vista in front of them.

The wind was starting to veer round more from a southerly direction, towards land. Ahead was The Manacles, a mouthful of canine teeth that had ripped the keels from many a hull over the centuries. Side-on seas were now lifting and dropping the boat without much alteration to her pitch. One particular bank of swell, coupled with a cross eddy, lifted and twisted the Goose on an axis that more or less passed through her midships and sheered across the exposed rudder. The spokes on the ship's wheel jerked in Bennett's hands. At the same time there was a clatter somewhere below decks, audible even above the din of slapping sails and wave impact, as the chain, operating the rudder, parted from its fixing and thudded against the stern timbers. The loose wheel signalled loss of steerage.

'We're in trouble,' Matthew Bennett shouted to his main deck hand and gave the wheel a spin to advertise the cause, as he stood back from the free-running wheel, 'run up a distress pennant and let's hope some o' them we pass on the headlands'll spot it.'

He was referring to the usual crowd of voyeurs who regularly collect to watch shipping coping with storm or near storm conditions around this busy stretch of coast. Sure enough, a group of coast watchers at Rosemullion Head had been following the passage of a number of vessels up and down these outer reaches of the Channel. The distress flag was spotted. A message was relayed to Falmouth from the one telephone possessed by a private house at Mawnan.

*

Nat, who had now been promoted to 2nd Cox status, heard the maroon and jumped aboard the Robert Ben-Hawk tied up below the foundry. He was followed by David Tresize and Sam Karslake who had, during the months the Ben-Hawk was being tested, assumed unofficial crew status. On one or two occasions Andrew Nancarrow had also joined them and suggested the two take on formal, RNLI membership. They both appreciated the opportunity to be part of trialling the new boat and needed no further persuasion to sign up for service. Their membership was welcomed by the regulars of the pulling lifeboat. The three cast off and one of the three raised the RNLI flag on the small mast at the stern.

They caught up with the man-powered lifeboat in the mouth of the estuary.

'What's the call for?' Nat drew alongside and shouted across to Andy.

'A brig a mile or so out below Helford. According to an eyewitness she's twisting about with no apparent direction but drifting towards the Manacles. We've got the current running one way and the wind another. Sounds like she's lost her steerage, by all accounts.'

'Right! I'll forge ahead. Seas like this and she's a goner if she drifts into Carn-du Rocks.'

Nat swung the Ben-Hawk away from the rowing boat carefully and set out in the direction of the Lizard. Outside St Anthony Head, beyond the shelter of the east and west reaches of St Mawes and Pendennis Point, the little boat hit the temper of a now fully developed gale. All three men were on deck wearing cork waistcoats and joined to a wire by safety harnesses. They were too focused at staying on their feet to experience sea sickness. It wasn't long before they caught sight of the stricken brig and a few minutes later they were close enough to pick out the four men on board.

'It's going to be a bugger getting a line on that one. Look, she's spotted us. Somebody's waving.'

In three or four minutes they were close enough to see the deck as the White Goose tilted first one way then another. Her hatches seemed secure and there still remained traces of the China clay over the decking on one side of each of the two hatches.

'Look out.' Nat called a warning to the other two as he tried to bring the Ben-Hawk round to face a huge breaking wave towering above them, just at the point of forming a tube. It was too late. The small craft rode up, side-on, the lower curl of the green bank of sea. As the wave propelled itself forward, the Ben-Hawk turned evermore onto its starboard side until the deck was vertical. The curl broke over a keel now higher than the wheel mounting. All three men, by this time, tossed overboard like so much jetsam, were running the grave risk of being keel-hauled by their safety harnesses. Slower than the wave, the Ben-Hawk's totally inverted hull reappeared as the surf raced past. The craft hesitated for a brief few seconds then tumbled back, as though to unwind itself, pulling the three harnessed men back on board. Coughing and retching they were merely shaken, having suffered a bit of a hammering but with no bones broken.

The engine was still running. Nat picked himself up, grabbed the wheel and looked back quickly in the direction of the running sea that had caused their capsize. There was no immediate replication, as far as he could judge, of the monstrous wave that had flung them overboard. He turned his attention to David Tresize and Sam Karslake. Both were back on their feet and hanging onto the side rail. They both grinned.

The White Goose had also taken the gigantic wave side-on but remained afloat. Nat looked across at her. Only the master was visible. He'd hung onto the useless wheel but one of her hatches had been ripped off by the chest-high surge of sea across her deck. Of the other three men there was no sign.

Nat shouted to Sam and David, 'I'm going to her landward side. Her crew must be in the drink. Get ready with the boat hook.'

Taking the rescue craft around the stern of the brig, the eyes of the three scanned the crests and troughs of the frothing maelstrom below the open side deck of the boat.

'Over there!' David Tresize pointed to three heads close together.

'That's a bugger. They're too close to those shore rocks.'

'Ase,' this was a Cornishman's way of saying yes in some regions of the county, 'but weme goin' t'have t'get the buggers.' Sam Karslake echoed the unspoken decision of all three.

Nat turned the boat towards the three men and was soon alongside. None of them appeared injured. Nat kept an eye on his proximity to the rocks as Sam tossed a rope across to the three men. David held the boat hook ready, the pole more of a hand-hold than a 'catch-all'. The sea decided to show some leniency and allowed a brief period of relative respite. With no raised gunnel but merely an edge to the deck, it was relatively straightforward to heave each of the three aboard.

'You're best staying on with us for the time being. Too risky to get you back on your boat yet.'

'What are you going to do? Throw her a line?'

'That's what I had in mind.' The answer Nat gave seemed to satisfy the eldest of the three crewmen.

'When the seas die down a bit we'll put one of you across. What I'm concerned about, though, is that open hatch. If we can get one of you across there's a chance you can get a tarp over the top but I don't rate the chances that high the way these seas are running. There's a pulling lifeboat on her way but she can't do much. Less, in fact, than we can and they'll be in as much danger of swamping as she is,' he nodded towards the disabled brig, 'more so. Anyway you best get into the refuge. We'll call you out when we need you.'

Nat swung the boat around and rode the swell fifty yards back from the White Goose. The Goose's master was still hanging onto the useless wheel but was obviously suffering now from the soaking he'd received earlier. His shivering was all too evident, even from that distance and did not augur well.

'What d'you reckon,' Nat turned to Sam and David, 'I don't like it but do we try to get across?'

Sam shook his head, 'Too risky. Another wave like that last one will swamp her hold. She'll sink like a stone. All we can do is hold off and hope the wind abates before she drifts onto The Manacles. I'd be more inclined to try to coax him across to us and ride out the storm with the chance of putting him back on later, for a tow, that's if she's still afloat.'

'Let's get alongside then.'

Nat guided the Robert Ben-Hawk closer to the White Goose. He shouted his intentions to Matthew Bennett who, by now, didn't need to be told he was in a desperate situation.

'If she gets swamped, she'll go down and suck you with her.'

Bennett nodded, took one sweeping look at her decks, fore and aft before making a dash for the brig's rail. To cross the gap between the two craft was impossible without a rope; was probably impossible even with. David Tresize held up a coil of a hemp line and waved it at the Goose's master who was trying to hold fast to the boat's rail. His hands were numb. Each rise and fall of the brig tired his aching muscles still further as he was swayed back and forth by the surging swell. A look of horror suddenly contorted his drained features. Nat and the other two had their backs to the scene that Matthew Bennett was facing. All three turned to see another gigantic wave bearing down on them. This time it was not quite at the stage of becoming a rip curl.

Nat swung the rudder just in time to line up, side on and ride up onto the escarpment of green water. The heavier brigantine just lay more or less supine, like some inert log trapped in a backwater. The rescue craft turned into an executioner's tool as it rose up over the brig's rail and knocked its master over beneath the cascade of surf. Nat and the other two managed to stay on their feet. The huge wave carried the Ben-Hawk over the totally submerged Goose. With both hatch covers now missing, the second ripped off by this monstrous surge of water, the holds inundated and the White Goose just vanished, silently, into the fathoms of water beneath.

Matthew Bennett was sucked down with it. The crew on the new RNLI boat looked at one another in shock. Some several seconds later the master of the brig surfaced, dead or unconscious.

'There he is.'

By this time the other three had emerged from the refuge to witness events. Nat pulled up alongside the limp body and several hands hauled the man onto the deck. There was a nasty gash across the master's scalp and blood was trickling down his neck into his shoulders. One of the men had experience of resuscitation from drowning. A technique known as Dutch Respiration, although it was more a form of pumping water from saturated lungs than of inflating the organ with life-giving oxygen.

'Get him over on his stomach.'

Bennett was laid out on the deck of the still heaving vessel. His arms were then bent each into a kind of triangle and the elbows raised and lowered by his crew mate.

'Hold his mouth open.'

Sea water began to 'pump' from his lungs with each cycle of lift and drop. This went on until no more liquid issued from his throat.

'Turn him on his side.'

The action resulted in a paroxysm of coughing. Everyone suddenly felt the tension fall away from muscles they had not known they were holding in check. Matthew Bennett opened his eyes. His vacant, dazed look left all in no doubt he was in a state of concussion. Gradually, the realisation of his lucky survival registered on his face and he smiled in gratitude at the sea of faces crowding round him.

'Right, get him into the refuge area. We're not out of trouble 'til we get into the harbour.'

With the injured man safely stowed Nat turned the Ben-Hawk round and headed back towards Carrick Roads. Just before Rosemullion Head they spotted the pulling lifeboat laid up in the relative shelter of the mouth of Helford River. Andrew Nancarrow, wisely, had realised he would be putting his crew in danger, serving no useful purpose by continuing in the impossible conditions that would only result in their capsize. Nat steered into the calmer waters. A rope was tossed to the bow man and the towing line secured ready for the short haul to Falmouth. The journey back was free from drama. They were navigating in a following wind and tide and both craft made a good eight to ten knots.

Back at the boathouse the Robert Ben-Hawk's seagoing performance was commented on by the three crew members from the White Goose. Their gratitude to Nat, Sam and David was almost embarrassing in its praise. The Turtle, coke-burning stove had been lit by one of the RNLI shore-based crew. Clothes were put to dry out on a waist-high fire guard whilst the owners of the wet togs were rigged out with an assortment of loose-fitting, spare garments always kept ready for returning crews. A still dazed Matthew Bennett was despatched to the local cottage hospital and appeared to be suffering from no broken bones. Concussion was the main concern of the doctor who treated him. The next twelve hours would determine the degree of seriousness the blow to his scalp had caused. But secondary drowning – the delayed effect sea water had on the walls of the lungs – could produce a discharge resulting in choking and death. Nursing staff, not familiar with the phenomenon, were alerted to the possibility. A week later, with a sore head, a few bruises elsewhere and a minor chest reaction, Bennett was declared out of danger by the doctor.

Later, at a celebratory meeting in The Chisel & Adze, conversation turned to the self-righting ability exhibited by the Robert Ben-Hawk together with comment suggesting additional improvements that could enhance further, her rescue capabilities. The little boat had stood a test no artificial conditions could have provided. Twenty to twenty five foot waves they had encountered had been endured with a remarkable, sea-going dynamic. Nat was more than reassured with her performance as a rescue craft and no less pleased by the gratitude shown by the crew he had rescued. The vote of confidence implied by the RNLI crew endorsing her adoption as an auxiliary, rescue boat, added to his pleasure. He felt justified in his obsession to create a piece of nautical history.

39

Young Robert Hawken was a big lad for his years. Physically he was athletic and inclined to investigate his environment in a way that made his mother concerned for his safety. He had a predisposition for climbing anything that invited his curiosity. The tunnel below the smoke house attracted his attention as soon as he became aware of his father and grandfather's interest in disappearing down into its depths through the granite chimney. Jim had a cheese production business in hand. The output of hams was also taking up more and more space in the cooler reaches of the priory pantry. As a consequence he'd taken on board Jenny's suggestion of enlarging and converting one of the two bays and the area below the smoke house, into rodent-proof, storage areas to stockpile the output of cheese and hams.

On one such day, watching them climb the dome of the smoke house with a load of bricks, Robert waited until they had dropped below the rim of the vent at the top and commenced the same climb to the granite surround of the access hole. It was child's play, literally. Clambering over the rim and into the well of the chimney presented no difficulty for him and he was down the granite footholds far more quickly than his father or grandfather.

At the bottom both Nat and Jim Bennallack were surprised to see him as he dropped the last few feet. They weren't cross, in fact both were impressed by the little lad's nerve.

'What have we here?' It was Jim who greeted his grandson with mock seriousness.

'Hello granpa. I just wanted to see what was down here.'

'And so you shall but not a word to anyone. Our secret! No one must know.'

The little boy was pleased he was not being scolded.

'Come with me,' Jim picked up one of the lanterns from the top of an empty cask in the middle of the drop area, 'we'll go to look for bats.' Robert was fascinated by these creatures ever since his grandfather brought a wounded one into the house to show him one day.

There were no bats, Jim knew but Robert was not to know this. The two set off down the tunnel. Robert looked about him in childish amazement. Part way down, at the first of the two storage bays, Jim swung the lamp for Robert to inspect the roof. They were both, particularly Jim, startled yet thrilled to see a row or two of bats hanging from the wooden slats supporting the roof. Serendipity! Jim could not get over it. He chuckled to himself, pleased his fiction had turned into fact.

'Why are you laughing granpa?'

'Oh, I told the bats you would be coming one day and that they must not go flying off until you'd seen them. We'll leave them quiet for now. They'll go out when it's dark to look for moths. Let's go onto the end shall we? Then you can see the river where the tunnel stops.'

The two went to the mouth of the tunnel where Robert picked up a few loose twigs and cast them into the slow eddies of the river. He asked a few questions about fish and bats, though his grandfather couldn't quite see any connection between the two, then signalled his desire to return to the main storage area. Back at the inland exit Jim put the lamp back onto the cask. Robert, still excited about this new domain, amused himself examining the quartz and other shiny bits picked out by the lantern in the wall of the enlarged tunnel. Tired of inspecting these crystalline 'treasures', he sat down against the cask to watch the two men lining up a cord as outline for one of the brick-built, storage areas.

His idle hands soon began to explore the floor around his body. He traced out the line of a groove by his side. Tiny fingers discovered a small, spherical object. He picked it up and held it between two fingers, allowing the lantern to give it form and colour.

'Look Granpa, I've found a marble.' Robert held up a lead ball to show them his discovery.

The two men looked at each other knowing immediately the significance of its existence in the tunnel. What Nat did not know was that Matthew Bennett, the man he had rescued days earlier, was the great, great grandson of the previous 'owner' of the 'marble', Roger Bennett.

Printed in Great Britain
by Amazon